The Hunted

VAL TOBIN

The Hunted

Copyright © 2019 Val Tobin

ISBN-13: 978-1-988609-11-9

DEDICATION

To my readers who keep asking for the next story. To Bob, Jenn, Mark, Chanelle, Savannah, and Jack, always.

ACKNOWLEDGMENTS

Thank you to Andrea Holmes; Val Cseh; Michelle Legere; John Erwin; Alis B. Kennedy; Wendy Quirion; Diane King, owner of The Hedge Witch in Sharon, Ontario; Melanie Smith; and Alice Swadner for beta reading, professional advice, and suggestions. Editing by Kelly Hartigan (XterraWeb) editing.xterraweb.com. Thank you, Kelly. Thanks to Patti Roberts of Paradox (paradoxbooktrailerproductions.blogspot.com.au/) for the amazing cover.

CHAPTER 1

The creature, a grendel, turned its pug-nosed face to the sky and sniffed the warm September air. Rachel remained motionless and alert, the beast's large, grey head framed in her rifle sight. One twitch and she'd blow its face off, but she could wait—for a moment or two anyway.

Where the hell is Hound Dog? No sooner had the thought breezed in and out of her mind than her earpiece blipped and Dog's voice rasped in her ear.

"Got two of 'em fifteen degrees from the alpha position. Firing in three … two …"

Rachel's rifle blasted, and the grendel's head burst like a rotting cantaloupe. The body dropped to the forest floor.

"Got 'im," she said into her mic. She'd heard the double blast nearby and waited for Hound Dog to report his kills.

"Two down, Frostbite. That's the nest."

Rachel no longer cringed at the Frostbite nickname; rather, she embraced it. If they wanted to paint her as a cold bitch, she'd be more than happy to freeze the chuckleheads out. At least they left her alone now, and she'd never have to contend with the frat boy antics other freshly minted protectors put up with.

Her teammates had learned on their first week together two years ago not to mess with Rachel Needham. She smiled, recalling Hound Dog's screams when he woke to find his pelvic region covered in fire ants. That little etiquette lesson came as retribution for sneaking into her room during the night on her first day as a full-fledged protector and dumping spiders in her bed. Initiation, the guys had called it, implying all newbies must endure it. Well, she had initiation rituals of her own. She promised them she wouldn't haze them if they left her alone. So far, they all behaved like good boys. At least, ever since the fire ants …

The snap of twigs and rustle of underbrush from the direction of the trees where Rachel's dead grendel lay brought her out of her musings. Silence no longer a necessity, her other two teammates clomped over to the body.

Code Master, tall and skinny and looking exactly like the nerd he was, squatted next to the corpse. He removed his glasses and wiped sweat and black curls from his forehead. "Yup, it's dead."

"You haven't even touched it," Foot-Long said.

"Don't have to. No head, no life." Code Master smirked and puckered his lips. "Or ya wanna give him mouth-to-mouth?"

"Like I give your mama every night?"

Rachel, having had enough of their juvenile banter, stepped from her makeshift blind in the shrubbery. "Can the chatter, boys. Let's get this fucker back to HQ."

The curses rolled off her tongue smoothly now, and Rachel no longer winced, even inwardly, every time she swore. She hated it, but it made her one of the guys—all in the name of career advancement and breaking through a glass ceiling that, in all honesty, wasn't as thick in the protector game as it was in the regular military or had been on the police force.

The force hadn't been too bad, and had life remained as it had been before the grendels appeared on the scene twelve years ago, she'd have continued through the ranks. Before she'd turned thirteen years old and the grendels ate her mother, she'd aspired to be a detective. After her mother's death, revenge drove her. From the moment the protectors were created, she hunted and killed monsters, and she was among the best.

She consoled herself over her lost career with the reminder that detectives couldn't kill their homicidal prey. Protectors won awards and recognition for doing so. Rachel snagged newcomer of the year her first year in, something her teammates might or might not have resented. She suspected Code Master and Foot-Long—for the subs he ate, not for the length of his dong, so she'd been told—didn't mind. Hound Dog, on the other hand, had probably added it to his list of grudges against her.

Fine with me. If he ever needed another lesson in manners, she'd provide one.

Rachel scanned the surrounding area, peering into the trees and brush.

"Where's Dog?"

She sometimes wished her rivalry with Hound Dog were friendlier. A coworker who helped and supported her efforts while giving her a decent rival to beat would have benefited them both. To their detriment, he undermined her at every turn. However, while Hound Dog behaved like an ass after hours, he was an excellent protector. It wasn't like him to take so long to appear in their designated after-kill meeting place.

"With his kills." Code Master's reply came too smoothly and automatically.

"You saw him or you're guessing?"

His grey-blue eyes, always piercing, met hers, but only for a moment. He flushed and looked away. "Sorry, boss, I'm assuming."

"Want I should search for him?" Foot-Long dropped a plastic bag next to the grendel's body.

"Nice try, grunt, but you're not getting out of corpse detail. You two bag the body. I'll find Dog." Rachel checked her phone to locate Hound Dog on the tracking app and melted into the trees, heading south-west.

When she spotted him propped against a tree smoking a joint, her first instinct was to tear a strip off his hide. When she registered his shaking hands and sheet-white face, she hoisted her rifle to ready and crept up beside him.

She spoke in a whisper. "What's the word, Dog?"

"A body, boss."

"Yeah. Two bodies. Why aren't they bagged?"

"No." He shook his head. "In the nest."

The grendels' nest. Grendels nested in groups of three or four, not always as families. Scientists specializing in grendel research, such as her younger brother, Jeff, reported that the creatures formed seemingly random groups. They nested together for safety and security, the way hunter-gatherers and cave dwellers had once done, Rachel supposed, but she'd never heard of grendels dragging a body back to their nests.

It must be bad if Hound Dog, a veteran hunter, became apoplectic at the sight of it.

She tilted her head, indicating the joint. "You're on duty, Protector."

"Sorry." He took a final drag and ground it out in the dirt. "It—" He breathed deep, gulping air as if he couldn't get enough.

"Okay. You puke?" It would matter, so she had to ask.

He shook his head. "Came close."

Relieved he had it together enough to keep his lunch down, she said, "Want me to bag it?"

Hound Dog shook his head again. "My job. Gimme a minute." His voice broke as he said, "A girl, boss. Just a girl."

"Christ, Dog. This will rain hot coals from hell on us." She crouched next to him and touched his shoulder. "Point me to the nest. I need to secure the scene and take evidence before we bag her. Finish here and then join me."

"Why?" The colour had returned to his cheeks, and his voice sounded stronger. *Good.* In a moment, he'd be back to his cocky self.

"You're assuming the creatures killed her. They probably did, but never assume."

"You just want to play cop." Irritation laced his voice.

"I'll always be a cop. That's why I'm team leader and you're not." She couldn't help needling him. Hound Dog's obvious resentment always brought out the nasty in her. He'd wanted the team leader job, but he didn't have the policing experience she did. It ticked one more box on his grudge list.

He waved toward what she assumed was the nest, and after reminding him he had two grendel bodies to bag, she slipped through the trees.

The girl was petite but older than Rachel had expected. The corpse lay beside the nest rather than in it—precision wasn't one of Dog's skills—and oddly, she appeared unmolested.

Since when do these creatures leave food unsampled?

Never, to Rachel's knowledge, yet here lay a body without a mark on it sitting at grendel-nest ground zero.

Drag marks indicated it had been in the nest, but they'd yanked it out and dumped it nearby. Why? This bugged her more than if she'd found the girl mangled inside the nest. The girl should be in pieces and should never have been in the nest at all. The throat and thighs, usually one of the first areas on the body these things chowed down on, remained intact.

"What happened?" she murmured. "What the hell happened?"

Uneasy, she studied the area first. The only footprints in evidence, aside from the grendels', were hers and Hound Dog's. All seemed quiet, but as her ears attuned to her surroundings, she picked up bird chatter in the trees. Behind her, plastic crackled, leaves rustled, and twigs snapped as Hound Dog bagged the two bodies.

Most groups nested well away from each other, so she didn't expect to encounter other monsters, but she never let her guard down anyway. The grendels wouldn't have read the manuals—they could do whatever the hell they wanted. She didn't trust them to remain consistent.

Rachel accessed the camera function on her cell phone and took pictures of the body, the nest, and the surrounding area. When she had enough photos of the scene, she pulled on a pair of latex gloves and squatted next to the body.

Rigor mortis had set in but hadn't completed, which meant the girl had been dead less than thirty-six hours. Rachel saw no obvious marks—no bullet wounds, stab marks, blood, or marks on the throat. After checking the eyes for petechial hemorrhages, she ruled out asphyxiation. The skin held a greenish tinge, a normal occurrence after death.

She rose. They'd have to comb the area for any evidence to show this was a body dump, cart the body back to the base, and then pass it along to the police. All protectors were trained in forensics to spare those not trained to hunt grendels from the risks of poking around in grendel territory.

After gathering evidence and taking photos, they'd need to get this body and that of the grendels out of the forest, but they had a Humvee for that, parked about a kilometre back. No roads, not even crappy dirt roads, led to their current location. The team had hiked in from where they'd left the vehicle.

She got to work.

CHAPTER 2

The girl's body was on its way to the health sciences offices in Peterborough, Ontario, where the nearest pathologist worked. Back at the base, on the outskirts of Lakefield, Ontario, Rachel and the rest of her team hit the showers and then gathered in the cafeteria for dinner.

The large room was deserted, everyone else on the base having already had their meal. Rachel ordered the chicken pot pie special with salad and a bottle of water and took her tray to the table where Hound Dog already sat.

"Looks like you recovered from your find," she remarked as she set her tray on the table and snagged a chair across from him.

When he shrugged rather than responded with a scathing retort, she changed her mind. "Still shook?"

"No."

"It's all right to be upset by what you found."

"I'm fine." He poked at his meat with his fork, spearing it and sliding it around in the gravy pooling around his mashed potatoes. As he continued to poke at it and not eat, Rachel studied him.

He appeared healthy enough. His colour was good, and his large brown eyes shone bright and clear. His eyes gave him the nickname, not any womanizing ways as she'd assumed when they were first introduced. He had eyes like a basset hound and a nose as adept as any dog's at sniffing out grendels. A large, burly man, Hound Dog had played football in high school and worked out as if training to compete for the Mr. Universe title.

Code Master joined them with his tray of chicken nuggets, fries, a bowl of chocolate pudding, a large cola, and three chocolate bars. No wonder he had raging acne.

Rachel scowled.

"What's with the face?" Code Master asked.

She grinned and waved a hand at his food. "You eat like a hormonal teenager."

"Gives me energy."

She shook her head in disgust. "You have no vegetables."

"Sure I do. Fries are made from potatoes. Potatoes are vegetables. Besides, you're not my mother."

"Someone apparently has to be." Now, why should she care enough to argue about his diet? The dead girl's face flashed through Rachel's head. "Sorry, Coder, I guess I'm still punchy from finding that chick."

"What did the cops say?" Foot-Long joined them, setting his tray down across from Code Master. At least he had a salad to go with his—surprise, surprise—submarine sandwich. Loaded with cold cuts and drenched in mayo, the sandwich shed hot peppers from all sides. His drink of choice was a large iced tea.

"Not much. The detective was as surprised as me that she was intact. The coroner's report will explain what happened to her, but I doubt they'll share the information with us when they get it. We're just the clean-up crew."

"But you'll find out, boss." Hound Dog levelled his gaze at her. "You always find out." Behind the even tone hovered a hint of accusation and, perhaps, annoyance.

"I take an interest. They like that."

"Well, maybe I want to take an interest in this one."

"Why?" Genuinely surprised, she waited for his reply.

"Because it's weird," Code Master said.

Foot-Long also threw his hat in the ring. "I want to know too."

"I can talk to the captain. Ask her to update us," Rachel said.

"Will they tell her?" Hound Dog asked.

"She could ask them to. They might want to interview us, ask us what happened out there. What we found—not that we found anything besides the body." She ate a few mouthfuls of food. At times, the four of them together made a comfortable group.

"And you're so special Cap will fill you in? Or is it because you're both women?"

Until Hound Dog spoiled the mood—and Hound Dog always spoiled the mood.

"Damn it, Jack, why must you do that?"

He licked his lips and grinned lasciviously. "I love it when you say my name. Say my last name, too, babe. I'll propose."

She gave him a bland look. "Let's stay on topic. We leave tomorrow. When we return to the base in two weeks, they'll have news—probably. You want me to get Cappy to share the info? She'll tell me because I'm asking. Any of us can ask."

"Yeah, but not all of us would get answers." Hound Dog's voice betrayed a touch of wounded ego.

"Maybe because you go around acting like you're king of the compound." Rachel had had enough of the conversation. She speared a bite of Hound Dog's roast beef with her fork and popped it in her mouth. "Good meat."

"I hear that a lot."

God, she'd walked right into that one. Without missing a beat, she said, "Too bad it's cold."

She rose and picked up her tray. "When we get back from break, I'll hunt up the captain and ask her what happened with the girl. Whatever she knows, we'll know. I promise."

Rachel left her team and went to her dorm room. With luck, no calls would come in during the night and she'd be home for her two weeks off by noon tomorrow.

***

Since the night remained quiet, Rachel got home to her townhouse in Peterborough by ten o'clock in the morning. When she arrived, she found the street as silent as her night had been. On this Monday morning, most of the residents were at work or school.

Rachel's shifts covered fourteen days on the base followed by fourteen days at home, and she liked the schedule. She brought home a good salary and lived below her means. The townhouse complex was in a decent area outside the downtown core but close to the hustle and bustle. It also resided far from the edges where the forests might encroach.

The grendel infestation that had exploded in the forests around Ontario twelve years before had forced people away from the woods, away from trees in general. No one went into the wilderness anymore alone and unarmed and never without hiring a protector to accompany them. Rachel frequently hired out her services on her weeks off, and sometimes, she and her entire team were recruited through the base to do special jobs.

She pulled her brand-new silver SUV into her driveway, rolling up the garage door with the automatic door opener in her vehicle. Arriving home and settling back into a house she'd left empty for two weeks but for a neighbour peeking in each day to check on it always felt a little strange. The base felt more like home to her than her house did.

Her furnishings looked as new as her car because she hardly used anything. The clean and shiny walls shone as if freshly painted. She always entered the house from the garage and made her way upstairs to her room to drop her duffel bag on the floor. Next, she'd fix herself a drink—it was five o'clock somewhere, she habitually joked to herself—and watch a show on a streaming service. Really, she spent most of her break running errands or biding her time until she could return to work.

As she measured an ounce of gin into a highball glass and topped it with tonic water, she used the remote to turn on the television. Most of the time, Rachel avoided the news when she first arrived home, but today, she wanted to see if the media had picked up anything on the body Hound Dog had found.

She snatched up her drink and strolled to the lounge chair facing the television. Setting her drink on the end table next to the chair, she sat down and released the footrest. On the screen, the news cycled through car accidents, shootings in Toronto and surrounding areas, robberies, assaults ... So far, it was people hurting people. No mention of grendel attacks.

Perhaps people had finally learned to coexist with the creatures. The thought made her smile. That would never happen. As if to prove her point, the news shifted, and a picture of a grendel displayed behind the newscaster.

"A local team of protectors, based in Lakefield, Ontario, eradicated a nest of grendels over the weekend. Hunters Rachel Needham, Jack Ainsworth, Dalton Morin, and Paul Fraser recovered three grendel bodies from the kill site and one female victim. They found the female's body near the nest. Details are unavailable at this time. We'll update reports as we receive them."

So, HQ had told the media the grendels had killed the girl, but they hadn't told them she'd not had a mark on her. The creatures couldn't have killed her. They didn't use subtlety to kill—they tore in with teeth and claws. Whatever had killed the girl wasn't readily visible. Poison? Drugs?

None of what they'd found made any sense.

She picked up her drink. One hand holding the cup steady on her thigh, Rachel watched the news and sipped.

A video clip played next, a voice-over explaining the contents.

"Protests at the Needham Scientific Research Facility near Peterborough, Ontario, turned violent yesterday when Jeffrey Needham, son of CEO Stefan Needham, rammed his car into the facility's gates. Bail was set this morning for Needham and two other protesters arrested along with him. Charges include destruction of private property and trespassing."

Rachel sat up in her seat, snapping the footrest back into place and setting her drink on the table.

"Oh, God, Jeff," she muttered. "What the hell have you done now?"

CHAPTER 3

Her heart pounding, more with anger than shock or fear, Rachel turned up the sound on the television. Her younger brother had apparently led a group of protesters to the facility owned by their father. When they found the entrance to the property barred to them—*of course it was, you idiot, it's a private research facility*—he'd rammed his car into the gates.

Rachel rose and paced the room. No one had called her. Why hadn't Dad called? Or Jeff? One of them should've let her know he'd been arrested. There he was on the screen, hands cuffed behind him, a smug expression on his handsome face, as a police officer guided him into the back of a cruiser.

She raced up the stairs to her room and fished her phone from her backpack. So much for unwinding with a G&T and watching television. She never should've flipped to the news. First, she tried Jeff.

Voicemail, which wasn't surprising given the recent revelations.

She called her dad. Her father's assistant gave Rachel a difficult time, but in the end, he put her through.

"Hi, Rache."

"Dad, why didn't you call me? I had to find out from the news."

"You mean Jeff?"

"What else would I be calling about?" She sat on the edge of her bed, changed her mind, and lay down instead.

"I was busy dealing with everything."

"Where's Jeff?"

"In jail."

"You left him in jail?" Her voice rose.

"What do you want me to do? He's a grown man. If he's going to do something this stupid, I'm going to teach him a lesson."

Yes, her dad loved lessons. Loved stepping back to let them cope on their own. She supposed the strategy had worked. Neither she nor Jeff ever relied on their father for anything.

"He's barely nineteen. He's barely old enough to drink." That reminded her she had a gin and tonic sitting on the end table downstairs. Rachel went to retrieve it. This conversation would require it.

"He's doing this shit sober. Imagine what he'd do drunk."

"That's not funny."

"It wasn't meant to be."

"Why was he there?" Back in her room, she stood in front of her trophy case, her gaze flitting across the awards for running, for martial arts, for achievements as a protector. She sipped from her drink, and it slid refreshingly down her throat.

"Protesting. You know how he is. We're the bad guys to him."

"Have you talked to him? About your work?"

"I can't talk to him about what we do. It's classified."

"No kidding." She enunciated each word, frustrated that he spoke as if she were an imbecile. She adjusted her tone to reflect his. "Talk to him scientist to scientist. He understands genetics. The kid graduated university at seventeen with a Ph.D. in it. You don't have to discuss specific projects. Listen to what he has to say. What if he's right?"

Stefan heaved a sigh so loud Rachel almost felt the breath

in her ear. "Sweetie, do you think I haven't tried? I invited him to work here. It could get him a Nobel Prize in genetics. He refuses every time. I'm out of ideas about how to deal with your brother. I've got nothing left."

"Will you bail him out? If you do, I'll talk to him. I've got time off. Please? I'd do it myself, but I don't have the money."

"What would it look like if I bailed him out? No, Rachel. You want to talk to your brother, go ahead. You can talk to him in jail. Perhaps that big brain of his will help him find a way out."

She heard a voice in the background, and Stefan said, "Yeah, on my way." To Rachel, he said, "I gotta go, honey. I'm sure you'll figure something out. You're my warrior, right?"

"Sure, Dad."

Before she could say anything more, he disconnected.

Rachel next called the police station in Peterborough to track down Jeff's whereabouts. The cop she spoke to, an old friend from her days on the force, told her someone had bailed Jeff out only moments before, but he wouldn't tell her who.

With some hope he'd answer, since he'd been released recently and would have his phone back, she called her brother.

"Jeff Needham."

"Jeff, thank God. What the hell, bro? What are you doing ramming your car into the gates at Dad's company?"

"Nice to hear your voice, too, Rachel."

"I'm not trying to judge you. It's all over the news. That's how I found out. Not from you. Not from Dad."

He chuckled. "I'd have called you, but I was a little busy. Besides, the cops took my phone. How did you expect me to call you?"

"You managed to call someone to bail you out." She didn't allow him a response and said, "Where are you? Want to come here? We can figure out what you need to do next."

"I appreciate the offer, sis, but you're not responsible for me anymore." Annoyance gave his words a hurtful punch to her gut.

"I'm not trying to be responsible for you. God, I'm worried about you. Can't you appreciate that?" Didn't he realize she'd do anything for him?

"Not really. I'm not a kid. We're not running from grendels anymore."

"Yes, we are. Everyone is." She sighed. "You think because you study them for a living and they're humanoid that they can be domesticated. They can't. They're monsters. They'll always be monsters. Wherever they sprang from, we must eradicate them."

"That's your job. You won't get my cooperation for it."

"They killed our mother. Why do you overlook that? They don't understand you're trying to help them. They'd kill you, too, if you stumble on them in the forest."

"So would a lion, but you don't see people trying to eradicate the entire species."

Before responding, Rachel tossed back the rest of her drink in one gulp. "Lions evolved naturally. These things aren't natural."

"I disagree. They're flesh and blood creatures. Just because we don't know where they came from doesn't mean they couldn't have evolved naturally. However, on that point, I agree with you. I think they're the products of genetic manipulation."

Rachel gasped. "Why?"

"I can't prove it yet, and I can't discuss this over the phone."

"Then come here. We'll talk about it."

"All right. It'll take me about an hour. I'm stopping by my house to shower and change, okay?"

"Sure."

They said their goodbyes and disconnected the call.

Two hours later, Rachel still waited for Jeff to show up. When she called his cell phone, it went directly to voicemail.

CHAPTER 4

Reluctantly, Rachel called her father's office. She didn't expect help from that direction but refused to let him off the hook. If something had happened to Jeff, her father needed to get involved in searching for him. He was their father, for God's sake. Why didn't he ever act like it?

"What? I'm busy." His exasperation came through the cell phone in waves.

"Of course you are. Do you think I'd call you for no reason?"

"I'm sorry. I didn't mean to snap at you. It's Jeff again, I assume?"

"He's missing."

"What do you mean? Isn't he in jail?"

"No. Someone bailed him out."

"Who?" The annoyance in his voice climbed to new heights.

"I don't know. He didn't tell me when we spoke."

"But you spoke. What makes you think he's missing?"

"I expected him here over two hours ago. He hasn't shown up and isn't answering his phone. I'm worried."

"You're overreacting. He probably stopped somewhere and hasn't let you know. I'm sure he'll show up soon. Give him time."

"Couldn't you at least, for once, sound a little concerned?"

"I'm not concerned because there's nothing to worry about. Look, if you must do something, call his friends. Call those maniacs he protests with. One of them will know something. He's probably with them." He paused, but when she didn't reply, he said, "I don't have time for this. Figure it out. Shoot me a text when you track him down so I can say I told you so."

As before, she didn't find his attempt at humour funny. "Sure, thanks. Bet you win Father of the Year this year." She disconnected the call.

Damn him—her father and, frankly, add in her brother, too. She'd only ever wanted a normal life. Grow up, become a detective, help people, get married, start a family ... and where was she now? Hunting monsters, arguing with her dysfunctional family, and living the single life—and not even really living it since she hadn't had a date in two years. Ever since she became a protector.

If cops had a difficult time having a family life, protectors had it so much worse.

She opened the contacts list on her phone. How many of Jeff's friends or partners in protests did she have on here? Not many.

Isabelle Marie Hodgkin—Jeff's friend and a member of his protest group. They'd met in university. She was older than Jeff by two years, but they were tight enough Rachel had added the woman's contact info to her phone though they'd never met. Isabelle Marie might give Rachel more names and numbers. Or Jeff might be at Isabelle Marie's. If so, Rachel planned to tear him apart grendel-style for worrying her.

The woman didn't pick up, making Rachel wonder if the two were together. She left a brief message on Isabelle Marie's voicemail saying she was searching for Jeff, gave her number, and disconnected the call. Jeff's friend might simply have turned off her phone, but then again, something might have happened to both her and Jeff. Rachel's worry deepened. Who could she call next? He wouldn't have gone to the university, would he?

Before contacting the police, she'd try one more thing: tracking his cell phone. Rachel chastised herself for not doing that immediately. She went upstairs to the room she used as an office and booted up her computer. Once online, she searched for how to track a stolen phone, followed the instructions, and entered Jeff's cell number into the online tracking app.

She located it in the woods outside of Peterborough.

**

Hound Dog lived in a much posher part of Peterborough than Rachel. His home sat on an acre of land on a cul-de-sac of exclusive homes. While not quite a mansion, the dwelling was, nevertheless, impressive. The door, set in a turret, swung open after Rachel rang the doorbell twice. Hound Dog stood before her, wearing only a towel wrapped around his waist.

"Making a house call, Frosty? Lucky for you, I'm naked under this towel."

"Get dressed. I need your help." Why had she picked Hound Dog to turn to? But she knew the answer. Next to her, he was the best hunter in the protector fleet.

Immediately, he turned serious. "What's wrong? Something happened? You okay? Is it the girl we found?"

"Are you alone?" She didn't want some woman he was banging to appear naked from a bedroom.

"Yeah. You interrupted my steamy session in the shower."

"All right, don't get disgusting." She almost smiled. Almost. "Without you getting skeevy about it, may I come in? I've got a huge problem, Dog. I don't know who else to ask for help."

A puzzled look on his face, Hound Dog stepped backward into the house and ushered her in.

"What's up? Sounds personal, so not about the girl I found."

"Right."

He led her into a large but cozy family room with neutral walls and warm-toned accents and waved her to a sofa in front of a gas fireplace.

"Sit. I'll be right back." He left the room.

She appreciated he'd turned all business. Perhaps ... no, he was nothing but a jerk underneath. Peel off the top layer, and you'd find he was as rotten at the core as he was on the surface.

He returned five minutes later, dressed in a black T-shirt and blue jeans. "Want a drink?"

"No, thanks."

"What's going on. You look nastier than usual."

When she gave him a stricken look, he shrugged. "Just trying to cheer you up. What happened, Rachel?"

As her name fell from his lips, tears sprang to her eyes, and she turned her face away. After taking a deep breath and pushing the emotions down, she met his gaze.

"My brother's missing. Jeff."

"I saw the news. Isn't he in jail?"

"He's out on bail. I tracked his cell. To the forest. I'm going after him, and I want you to come with me."

CHAPTER 5

They took Rachel's vehicle because she insisted and Hound Dog understood she needed to have control. He could relate. If it were his brother—he'd had three, so he knew what it was like—he'd have done the same thing.

As she drove, he studied her with furtive glances.

She had a fierce expression that enhanced the warrior aura she always radiated. Her long, goth-black hair was tied back in a single braid and topped with an army-green ball cap. The denim jacket she wore hid her muscular arms. Not that it mattered. Hound Dog could picture those ripped biceps. He'd felt the force of them whenever they trained together. She'd learned martial arts from the time she was fourteen and had even won a few competitions.

He tried to spar with her as often as possible, not just for the challenge but because he enjoyed being around her. Self-aware enough to realize the inauspicious start to their relationship was his fault, he nevertheless continued to allow his ego to dictate their interactions. That didn't stop him from seeking out more contact. He swore to himself he'd stop coming across as a sexist lout, but his mouth and body refused to listen to his brain. One day, he'd outgrow the need to annoy her.

But not today. Not now. Now, he wanted to ease her

anxiety, and the best way to do that was to piss her off.

"Couldn't stay away, could you, babe? We got a week off, but you had to have more of the Dog." He produced a lusty howl to punctuate the words.

She gave him a satisfying scowl. "Don't start with me. I'm not in the mood."

"It's okay. Actions speak louder than words. You needed a knight in shining armour. I get it. Who you gonna call? Hound Dog, baby."

"Oh, my God. I should've gone alone. What the hell was I thinking?" A grin flashed across her lips, and her brow lost its frown, smoothing out the lines. Her breathing also returned to normal, but her hands remained gripped tightly on the steering wheel.

He hoped she was joking, but just in case, he said, "You never go alone." When she didn't reply, he said, "He's family. I understand. You never said, but I'd bet you didn't file paperwork on this little jaunt."

Her neutral expression changed to guilty. "I should've told you that. It was an oversight. If you don't want to go, you don't have to. I'll drop you at a bus stop or let you out and you can call a cab." The car slowed.

"Oh, no you don't. What did I just say? You don't do this alone." Annoyed she assumed he'd abandon her and she believed his issue was over regulations, he scowled and said, "You think we're coworkers, don't you?"

Puzzlement crossed her features, but the car picked up speed. "What?" She shrugged. "We *are* coworkers."

"We're a team. Close as family—closer. Family isn't always blood, Frostbite, but those who have your back."

"Sure." Her tone was placating.

"I'm serious. We face grendels almost every day. I know I don't have to worry about what's behind me when you or Coder or Foot-Long are back there because you got it. We might not agree on everything, we might dick each other around, but out in the wild? Boots on the ground? We're family and we got each other's backs."

"We're not out in the wild right now."

"But we're heading there. No way would I let you go alone." He sat rigid in his seat and glared at her.

She met his gaze for a second before returning her attention to the road. "Fine."

"Isn't that why you asked for my help?"

"Yes," she hissed.

"Then what's your problem?"

"I don't have a problem. Look, I was joking. I came and asked for your help. I'm not going alone."

He didn't point out she'd slowed the car and threatened to dump him on the side of the road. "Don't ever lone wolf it."

"I wouldn't. Protector training too ingrained." She paused and then said in a voice filled with surprise, "I found myself at your door without even thinking about it."

"All right." He relaxed in his seat. "Where exactly are we heading?"

"Buckhorn Road. Toward Lakefield. It's a forested area and Jeff's phone is giving off a signal in there. Why the hell would he go there?" She answered the question without giving Hound Dog time to reply. "He wouldn't. Something happened to him; I know it."

"Calm down. Maybe he's not alone. Something came up he had to attend to, and he had no chance to call you."

"In the woods? I hardly think so." After a moment, she glanced at him, an expression of mild amusement on her face. "Thanks, Dog."

"What?"

"You're trying to make me feel better, and I appreciate it." She grinned as she returned her attention to the road. "Even if it's not working."

"You're welcome. I think." In an exaggerated gesture, he gripped the door handle. "Just keep your eyes on the road, Andretti. I want to arrive in one piece."

If Jeff really had entered the woods alone, unarmed, as Rachel had said, they likely wouldn't find him in one piece. In that case, she'd need all the strength and support Hound Dog

VAL TOBIN

could give her. As the scenery sped by—she hurtled well over the speed limit—Hound Dog's anxiety ratcheted up several notches.

***

Rachel parked the SUV along the side of the road, and before they jumped out, they armed themselves. Each carried a rifle at the ready, and each had a knife in a sheath hanging from a belt at the waist. In a duffel bag slung over her shoulder, Rachel carried more weapons and extra ammo. On her back, she'd strapped a collapsible litter in case they needed to transport a wounded Jeff. Hound Dog wore a backpack containing food, water, first aid supplies, and a body bag in case the worst happened. Strapped to his calf was another holster with a pistol. Rachel had the same.

To get to the woods, they'd had to cross a checkpoint, and Rachel had lied to the protectors manning it. She'd told them they were on a search and rescue mission—which was true, as far as it went—but the mission was personal, not sanctioned. As Hound Dog had guessed correctly earlier, they had no paperwork to back it up had they been asked for it.

Luckily for them, their IDs got them through the gate. Most cities and towns had put up barbed wire fencing around their borders, which kept the grendels out of populated areas. Not a foolproof solution—occasionally, a creature would get through the barriers and mangle some innocent soul before protectors put the creature down—but it helped. Deaths caused by grendels had gone down since the fences went up.

The city of Peterborough had been all Hound Dog had known until he'd gone to university. He'd hightailed it out west and earned a degree in engineering from the University of Alberta. After that, he'd returned to Ontario, but the desire to actually go into engineering had left him, replaced by the burning desire to hunt down and kill grendels. For revenge— they'd killed two of his brothers while he was away.

The senselessness of the deaths and how preventable they

were stoked Hound Dog's fury the most. It'd happened well after the creatures had first appeared on the scene. His brothers, unarmed, had taken a shortcut through a wooded lot within city limits. A grendel had breached the fencing and dropped on them from a tree in which it hid. It never should've happened.

In the early days, this happened frequently. Many people had lost their lives because they had no idea such predators had appeared in previously safe locales. Sure, parts of Ontario had potentially dangerous wild animals—wolves, bears, cougars—but none of them went out of their way to hunt down and eat humans. Most of them were more afraid of people than people were of them. Then, out of nowhere, the grendels had appeared, slaughtering not just humans but pretty much anything that breathed.

After the first five years, some animals, already becoming scarce, teetered on the brink of extinction. Hound Dog hadn't followed the scientific reports, but he was sure a number of species had disappeared altogether. At first, the police and select military personnel had mobilized against the monsters, and then the protectors had formed.

Trained specifically to hunt grendels, protectors were recruited from police forces and from military personnel— and, as in Hound Dog's case, from civilians who had a burning desire to kick grendel ass. Hound Dog signed up, trained, and never looked back. Every time he killed a grendel, he noted it in a journal. So far, he'd tallied two hundred thirty-four.

Rachel held up her fist, ordering him to halt.

Hound Dog froze, listening. Birds chirped. Since fall approached, a tang of rotting leaves and mouldering wood permeated the air. A subtle breeze blew from the west. Something small and fast scuttled in the underbrush—not a grendel. Animal activity boded well. With a grendel nest nearby, most of the wildlife would be gone.

Rachel pointed south-east and resumed walking. Rifle up and ready, Hound Dog crept after her. Neither made a sound as they walked across the ground, avoiding branches, twigs, loose rocks, and dry leaves.

When Rachel halted again, she inclined her head toward a grove of widely spaced trees ahead of their current location. Hound Dog nodded, understanding her brother's phone, if not her brother, was up ahead.

With his eyes and hand gestures, he suggested taking the lead. She shook her head and motioned he should enter the clearing from behind. He nodded agreement, because this was her party and he'd follow her lead, but he didn't agree. If her brother's body lay in that clearing, it might freak her out enough to get them on a grendel's radar.

Even so, he crept forward, slow and steady. In his periphery, Rachel approached the semi-clearing. The sun remained high enough overhead that, if Jeff was there, the grendels wouldn't leave the cover of the forest to attack the two protectors as long as they kept to the areas of full sun. Sunlight burned the creatures' skin. At least the evidence of the phone's location gave them hope of finding Jeff alive.

But if he was alive, why didn't he answer his phone?

Hound Dog's belly twitched. They wouldn't find anything good in the clearing beyond the copse. His gaze met Rachel's, and at her signal, they approached the clearing and peered into it together.

CHAPTER 6

At the sight of the body—her brother's, she could see that immediately even though blood from a wound in his throat covered his face and chest—Rachel went numb. She forced herself to keep still and not rush to his side.

A glance across the clearing at Hound Dog told her he recognized what they'd found, but he maintained caution and remained in place. He'd wait for her command.

She was grateful now she'd brought him—not because the others wouldn't follow protocol but because Hound Dog wouldn't let her wimp out. His presence alone reined her in, prevented her from losing her shit.

After scanning the area, Rachel waved Hound Dog to join her by the body. She took her first steps over to her brother in cautious haste. Once beside him, she dropped to her knees.

"Guard us," she ordered.

He nodded and kept his rifle up. His glance never strayed to the body but focused on the woods.

"I have to treat this as any other find." If she talked it through, she'd cope.

"Yup. We're here to do a job, boss. Best for him if we do it well."

"Agreed." Grateful her voice hadn't betrayed her emotions, Rachel used her cell phone to take photos of the

27

body. *The body.* Her brother. Grief stabbed her heart, and tears welled up in her eyes. With a surreptitious glance at Hound Dog, busy scanning the area and standing guard, she dabbed at her eyes. After completing the photos, she slipped on gloves and, for the first time, registered what she witnessed.

"Dog."

The urgency in her voice snapped his head around. "What's wrong?"

"Grendels got him, but they went no further than ripping out his throat and biting one thigh."

Hound Dog maintained his position, but his expression changed from worried to confused to interested. "Why?"

"Why would grendels toss a body from their nest without tearing it to pieces and eating most of it?"

"The girl," he said, contemplating.

"Something's weird here. Like it was weird there. They bit him. They never bit her."

"Could be the sun drove them off?"

"They would've dragged him with them. Into the trees. We should've found him in pieces deep in the forest, not here with his throat gashed in this sun-dappled clearing."

"We should've tagged Coder and Foot-Long. The nest could be around here."

"We've handled retrievals alone before."

"I know, but I have a bad feeling about this."

She smirked, attempting to tamp down the rising fear with brevity. "Scared, princess?"

"Only of you, Gothzilla," he quipped but then sobered up. "Bag him, Rachel. Let's get out of here."

Afraid delays would cost them and trusting Hound Dog's instincts, she bagged any evidence she found, including Jeff's cell phone, wallet, and keys, in case this was a body dump made to appear like a grendel kill. She'd seen more than one of those since her career as a protector began.

When she finished, Hound Dog retrieved the body bag for her, and she quickly wrapped her brother in it. As she worked, she forced her brain to view him as a stranger. If she didn't, she'd fall apart, and that could get them killed. Perhaps, alone, she would've indulged in tears and inattention, but Hound Dog and Jeff counted on her to be professional. She wouldn't let them down.

She unfolded the stretcher, locking the parts in place, and strapped Jeff's body on it.

"Stay on guard. I'll drag the litter," she said.

"You ready?"

"All set. Take it slow. No surprises."

He acknowledged her with a thumbs up and led the way. The hike would be a short one so long as nothing interfered with their progress. As they walked, Rachel kept her ears attuned to the forest sounds and watched the surrounding trees. Part of their trek would take them through dense brush.

Alert though she was, Hound Dog spotted the grendels first and raised his fist, halting her.

"Two at ten o'clock." His voice remained calm, even.

Rachel dropped the litter and readied her rifle. "I see them. Sitting against the tree."

Movement in the bushes to her right had her veering her rifle at whatever approached. She spotted two more grendels. "Nest of four. I got these two. You take the first two."

"Gotcha, boss."

They counted down. Fired. Twice. Rachel fired a third time when her second target shifted out of the way and she missed it. At the edge of awareness, she sensed rather than saw Hound Dog rounding toward the rapidly approaching grendel. Howls came from the creature, drool streaming from its open mouth.

She fired before Hound Dog could and dropped it.

"I had it. I didn't need your help."

"Easy, Frosty. I wasn't trying to one-up you. Your two behaved normally. Mine didn't move," he said.

She huffed out a breath, and her shoulders dropped along with the tension she'd held. "You're right. Sorry." After a pause, she said, "We'll have to call this in. We can't take them all back along with Jeff's body. Not enough bags. I need to let HQ know what happened."

"Agreed."

"I want to examine the two you hit before we bag them. Why the hell did they just sit there and let you shoot? You ever see anything like that?"

"Nope. They saw us—I know they saw us—but they didn't move. You think they're sick?"

"Stay alert. I think we got the nest. These four probably all live together …"

"… but you never know," he finished for her.

"Yeah."

Vigilant, the two set their packs beside the stretcher and walked to the pair of grendels slumped against the tree. Hound Dog had neatly dispatched each one with a shot to the head. Rachel squatted next to the bodies and studied them without touching them.

"No drool," she commented.

"Weird."

Grendels drooled when they caught a scent of humans, an autonomic reflex that occurred when they spotted food. Rachel had always found the trait disgusting, and whenever she saw a slavering grendel, she took particular delight in firing at the mouth.

"Skin looks dry." She glanced up at Hound Dog. "Why would their skin be dry?" Typically, a grendel's skin was tough, like leather, but moist and slimy.

She pulled out her cell phone and took pictures.

"Maybe they're allergic to humans." He chuckled, but the effort was half-hearted, as if he believed it might be possible.

"The ones we caught the other day where we found the girl, they all seemed normal. The two I shot seemed fine—from a distance, anyway."

He shrugged. "Let's verify. But then we'd better book."

She paused to look and listen but heard and saw nothing sinister.

"All right." Rachel stood. "Let's check out the other two.

Once the on-duty team comes in, they'll take over and we won't hear anything more."

"You mean you won't ask Cappy to keep you in the loop?"

"You know I don't mean that. She'd tell me—us—whatever we want to know. This isn't a top-secret investigation. As soon as the bodies leave our facility the information no longer streams to us. Assuming there's information to stream. Likely, they'll burn the bodies the way they always do."

"You think they should keep these bodies? Do tests?"

"I'll recommend it. Even if they do as I suggest, we won't hear what happened. We're just the grunts who pick up the trash. If it wasn't my brother in that body bag, I'd be okay with it. You know? Maybe not even then. Something's wrong with these grendels. If they're carrying a virus, it could affect us all."

He stared at her, horrified understanding dawning on his face. "Should we get the government involved?"

"That's the captain's call, but yes. We have to find out if they've got a disease and if it's transmissible from grendels to humans."

"Christ, Frostbite, what'd we stumble onto?"

She shook her head. "I don't know, but it's nothing good."

CHAPTER 7

Once they returned to Rachel's SUV, they loaded up the body, stowed their equipment, and contacted HQ. Dispatch got a fix on their location and mobilized a team to come out and retrieve the grendel bodies Rachel and Hound Dog had left in the woods. The two protectors met the team, guided them to the remains, and then left them to their work. Back at the office, a dressing down from the captain awaited them, and they wanted to get it done.

Captain Kim Pattenden had them sent to her office the moment they arrived. Her assistant ushered them in immediately. Rachel opened the door for Hound Dog and he walked in ahead of her. They took seats in front of the captain's desk.

Pattenden got right to the point. "I hear you two did some off-the-clock hunting."

Rachel took the lead since it was her brother they'd set out to retrieve. "It's my fault, Captain. Hound Dog had nothing to do with it."

"I'd say he had a lot to do with it—he accompanied you."

"Yes, because I asked him to."

"Don't defend the indefensible, Needham. He should have either insisted you contact HQ or done it himself."

Hound Dog had remained silent through the back and

forth between his captain and his team leader, but the moment Pattenden finished speaking, he cut in.

"Extenuating circumstances, Captain. I went along with her because, to begin with, it wasn't a hunting expedition."

When he fell silent, the captain said, "Then what was it?"

"Search and rescue," he replied. He faced Rachel with an expectant expression as if prodding her telepathically to come clean.

They had nothing to lose by being honest. She said, "My brother went missing. I tracked his cell phone to the woods outside of Peterborough. He'd spoken to me two hours before that. I didn't expect to find a body or grendels."

"You went to the woods. What else did you expect to find?"

"He hadn't been out there long—he couldn't have been out there long. And he studies grendels for a living. He's not stupid. No way would he have gone without protection."

"Did you find a weapon on him?"

"No."

The captain leaned forward in her chair and pressed her hands flat on the desk. "What do you make of that?" she asked, her voice muted, gentle.

"I don't understand it."

Captain Pattenden turned to Hound Dog. "What do you make of it, Ainsworth?"

"I can't explain it. What we saw with Jeff Needham, his behaviour, the condition of his body, none of it makes sense. The grendels' bodies look wrong, too."

"How so?"

With a glance at Hound Dog, Rachel said, "Jeff's body was in one piece. They'd killed him, or so it appears, took a bite from his thigh, and then left him." She described examining the bodies and what concerned her about the findings.

Pattenden folded her hands on the desk. "I'll expect a detailed written report. I'll advise the coroner's office, and it'll be up to them to contact Health Canada and the Centers for Disease Control's office up here."

The CDC was US-based but had offices in Canada since the two countries had a vested interest in partnering on health issues. A communicable disease on the loose in Canada would impact the US, eventually.

"Thanks, Cap," Rachel said. "If you hear anything about what the ME finds, will you let me know? Especially regarding my brother." She hoped adding that last bit would compel Pattenden to more readily keep her in the loop.

"Whatever I can, Needham. Now, let's talk about protocol and why you don't cowboy in my unit."

*****

Even though the lecture from Pattenden seemed to last forever, in reality, it took only another five minutes of their time. Pattenden released them with instructions to go home and stay there, an order Rachel fully intended to follow. Hound Dog, on the other hand, had other plans. No sooner had they settled into Rachel's vehicle than he suggested they go for a bite to eat.

She slanted him a look. "I don't think so."

"You're not hungry?"

"My brother died." Her breath hitched on an inhale. "I have to tell my father. My relatives. Friends ..." She fell silent, everything she had to do filling her mind.

He put a hand on her arm. "I know. That's why we should go out for dinner. Put it off a little. Strategize it. I can help you with that."

"I have to tell my dad. He can't find out from the media. After what happened at the labs, they'll be all over it." She frowned. Her brother had planned on visiting her. Something had sidetracked him and led him to the woods. Perhaps something related to the protests he instigated. She shivered, suddenly chilly.

"What are you thinking?" Dog dropped his hand from her arm.

"The whole thing is shady. It stinks." She shook her head.

"Even so, I have to tell my dad."

"Then let's go back to your place. We'll order pizza, and you make your calls while we wait for the food."

"I want to be alone." She tried not to sound harsh and doubted she pulled it off.

"You shouldn't be alone." He punched the dashboard lightly with his fist. "You gonna make me say it, Frosty? Fine. What if whoever lured your brother to the woods comes after you next?"

She laughed. "Why would anyone do that? If someone murdered Jeff, it had to do with his work on the grendels or his protests about the grendels. Those have nothing to do with me."

"Unless it had to do with your dad's company."

She tilted her head, considering. "I doubt it. I have no involvement with his company or with anything Jeff did. I'm not on anyone's radar." She started the car. "I want to go home. I'll drop you at your place first. Thanks for coming along."

He shrugged. "Fine. Have it your way. But for the record, watch your back. You already think something's hinky here. I agree. This shit stinks. What if you know something you don't know you know?"

"That's convoluted even for you." She smiled. Dog loved his spy novels. Obviously, he'd been reading too many and they'd clouded his judgement. "I'll be fine." She pulled the vehicle onto the highway and headed for his home.

When they arrived in his driveway, he suggested she come in and they order food. Not sure whether to feel touched or irritated, Rachel declined. She had to call her father. Maybe he'd regret not helping when she'd asked him to that morning, which now seemed so long ago.

"I have to go home. Alone," she added quickly before he suggested following her in his car.

"Fine." He put his hand on the door handle as if to open the door but stopped short of tugging on it. "If you need anything, call me. All right?" He faced her, looked her in the eyes. "I mean it. I know we've had our issues, but we're a team. We support each other."

"Thanks." She refrained from mentioning the night he'd dumped spiders into her bed while she slept. They'd never talked about it again. He'd never apologized to her for the prank, but then, she'd never apologized to him for setting fire ants loose in his bedding. The memory brought a smile to her lips.

Two years later, she supposed part of the problem she had with him stemmed from that awful stunt. He saw it as a joke. She saw it as borderline misconduct and possible sexual harassment since she'd been sleeping naked at the time. That he didn't get it infuriated her and didn't allow her to forgive him for it.

Add to it the times he seemed to resent her or displayed envy or bitterness for her accomplishments, and they had too much bad blood between them. How could she ever consider him as a friend or turn to him in her time of emotional need? They maintained a professional relationship, and it would remain so. She refused to allow a guy like that into her personal space.

She'd only asked him to help her with this search and rescue because of his skills. His experience. His knowledge. She could trust him as a protector. That was all.

"Thanks," she said into the drawn-out silence. "See you in two weeks."

He stared at her for a moment longer. Just when she thought she'd have to open the door herself and push him out, he swung the door open and sprang from the car.

She watched him head into his house and sat there long after he'd shut the front door.

***

She noted the Mercedes parked in visitors' parking the moment she pulled into the street leading to her section of the townhouse complex. Out of habit, Rachel scanned the cars in the lot. She'd never spotted anything suspicious but always checked anyway. This car didn't put her radar on high alert, but something about it made her take notice. Perhaps it was just that an unfamiliar car sat here during a time when most people were at work.

After parking her car in the garage, she grabbed her duffel bag and went inside, closing and locking the door behind her. Immediately, she sensed an anomaly. She set the bag down quietly, slipped her keys into her jacket pocket, and removed the gun from the holster above her right ankle.

Her footsteps stealthy, gun cocked and ready, she made her way from the front hallway to the living room.

When she saw who sat on her sofa, she set the gun on an end table and opened her arms wide.

"Get over here and give me a hug. Damn, Peter, I could've shot you."

Peter, her old friend and the man who'd saved her life and Jeff's life from the grendels twelve long years ago, rose and approached her. He looked great despite his prematurely grey hair. His hair was white rather than grey and gave him an ethereal aura. His fashion sense had improved since she'd last seen him. The charcoal-grey suit he wore looked expensive, not that she could identify a designer suit. It fit him well, making her appreciate the solid lines of his slender yet muscular physique.

"Rachel, so wonderful to see you." He grabbed her in a bear hug, squeezing the breath out of her.

"You broke into my house. Why'd you break into my house?" she huffed out when she could speak.

"I didn't. Jeff gave me his key."

Immediately, Rachel's back stiffened, and she extricated herself from his arms. "What do you mean? When did you see Jeff?"

"This morning. I bailed him out of jail."

CHAPTER 8

"What's wrong?" Peter asked. "Rachel? You okay?"

The blood drained from Rachel's face. A low moan escaped her, causing Peter to grip her upper arms to steady her.

Jeff was with Peter? Peter sidetracked Jeff?

"Oh, God." She shrugged off his hands and snatched her weapon from the end table. Feet planted hip-distance apart, she pointed the weapon at him. "You son of a bitch. You lured Jeff out to the woods. Get on the floor. Legs spread. Now."

Peter's face went white. "What are you doing? What are you talking about?"

"Get down," she shrieked. "I won't ask you again."

"You'll shoot me?" But, slowly, he kneeled and then lay face down on the floor.

Rachel snatched her phone from the holster at her waist and called Hound Dog.

"Hey, Frosty, changed your mind about dinner?" His tone aimed for jovial, but it sounded forced. His voice held an undercurrent of concern.

"I've got the person who killed Jeff. Found him in my house when I got home."

From the floor, Peter shouted "What? No, Rachel, listen

38

to me!" From the phone, Hound Dog yelled, "Jesus! Did you call the police?"

"Shut up, Peter. You'll speak when I tell you to speak." To Hound Dog, she said, "No cops. Not yet. But I need you as backup. Can you come over? I want you to search his car while I question him."

Without hesitation, Hound Dog said, "I'm there. Be careful. Don't let him get the drop on you."

"As if," she replied and disconnected the call.

Gun trained on Peter, she backed into the kitchen—thank God for open-concept layouts—and retrieved zip ties from a drawer. She returned to the living area and ordered Peter to put his hands behind his back. When he did, she kneeled, one knee on his back, set her gun on the floor out of his reach, and zip-tied his wrists. That done, she snatched up her gun, hauled him to his feet, and shoved him onto the couch.

"Rachel, what is this? What's going on?"

"I'll ask the questions."

He looked genuinely confused, and it bothered her, but she refused to trust him. That might have been Jeff's downfall. He would've trusted Peter even though neither she nor Jeff had seen him in years—not since he'd rescued the two from Storm Lake Marina twelve years before.

"What are you doing here?"

Peter huffed, his face red from exertion. "Why are you doing this? What do you mean 'killed Jeff'? I just saw Jeff."

"What are you doing here? Why are you in my house?"

"Jeff sent me here. After I bailed him out," he replied.

"That doesn't explain why he gave you a key. Why'd he send you here?"

"I wanted to meet with you both and tracked Jeff to the jail. He was simple to find—I caught the arrest on the news. We talked, I bailed him out, and he sent me here."

"You came into my house."

"You weren't home." He raised his chin, and his voice dripped with defiance.

"Why'd he give you his key? Why didn't he come with

you?" She frowned. "And why the hell did it take you so long to get here? You left him at least two hours before you arrived here. I waited here for him at least that long."

He eased back into the sofa, getting more comfortable. Clearly, he didn't believe she'd shoot him or have him arrested.

"He said he needed to do a few things before he came over. He wouldn't let me tag along with him. I'm working on a story and wanted to follow a lead anyway. On my way here, I detoured to talk to someone I've been trying to interview for a long time. So, where's Jeff? What you say can't be right. I saw him not five hours ago."

"Dead. I wasn't home when you got here because I traced Jeff to the forest. Then I found him dead and had to bring his body out. Why the hell did he go there?" she shouted, unable to control the rage. Her hands shaking, she levelled the gun on him. "The truth."

Peter's face drained of blood again. "I wouldn't hurt your brother. It's me, remember? We survived the grendels together."

"That was years ago."

The doorbell's ring interrupted them.

She sucked in a breath and steadied her hands. "Get up. We'll answer the door together. It's probably Dog, but I'm taking you with me."

When he rose, awkwardly, from the couch, she waved him into the hall and followed him to the door. Through narrow windows on either side of the door, she glimpsed Hound Dog standing on her front stoop.

"Stand back," she ordered, and Peter backed up against the wall.

"I'm not here to hurt you. I'm here to ask for your help."

"We'll see." One hand holding the gun on him, she used the other to open the door. "Come in, Dog. Join the conversation."

Hound Dog stepped into the hallway and gave Peter the once-over. "Who's this guy?"

"An old friend." She spat the words out as if they tasted bitter in her mouth.

"What happened? Did he hurt Jeff?"

"I didn't," Peter cut in. "I swear I didn't. Please. Believe me. I wouldn't hurt either of you, Rachel. You're the only ones who can help me."

She didn't respond to that. Instead, she said, "I assume the Mercedes in visitors' parking belongs to you?"

When he muttered "yes," she asked him where she could find his car keys. He directed her to his pants' pocket. She used her free hand to retrieve them, and Hound Dog snatched them up with a giant fist and headed for the door.

Her gaze steady on Peter, Rachel said, "Search his car, Dog." With a wave of the gun, she motioned Peter back into the living room. "We won't call the police. Yet. We'll hear your story first, check your car. If I don't like what we find, my friends on the force will investigate whatever you're up to. And if you're responsible for Jeff's death, they'll make sure you pay for it. Sit on the couch."

Peter did as told and Rachel sat across from him on the edge of the recliner, watching him with blazing eyes. "What happened when you saw Jeff?"

"After I saw his arrest on the news, I wanted to talk to him. I'd heard you were a protector and hired your services as a guide. I need a guide." When she opened her mouth to speak, he cut her off. "I'll explain later. First, let's talk about Jeff. I went to the jail, and he agreed to see me. He seemed happy I was there."

"Is this the first time you've seen him since ... back then?"

"Yes. We'd kept in touch over social media—you know how it is—but we haven't seen each other in twelve years. It felt good to see him even under bad circumstances. He's really grown up ..."

His voice broke, and the faraway look in his eyes brought tears to hers. Rachel lowered her gun, doubt creeping in. Peter wouldn't have hurt Jeff. They'd been through too much together. They were friends—distant friends but friends nevertheless.

"What happened next?"

"Jeff said he'd been arrested for crashing his car through the gates at Needham Scientific Research Facility. I already knew that, of course, because that's how I tracked him to the jail. He wanted to talk about it, I guess. He said your father's company conducts unethical research. I assume he referred to the GMO research they do. He didn't go into detail. He begged me to put up his bail and promised me if I did that then he'd get me into the facility."

"Why do you want to do that?"

Peter leaned forward. "Did you know I'm a journalist?"

"Yes. I saw it on your social media pages. Are you investigating genetic research? My father's company gives tours to reporters. They have nothing to hide. You don't need Jeff to get you in." She paused a moment and said, "If you want a way in, Jeff isn't—wouldn't have been—it. As you can imagine, my father doesn't feel warm and fuzzy toward him these days."

"We wouldn't have been going in through the front doors."

Surprised he'd admit that, she said, "Then what? What did he promise you, exactly?"

"A way into the lab. To prove to the world they're doing illegal experiments using unethical means."

"Specifically, what?"

"He didn't go into it."

"Why were you even discussing it? What's your story? Why are you pursuing this?"

"I wasn't, at first. The grendel research your brother does interests me, his take on how to domesticate them interests me, and your role as a protector who hunts them down interests me. I wanted to commission you to take me on your next hunt."

She rose and went to the kitchen. A pair of scissors hung from a hook above the stove and below the microwave exhaust fan range hood. She returned to the living room, set her gun down on the end table once more, and went to Peter.

"Give me your wrists."

When he shifted so his back faced her, she snipped the zip tie and set it and the scissors next to her gun.

"You believe me?"

"I'm starting to. Tell me more. How did you leave Jeff? Why did he end up in the woods—dead?" She still hadn't told her father. The police would've notified him by now, surely, but she needed to contact him.

"When I left him, he told me he had an important errand to run. Didn't say what, and I didn't ask. I assumed he wanted to get his car back. The cops probably impounded it. He didn't seem bothered by anything—not anything more than the bother of being in jail."

"He brought that on himself."

"Yeah, which is why he wasn't upset. He'd expected to end up there."

"Did he explain why?"

"He wants to trigger an investigation into your father's company."

"They won't investigate Dad's company over that stunt. They'd just charge Jeff with a misdemeanour or two. The company wouldn't interest them at all except that the crimes were committed on company property."

Peter rose and crossed the room to stand in front of Rachel. When she shot a worried glance at her weapon, he crouched in front of her and took her hands.

"I'm not here to hurt you. Jeff had plans to escalate things and keep the spotlight on himself and the company. He figured if he made enough noise people would want to see the truth. I'm investigating a story about the grendels and research Jeff had done. That's all. I still want to take the hunting trip with you. Rachel, I want to learn how the grendels originated."

CHAPTER 9

"Ahem." The sound made Rachel and Peter look to where Hound Dog stood scowling in the doorway. "Am I interrupting something?"

Peter released Rachel's hands and stood. "No. We're just talking."

"He give you a good enough reason to release him, Frosty?" Hound Dog walked into the room and tossed Peter back the car keys. Peter snatched them from the air with one hand.

"Thanks," he said. "Dog."

"That's Protector Ainsworth to you," Hound Dog responded.

"You rooted through my car. I'm not under arrest. Protector." He returned to the couch and sat down. "Did you lock it up?"

"I'm not your valet," Hound Dog snapped. He glanced at Rachel. "But yeah, I locked 'er up."

"Take anything?"

Hound Dog held up his hands. "Nothing in my hands, dude." He rolled up each sleeve. "Nothing up my sleeves."

"Anything to report?" Rachel asked.

Hound Dog strode across the room and took a seat on the couch farthest from Peter. "Looks as if he's living in his car.

44

Lots of luggage, food, cases of water. Electronics."

"I'm working on a story. I drove up here from New Jersey."

"You a Jersey boy, Pete?"

"That's Mister Sanderson to you, Protector Ainsworth."

"Fair enough." Hound Dog laughed. "This clown talked you into letting him go?" His expression sobered. "What happened to Jeff, Mister Sanderson?"

Peter shook his head in sorrow. "I don't know. We parted company. I had an interview to chase down; he had an unknown errand to run."

Hound Dog continued the questioning as Rachel remained quiet, observing. "He say anything about where he headed, what he wanted to do?"

"No. If I'd have known he planned to go into the woods, I'd have stopped him. He was alone when I left him. I went to my interview and then came right here. When I discovered Rachel gone, I let myself in and waited. Since I knew she expected Jeff to show up here, I figured she'd be back soon."

Rachel opened her mouth to point out the discrepancy in Peter's story, but he jumped in before she could speak.

"You called him as soon as he left the jail. I assumed you'd heard he'd been released. We made plans to meet here after he spoke to you. I listened in on his end of the call. He told you he needed to go home and shower and change. That's true, I guess, but he didn't tell you he had one other stop to make, and he didn't tell me what that was either."

That he'd listened in on her conversation with Jeff gave his story a greater ring of truth and eased the knot of tension in her gut.

"Did he call anyone else while you were with him? Or did anyone else call him?"

"He tried to call a friend but didn't reach her."

Rachel turned to Hound Dog. "We need to visit his place. Dog, you can go home. Thanks for your help, but I've got this. Peter can come with me."

Hound Dog studied the tall, skinny man and apparently

found him lacking as backup. "The guy's a beanpole. A strong wind could take him down." He turned to Peter. "No offence."

"How is that not offensive?" Peter asked. "Muscle Head—no offence."

"Because I'm stating a fact. Have you any training in self-defence? Do you have a permit to carry a weapon? I can answer that one myself—no, because you're not in law enforcement."

"I have a gun permit—and a gun."

Rachel silently watched the back and forth between her partner and the man who'd saved her life when she was a thirteen-year-old child, hoping they'd sort it out. Finally, she had enough.

"Guys. Stop." She rose from her chair and paced the living room. The distance she covered with her long strides meant a short run, but the movement helped ease her stress. "Dog, I can take care of myself. I'm taking Peter with me for personal reasons."

When Hound Dog's brows furrowed and his lips curled into a snarl, she said, "Don't get offended. I'm not leaving you out of any big loop. I just don't have time to explain. If there's anything to find in his house, I want to get to it before anyone else does."

"Like who?" Hound Dog asked as Peter said, "Who'd do that?"

She stopped in front of the couch and glanced from Peter to Hound Dog. "Investigators. Whoever killed him. They might've gone through Jeff's place already. Maybe they kidnapped him from there, which, if they did, could have evidence to indicate that."

"The hell with this, Frosty. You're not going alone."

"She won't be alone," Peter said instantly.

"With you, she might as well be."

Rachel ignored the pissing contest. Still facing Hound Dog, she said, "It's your week off, Dog, and I don't want to drag you into anything more than I already have. The investigators will take over, but I have to do what I can to get a jump on them. I need to know what happened to Jeff."

This time, Hound Dog ignored Rachel and talked over her to Peter. "She's a perfectionist. Has to control everything." To Rachel, he said, "Don't insult me. I'm coming with you. If you've got a problem, boss, I've got a problem."

In the end, all three of them piled into Hound Dog's pickup truck and headed to Jeff's house.

***

Jeff Needham lived in a two-bedroom bungalow on the edge of what was technically the town of Cavan-Monaghan, Ontario, on the outskirts of Peterborough. It'd been a while since Rachel had visited him there. Most of the time they got together, either he came to her place, or they met at a restaurant or bar.

They rolled up to his driveway after sunset, which at this time of year was a few minutes past seven o'clock. Leaves covered the front lawn, deposited by the maple, elm, and birch trees scattered around the yard, and the various bushes growing across the front of the house.

"You going to break in or you got a key?" Peter asked as Hound Dog parked in front of the garage.

"Key," Rachel replied. "You and me first, Dog." She wouldn't allow Peter to step foot from the truck until they knew the house was clear. Hound Dog nodded his understanding but Peter protested.

"I can help you."

"You're in here until I tell you. Got it?" She hated to sound abrupt, but her senses were on high alert. The dark house appeared deserted, but that didn't mean it was empty. If an intruder had heard the vehicle pull up, he or she could've cut any flashlight and hid.

The understanding finally dawned in Peter's eyes. "Yeah, okay. Be careful."

"Take this gun," she said, handing him the weapon she'd

brought for him to use.

"Okay."

"Don't shoot. It could be me or Dog running out. You need the protection in case things go south in there."

"Got it." He took the Smith & Wesson Model 29. "That's a big gun."

"Try not to shoot yourself."

"Let's go, Frosty." Hound Dog opened the driver's door and hopped out. He left the keys in the ignition.

Rachel exited the front passenger seat and beckoned Peter from the back. "Turn the vehicle around so it faces the road. If we need to haul ass, I want you ready to drive us out."

He jumped out and climbed into the driver's seat without comment, slamming the door shut as Rachel waved for Hound Dog to cover the back. They both carried night-vision goggles and put them on. As soon as Hound Dog rounded the corner of the built-in garage, Rachel scurried to the front door.

She tried opening the door without the key first and verified it was locked. She unlocked it and tucked the key back in her jacket pocket. With her left hand, she turned the doorknob, keeping the weapon in her right hand raised. She flung the door open and scanned the room. When the door banged against the wall, she stepped back from the entrance, listening, scanning.

Nothing stirred.

"Police. Freeze," she shouted into the dark. A lie, sure, but anyone in the house illegally wouldn't know it, and it might flush them out.

The house had an empty feel. She quickly stepped into the entryway and scanned the living room. Room by room, she searched the house. Nothing had been disturbed. Had Jeff come home at all after he left the jail? When she checked the master en suite bathroom, she ran her fingers along the shower walls. They were dry.

Without the need to turn on lights, she moved quickly and confidently. When she reached the sliding doors in the dining room off the kitchen, she unlocked and opened them. After giving Hound Dog the all-clear, she waited for him to step inside. Once he was in and ready, she said, "Main floor is clear. There's a basement. Let's take it together."

"Roger that."

She let him lead, and together they made their way down the stairs. All seemed dark, quiet. They found nothing until they reached a locked door off the rec room.

"His lab," she whispered.

"He has a lab in his house?"

"Relax. He doesn't keep live animals or anything in it. It's similar to a home office but with microscopes."

"We'll have to break it down unless you have the key for it on you," Hound Dog said.

"He didn't give me a key to his lab. I'll do it." Who broke down the door to Jeff's lab didn't matter, but for some reason, she felt as if letting Hound Dog bust in was a betrayal. Jeff would want her to do it—at least, that's what her conscience told her.

"Stand back."

As soon as Hound Dog stepped away, Rachel kicked the door. The first attempt caused a splintering sound, so she reared back and tried again. This time, the door swung inward.

She'd been wrong when she'd told Hound Dog Jeff didn't keep live animals in his lab.

"Dog," she said, "we've got a problem."

CHAPTER 10

On the far side of the room sat a large cage containing a grendel. The creature slammed its body repeatedly against the bars, baring its teeth and snarling at the two protectors. Drool sprayed from its lips.

"Christ, Frosty, I thought you said he didn't do live experiments here."

"He didn't the last time I was here."

"What'll we do about this?" He placed a hand on her shoulder. "It's illegal."

"Yeah, Captain Obvious, I know."

Damn it. What the hell had Jeff been trying to accomplish and why hadn't he been trying to accomplish it at work? He had a fully equipped, completely legal laboratory at the university in Lakefield, constructed specifically to study grendels.

"We'll have to report it," she said.

Hound Dog pulled out his phone, but before he could place a call, she stopped him. "Hold up. I want to search for his notes first."

"We can't take anything."

"Right. But we can look and take pictures. I want to know what he was doing here with that thing. This might be what got him killed."

50

She yanked her night-vision goggles off and flicked on the lights.

"You going to let the reporter in on it?" he asked as he removed his goggles.

She considered. "Yes. I trust him."

"No kidding? You haven't seen him in how long? And you trust him more than you trust me?" The hurt in his tone seemed genuine, so she refrained from jumping on what he'd said.

"I trust you, which is why I called you when I couldn't find Jeff. Why I brought you along. I could've sent you home."

"No, I insisted on coming along. You had no choice."

"We're not arguing about this now. A monster's in that cage. We can't kill it. If he experimented on it, there's no telling what he's done to it." She smoothed a hand across her forehead, trying to tame a pending headache. "Go get Peter and tell him what we've found. I'll scour through Jeff's stuff. So far, it looks as if no one searched this place yet, and that's a bonus, but they might be only minutes behind us. I want to see what we can find and then report it. Once we do that, this place will be crawling with investigators."

"Yeah, and the captain will be all over us again."

"We aren't cowboying. I'm allowed to enter my brother's house. If the cops aren't investigating his death as a murder, someone has to."

Hound Dog left the room, his footsteps pounding up the stairs. She heard him bang through the front door and thud across the wooden front porch. In the meantime, she commenced her hunt through whatever files and notes she could find, snarls and howls from the grendel serenading her.

At first glance, she found only a few sticky notes, reminders to perform certain routines at certain times—why he didn't use his cell phone for that, she couldn't explain, but that was Jeff. One note was a grocery list. She didn't know why he hadn't used his cell phone for that either.

She sighed, loudly and long. *God, Jeff, why didn't you confide in me? What were you doing?*

She craved answers to those questions. He'd always been such a cute, lively boy. She still thought of him as a boy even though he was technically a young man. A tear trickled down each of her cheeks, and she swiped them away. No time yet to grieve. She must hurry and then call in the grendel's existence.

At the thought of the creature, she stopped her hunt through cabinet drawers and examined it from a distance. It looked like any other of its kind she'd ever seen: broad feet that slapped the ground when it walked; hard, grey, slimy skin and sharp teeth; a mouth that emitted hisses and snarls that sounded like a cross between a cat's growl and a dog's bark; long, skinny arms and legs; large, luminous eyes; spikes protruding from its back; sparse patches of hair covering its scalp; long, fleshy fingers; small, suction-like protrusions on its finger pads; and a pug nose that was a bump on a large head.

If Jeff had tampered with this creature, it didn't show in any way she could discern. She resumed her hunt, opening drawers, rifling through them and then closing them. Footsteps on the stairs alerted her to Hound Dog's and Peter's arrival. Peter entered the room first. He froze, jaw dropping, at the sight of the snarling, slavering grendel.

"Oh, my God, Hound Dog told me it was down here, but I wasn't prepared to actually see it so close. So real."

Rachel noted the use of Hound Dog's nickname and that the protector let it slide. Perhaps the two had declared a truce.

"Boss, here," Hound Dog called out. He waved her over to the closet next to the door. "It's locked. I assume anything useful would be stored in here."

"Yeah, I'm sure he's not locking up his winter boots." She hunted down a paper clip from Jeff's desk next to the closet and unbent it. In a few moments, she had the door open. Shelves inside held neatly labelled storage bins.

"This is helpful."

One box held tax files from previous years. Another was

folders containing research notes. She lifted that box onto a nearby table and opened it up.

"Help me go through these. Take pictures of what's relevant."

"What would that be?" Hound Dog asked.

Rachel and Peter exchanged glances.

"You'll know it when you see it," Peter replied.

"Where's his computer?" Hound Dog scanned the room.

"Good question." Rachel checked the counters, the desktop. "He used a laptop. Probably carried it with him." She turned to Peter. "Did he have one with him when he was arrested?"

"If he did, they probably impounded it with his car. Evidence."

"He probably has a computer he uses at the office strictly for work," she said.

"They'd take that, too," Hound Dog put in.

Rachel agreed and pushed thoughts of computers and Jeff's arrest from her mind. She focused on learning what they could from the hard copies of files he had in the lab. Together, they searched in human silence while the grendel continued its snarling tirade.

A few minutes later, Peter spoke. "He's trying to domesticate it." As soon as the words were out, he corrected himself with a sorrowful glance at Rachel. "Was trying to domesticate it."

"How?" Rachel asked.

"Talking to it. Feeding it dog food, rewarding it with treats. Tried to play with it using cat toys."

Rachel swallowed past a lump in her throat. "Does he say he had any success?"

"Not according to this, but he wasn't at it for long enough to draw any conclusions, and results on one subject don't mean much. Plus, if Jeff's been gone for two days, this creature must be starving."

They all stared at it. It continued to rave.

"Don't those things get tired?"

No one replied to Hound Dog. The question had no answer. The creatures seemed to have inexhaustible energy, which was why the two creatures resting against the tree near where they'd found Jeff's body made no sense.

"They must rest sometime. Right?" Peter used his cell phone to take shots of the documents he viewed.

"Yeah, when the sun hits its peak in the daytime," Rachel replied. "They don't seem to require much—not the eight hours humans supposedly need. Any studies done suggest they sleep between ten and two during the day. Other studies have found that's only on bright, sunny days."

"Impossible," Peter said.

"We don't know what they are or where they came from. What if ..." She trailed off.

"Surely you're not thinking they're extraterrestrial creatures." Peter's tone betrayed his contempt for that theory. It had been a popular one, on and off, since the grendels first appeared.

"How'd they get here? Can you picture these things piloting a spacecraft?" He snickered.

"What if they originated as organisms on a meteor?"

"Do you know where ground zero is? They burst from the trees twelve years ago. In southern Ontario. We're ground zero. No meteors crashed here then. You know where their population fans from? Storm Lake."

"Is this based on research you've done?"

"It's based on investigating I've done. The information exists. We need to verify it."

Rachel paused in the search through the files. Most of them were printed up from spreadsheets or word processing documents. She took photos of everything, unsure what might be relevant. Hound Dog and Peter did the same.

After they finished, they returned the files to the closet, leaving it unlocked since they didn't have a key. Rachel called HQ and reported the grendel. She spoke directly to Captain Pattenden, putting her on speaker.

"We had to break down the door, Captain. I have a key to

Jeff's house but not to his lab."

"Were you aware he kept that thing there?"

"Of course not. We rarely discussed his work. I understood he worked in grendel research, but I had no idea he was involved in anything illegal. As a matter of fact," she said, a realization dawning, "it's what he accused my father's company of doing."

"Anything else I should know?"

"No. I'll wait here for the team you're sending out to retrieve the subject. What will you do with it?"

"Take it to the university in Lakefield and have them examine it. They have the facility to work with live ones."

After a brief exchange where Rachel had to swear to her captain she wasn't involved in anything off the books, they disconnected the call.

"How will they get the creature to Lakefield," Peter asked.

"They'll tranquillize it and take the entire cage. No one wants to mess with one of these monsters." She glanced from one to the other, staying with Hound Dog. "We're done here. You can go home. I'll wait for the team to get here. Peter and I can call a ride-share vehicle when they're gone."

Hound Dog brushed a hand across his crewcut. "I'm not leaving. I'll stick around and see this through." He scowled. "Can we take this elsewhere? I'm getting sick of all this racket."

Rachel ushered the two men from the room and upstairs to the living room, closing the lab door and the door to the basement behind them as they left.

Hound Dog dropped into a recliner, Peter sat on the couch, and Rachel positioned herself on the love seat. When they'd all settled themselves, she said, "Peter's working a story."

"So?" Hound Dog asked.

"You don't need to get involved in this."

Understanding flashed in his eyes. "You told the captain you weren't going off book."

"I'm not. Peter's hiring me to take him into the woods."

She turned to Peter. "That's what you wanted to discuss with me before we discovered Jeff's body. Right?"

"Correct."

"You need a team for that," Hound Dog said.

"We're returning to Storm Lake. I can do this without involving the team," Rachel insisted.

Hound Dog's mouth opened in a perfect oval. He clamped it closed and then said, "Why the hell would you do that?"

"I have a theory about where the first grendels originated," Peter said.

"Yeah, I heard ya. Storm Lake." Hound Dog said. "How'd you figure that?"

"Logic, some investigating."

"What investigating?"

The rumble of vehicles pulling up in front of the house reached their ears.

"Save it," Rachel said. "Let's get that thing out of here first."

She rose and went to the door to let the team of protectors into her dead brother's home.

CHAPTER 11

The team worked quickly. They secured the tranquillized grendel inside its cage in the back of their truck. A pair of scientists from the university had accompanied the protectors, and Rachel turned over all the research files they'd found in Jeff's closet.

After the team finally left, she locked the door behind them and returned to the living room. Peter and Hound Dog had returned to their original seats, and Rachel sat once more on the love seat.

"I haven't spoken to my father yet." She wasn't sure why she led with that except it had popped into her head. Why hadn't he called her? By this time, news of Jeff's death had probably hit the media.

"Call him," Peter said.

She hesitated but not for long. If her father knew something she didn't, perhaps she could draw it out of him. Rachel made the call. With a glance at her two partners in crime, she put the phone on speaker and set it on the coffee table between them. She held a finger to her lips, signalling them to remain silent.

"Stefan Needham."

"Dad."

"Why do you always block your call when you call my

cell?"

"Is that your biggest concern right now?"

"No." His voice softened. "I was about to call you."

Sure you were. She waited for him to continue.

"Honey, something happened to Jeff." He exuded sorrow, compassion.

Rachel doubted it, but the ice around her heart melted a fraction. "I know."

Silence lingered for a moment. She assumed her father was digesting this revelation.

Finally, he said, "What? How?"

"I found him."

From the phone came a sharp intake of breath. "What do you mean you found him? Where? Rachel, what have you done?"

An interesting way to phrase it. "Me? What could I have done? I waited for Jeff to come to my house. When he didn't show up, I tracked him to the woods. The grendels had caught him." She didn't mention the anomalies in Jeff's body and in two of the four grendels they'd found in the vicinity. The lab would examine each monster's stomach contents to verify they'd killed Jeff. Odds were good they had, but the investigators couldn't assume anything. Tests had to verify.

"Why was he there?"

Something about her father's tone perplexed Rachel. He'd said it smoothly, as if asking the question was more important than any answer she might give.

"No idea. He wasn't supposed to be anywhere near the woods."

"He was supposed to be in jail." Again, his tone seemed off: smooth, conversational, when it should have been aggrieved or even frustrated and angry at the injustice of it all.

Rachel had gone through all the what-should-have-beens and the if-onlys in her head, struggling to accept that events had played out the way they had. While searching her brother's lab, she'd by turns cursed him out for stumbling into death and lamented him for being a hapless victim. What she hadn't done was reach a point where she could discuss Jeff's death as if it were long past.

Perhaps she read too much into it. Everyone grieved differently. She filed the information away in the back of her mind to give him the benefit of the doubt but kept it on her radar.

"A friend bailed him out. No clue how he ended up in the forest. The friend and Jeff parted company after Jeff's release." Her gaze met Peter's as she talked.

His face bore a look of anguish, and she gave him a half-smile and a slight headshake to reassure him. He should assume no blame for what had happened after he and Jeff had separated. Whoever had taken Jeff to the woods should bear all the responsibility for his death.

"How do you know this so-called friend didn't lure him out to the woods? Feed him to the creatures?"

Peter's expression became stoic, and Rachel immediately shut down that line of questioning.

"I know this person, Daddy. He wouldn't have done that. He saved our lives twelve years ago. No way would he do anything to hurt me or Jeff."

Hound Dog, looking as if a million questions rolled around in his head, stared at Peter. Rachel shook her head at each of them and held her index finger up, begging them to maintain their silence. Both the men would provide unique and objective perspectives on the conversation. As long as her father assumed it was private, he'd speak more candidly.

Part of her felt guilty for tricking him, but another part of her wanted to prove he knew more than he let on. In the darkest corners of her mind lurked the suspicion he was somehow responsible or at least involved. Whenever that idea surfaced, so did rage and a desire for vengeance.

"That was twelve years ago. You don't know him anymore. Is he the guy who showed up at the house with you in the delivery van?"

"Yes," she whispered, suddenly wondering if he was right.

She'd risked everything by trusting Peter, and he'd been

the last one to see Jeff alive. He'd shown up at her house with a key he'd received from Jeff. But a key that would've been the only one missing from the ring he had on his body when they'd found him. Peter wouldn't have known which key belonged to her house. He couldn't have gotten the key without Jeff identifying hers—unless it'd been done at gunpoint.

"I'm grateful for what he did then, Rachel, but how do you know he's okay now?"

"I've spoken to him. Jeff was alive when Peter left him."

"Glad you think so. I've contacted the investigators. They're turning the bodies you found over to the company. We'll examine them here."

"What? Why? When we find human remains among the grendels, they're all supposed to go to the university lab where a specialist can examine them."

"We've got better facilities, and I want to make sure nothing's overlooked. We're experts in this type of research."

"The grendel department at the university in Lakefield specializes in this. They have everything they need. You shouldn't be allowed to go near it."

"I'm not. My staff will do all the work. They'll remain objective."

She doubted that. They might provide Stefan with unbiased results, but the company could spin the reports anyway he wanted them to when it came down to releasing the findings to the investigators.

"Your captain and the investigating officer will oversee it. We've done this before. They often need us to handle the overflow or high-priority cases."

"Is that so?" First she'd heard of it. "It's your son. How can they overlook the conflict of interest in this? Doctors can't do surgery on their own relatives. This is the same thing."

"I'm not working on it directly. The reports will automatically go to the investigators. I'll receive a copy. Do you want to know the results or not? I'm doing this for you too. You'd never learn the results if I didn't have the autopsies conducted here."

His suggestion was illegal. She had no right to those results. Uneasy, she said, "Was this your idea?"

"Of course. I haggled for it. As soon as the cops called to inform me they had your brother's body, I insisted they bring it, and the grendels' bodies, here."

The information didn't reassure her, but at least this way she'd learn whatever came out of the autopsies—as long as Stefan told the truth. "Okay. Yes, I want to know the results. You'll send them to me?"

"As soon as I get them."

"Will you plan the funeral with me?"

"I have staff who can put together something nice for him. We won't have to do anything."

He probably thinks he's doing me a favour taking this off my hands. "No, Dad. I want to do this."

"Why? Don't be silly. I'll have my assistant take care of the legwork and send you options to approve."

"You don't get it, do you?" she asked. "We never got to bury Mom. No one ever recovered her body." Agony seeped through her words. "When Jeff's body is released, I'll plan his funeral. Select an urn. Find a caterer and buy flowers and do whatever the hell else needs to be done to lay him to rest. It'll be personal. Your assistant barely knows him, and your company threw him in jail." She added that last as a stab at him for not helping Jeff in his hour of need—any hour of need, not just today.

"He broke the law and trespassed on private property. He vandalized the gate. Are you forgetting he brought that on himself?"

"No, but you could have prevented this." A sob caught in her throat. "You could've supported him. Helped him work through his confusion and worry. You know: been a dad?"

"Enough of this. You're grief-stricken. Sounds as if you need someone yourself."

For a moment, she thought he might reach out to her the

way a father should. The moment didn't last long.

"Why don't you call a friend, okay? I've got to go. This stuff with your brother has wreaked havoc with my schedule. Tell you what. When they release his body, send whatever you want done to my assistant. He'll make sure it's implemented. Okay?"

"Fine. Whatever. I'll be in touch. Goodbye, Dad." She disconnected the call.

CHAPTER 12

Silence hung heavy over the room. No one wanted to be the first to shatter it. Rachel regretted allowing Hound Dog and Peter to listen to the call. They had a clear picture of the relationship she had with her father. Peter had already had an inkling, perhaps, based on her father's reaction to their arrival at his home twelve years before, but that was a snapshot taken long ago. Peter could've assumed it was no longer valid and the product of stress and horror from the sudden emergence of the grendels.

Not that her father had been nasty to Peter—on the contrary—he'd thanked the young man profusely for rescuing his children from deadly predators. But Peter had likely read between the lines when neither child had displayed overwhelming affection for Stefan. Rachel and Jeff had clung to one another, had clasped Peter's hands. To their father, they'd shown relief at finding him alive and hope, but not trust, he'd make everything better.

"What's your take?" She looked from one man to the other. Her gaze settled on Peter.

She studied him, gauging his reaction. As the conversation with Stefan had wrapped up, Peter's scowl had deepened, and he looked pissed beyond words.

"I don't like what he implied about me."

"Clearly."

"Jeff was so young …" Peter pressed his palms to his face for a moment. When he removed them, his eyelashes were damp.

"Peter," Rachel began, "what happened to you? I know you posted some things on social media, but you've never said how you went from majoring in business to investigative journalism."

He leaned back in his seat and tilted his head, resting it atop the backrest. When he spoke, he directed his words at the ceiling.

"My girlfriend. The grendels got her. At least, I assume so. It was the long weekend—the Victoria Day weekend—when they appeared."

"That May two-four weekend seems to be when they first appeared anywhere," Hound Dog commented.

Rachel remained silent as her ordeal that same weekend flashed through her mind.

Peter kept his gaze on the ceiling and continued his story. "She disappeared. I had to work that weekend. Holiday pay paid double-time-and-a-half. I needed the money." His eyes squeezed closed, but no tears slipped out though his hands balled into fists. "I needed the money, so I didn't go camping with her."

A chill raced up Rachel's spine. She'd seen tributes to Peter's former girlfriend on his page and assumed the young woman was a victim of the grendels, but hearing him tell the story made it real.

"No one who went camping returned after that weekend," Peter said.

"Where did they camp?" Rachel asked.

"Near Algonquin. Not in the park itself but on someone's privately owned land on a river. They planned to canoe and hike." He heaved a sigh and sat up straight, aiming his gaze into a spot somewhere on the wall between Rachel and Hound Dog. "I searched for her. Tried to, anyway. No one was permitted to go into the woods when the news of the grendels spread—not even cops."

Rachel remembered that time well. As a thirteen-year-old child, she hadn't understood everything that went on, but she knew from experience why entering the woods had become dangerous. She was happy the government made it illegal to everyone except those in the military. Since no one knew anything about the creatures they fought, even military personnel who went after them sustained high casualties.

Shortly after that, the protectors formed. After six months in boot camp, protectors could go into the forests in teams and hunt the grendels with fewer human lives lost.

Peter continued his story. "Business and making money lost all meaning for me. I lost my drive for it. The first civilians they allowed to enter the forests were journalists. I wanted in—not just to find out what had happened to Sylvia but to dig into how this happened in the first place. Where did the grendels come from? Why did they suddenly appear throughout the forests in first Ontario and then everywhere else?"

"What did you find?" Rachel hadn't followed the news and studies about the grendels. She hadn't cared where they came from. All that had mattered to her was wiping them out.

"Nothing about their origins, which is why I'm here. I found traces of my girlfriend's camp. Where she died." His voice choked, and this time, tears leaked from his eyes.

Rachel's breathing shallowed and her eyes welled up. A glance at Hound Dog showed him staring intently at the floor, his expression neutral. His face had gone pale, and his palms braced against his thighs. As she watched him, he bit his lip but released it when he raised his eyes and discovered her watching.

"I found their belongings. Most of them were scattered or gone, but a few items remained. I went in with a team of protectors." Peter turned his gaze to Rachel. "You weren't a protector yet. I think you were a cop then. This happened a year after I became a journalist. I hired a team to take me into the woods where Sylvia's group had camped."

"Couldn't you track her phone?"

"I tried, but it didn't work. It was probably destroyed in the attack or by the elements."

"Are you sure it's their gear you found?" she asked.

"I found her journal." He scrubbed his face with his palms. "She wrote that they'd barely arrived at their camp when one of their party disappeared collecting firewood. That's the last entry she made. I guess, after that, they fought for their lives. And lost."

Peter's final words lingered in the space between them. They'd all lost loved ones in those first horrifying months after the grendels appeared. Every person Rachel had met since then had lost someone. Hound Dog, too, had lost loved ones.

"Have you ever returned to Storm Lake?" Rachel asked. In all her forays with the protector teams, she'd never gone back there. Her father had paid to have the cottage maintained, sending in protectors to guard the maintenance people the two times per year he sent them out. Rachel had never been part of those teams. She never wanted to return to the place where her mother and her beloved pet dog had died.

"I did. Once. To see what was left of it," Peter replied.

"What happened?"

"All the buildings I came across were abandoned, falling into disrepair. No one lives there anymore, which isn't surprising. The small towns in the area have electric fences around them. They've cleared the trees away from them. You remember Ridley? The town closest to Storm Lake Marina?"

When she nodded, he said, "It's gone. Wiped out."

"The police station?"

"All of it. We're lucky we didn't stay. If anyone survived the attack, they left. The houses, the stores, the town are all abandoned."

"Why do you want to return?" Hound Dog asked, frowning. "If nothing's there, what do you hope to accomplish? Sounds like a suicide mission." He glared at Peter. "You want to drag Rachel out there for what?"

"Not Rachel. A team. With Rachel."

"That's not what she told me."

Peter shifted his body so he faced her directly. "What exactly did you tell him?"

"We're going to Storm Lake. You and me."

"Not alone, Rachel. I trust you, but we can't go alone."

"You want to explore the area—see what we can find about where the grendels appeared and how. We don't need a huge team. It's not a hunt."

"It'll turn into a hunt if you stumble across a nest. They'll come after you," Hound Dog insisted.

"Other teams have gone in. They've cleared nests from the surrounding forests. A team went through last month. My father sends teams in at least twice a year."

"How long does it take them to repopulate once you've cleared them? The trees weren't cut down," Peter said.

"A couple months at least," Rachel replied.

"Why the reluctance to call the rest of the team in on it, Frostbite?" Hound Dog gave her no chance to respond but turned to Peter. "You have the funds for a whole team? They don't come cheap."

"He doesn't have to pay me. I want to do this for my sake. For Jeff's sake," Rachel said.

"I want to hire you, Rachel, and your team. I have money."

"We'll go together," Hound Dog said. "Or not at all."

She closed her eyes, and memories of the past twelve years flashed through her mind. Her mother's remains were out there somewhere—probably in the lake since she'd been killed in a rowboat. They could visit the cottage, stay there. Her father had paid to put a metal roof on it, making it impenetrable to grendel invasion.

What would this do to her plans for Jeff's funeral? She'd have to work around it. If she knew when they'd release his body, she could plan it for when they returned. They'd be gone at least three days, she estimated. That might give them enough time to see what there was to see.

Rachel opened her eyes. "Okay. But it's my party. You follow my orders. Dog, you contact Foot-Long and Code Master. The weather's not getting any warmer. We'll leave the day after tomorrow."

CHAPTER 13

The three left Jeff's house, Rachel locking it up securely behind them. Hound Dog dropped Rachel and Peter at Rachel's place. Hound Dog pulled up on the road in front of the house and waited while Peter went to visitors' parking to move his Mercedes into the driveway for the night. She got the impression her teammate was stalling and hesitated to leave her alone with the journalist.

She stepped from the vehicle and slammed the door. When Hound Dog rolled down the driver's window and waved her over, she obeyed but said, "I trust him. You can quit hovering."

"Yeah, no problem. I just want to verify a few details," he replied. "To tell the guys," he added hurriedly.

"Like what?"

The grin he flashed her looked sheepish. "Okay, fine. I want to make sure you know you can call me if he gets out of line."

She laughed, making him scowl.

"I'm not laughing at you. Relax."

"You're not laughing with me. I'm not laughing."

"He'll sleep in my guest room. I'll be up and out early in the morning. I have calls to make and errands to run to set things in motion for Jeff's funeral."

"Anything I can do to help?"

"No, thanks. My dad offered to have his assistant do the grunt work, and under the circumstances, I'll let him. I want to make all the decisions, though." She sighed. A great deal of work and stress loomed over her.

"Did Jeff have a girlfriend?"

"Kind of." At the reminder she hadn't contacted Isabelle Marie to tell her they'd found Jeff, Rachel's shoulders slumped. "Oh, God, Jack, she'll be devastated. I'll call her when I get inside."

"Sorry for your loss, Rachel."

She stared at him, puzzled.

"I don't think I said it before, but I am very sorry. Your brother and I never met, but you've talked about him often." He reached out and raised her chin with a finger so their eyes met. "You're tough, boss. It'll be all right." He dropped his hand, resting his arm along the ledge of the open window.

She grinned, unable to stop herself. "Who are you and what have you done with Hound Dog?"

"Yup. Just don't hesitate to call me. Listen"—he leaned out the window, and at first, she thought he wanted to kiss her—"whoever killed Jeff might target you next. This might've had nothing to do with his research and everything to do with your father. Right?"

She nodded. "Don't worry. No one will get the jump on me. I don't care what it has to do with. I protect myself."

"Stay on your toes." He stared in the direction of the driveway where Peter exited his parked Mercedes. "Keep an eye on the civilian, too. He appears; Jeff dies. The two may be connected."

She scowled and opened her mouth to vent her anger, but Hound Dog cut her off.

"Relax. I'm not accusing Peter of anything. I'm saying perhaps he brought the danger with him. What he's investigating? Some might not want that information to get out. So, yeah."

She hadn't considered that angle. "All the more reason not

to drag Coder and Foot-Long into this."

"We have to. For safety. They're tough too, and we'll fill them in on the risks. They can decide if they want to participate."

Peter arrived and stood beside Rachel.

Hound Dog said, "Gotta split. Stay paranoid." He wagged his chin at Peter and then turned to Rachel. "All good?"

"Five by five, Dog."

"All right, then." He rolled up his window and drove away.

When he disappeared, Rachel turned to Peter. He had a duffel bag slung over his shoulder, and it looked stuffed.

"You have everything you need for tonight?" She grinned. "Or for the entire excursion?"

"Ha-ha. I got stuff I don't want to leave in the car too long."

"Right. Let's go in. I'll show you the guest room."

***

Rachel ushered Peter into the house and showed him the spare room. He dropped his duffel bag on the floor and followed her back downstairs to the living room. When they realized neither had eaten dinner, they ordered a pizza. Rachel grabbed two beers from the fridge, and they sat in the living room to wait for the food.

"Hound Dog doesn't trust me," Peter said, accepting the bottle of beer Rachel held out to him.

"He'll be fine. He's being cautious."

"And a knight in shining armour?"

"Don't be ridiculous." She chuckled. "He's one of those guys who doesn't understand how to deal with women in the workplace." She paused and reconsidered. "Come to think of it, he might have improved on that front these last two years. He was kind of a dick when I met him—pulled a stupid prank on me."

"I bet you've taught him appropriate behaviour." Peter

smiled at her with obvious affection. "You've always been a strong person, Rachel. You're a leader, but you lead with finesse."

Rachel laughed, recalling the fire ants. "Not always."

His face sobered and he tilted his chin at the gun still strapped to her waist. "You having second thoughts about me too, or are you expecting an invasion?"

"Someone murdered Jeff. I don't know what it related to, but Dog reminded me it might have something to do with either our family or your mission rather than his work. I'm not letting my guard down until I figure it out." She leaned back in the recliner, pulling the lever to pop out the footrest. "Tell me about your investigation. This might be a good time to figure out if what happened relates to that."

"You think someone killed Jeff because of me?" His eyes widened and horror laced his voice. "Who'd do that? Why?"

"I don't know. What've you done and who else knows about it?"

"My editor at the newspaper knows. I've investigated grendel-related deaths in the past, have written features on protectors and hunting grendels ..."

"What's different about this story?"

"It'll be more in-depth. I'll dig into the origins of the creatures."

"Who have you interviewed for it?"

"A few scientists." He took a swig of his beer and gazed off into space. "Two from the university. I talked to a guy from your dad's company, but he wasn't too forthcoming, if you know what I mean."

"Yeah. They play it close to the vest. Proprietary research, Dad calls it. They sign confidentiality agreements. Since it's a privately owned corporation, they can keep things from the public and call it a matter of national security or trade secrets."

"The university lab could use the national security excuse, too, but they don't. At least, they haven't so far."

The doorbell chimed then, and Rachel stood. Peter

jumped up to stop her, reaching into his pocket for his wallet. "I'll get it. I owe you."

"Okay," she said, "but wait for me to verify it's the pizza guy." She strode to the door, gun drawn, and peeked through the peephole. She glimpsed the orange cap and orange jacket all the delivery guys from this place wore.

"It's fine." She waved Peter over and stepped away from the doorway so he could open the door. He took the boxed pizza and bag of wings from the young man and handed them to Rachel, who holstered her gun and accepted them.

When Peter had paid for the meal and they'd served themselves, they sat in the living room again with a second beer.

"A little dramatic, don't you think?" Peter said.

She threw him a puzzled glance, and he said, "The gun."

She shrugged. "Just being careful."

"Should we check the food for tampering?"

"Very funny. I know the guy. He's my regular, so I'm sure the food's fine, but you make a good point. We'll have to be more careful."

"You can't be serious."

"No. Yes. I don't know. This is new territory for me. Someone wanted my brother dead. Until I know why ..."

"Do you have an alarm system on your house?"

"Yes."

"You'll arm it when we go to bed?"

"Yes. Don't worry. That's a precaution I've always taken."

"I notice your brother didn't."

She tilted her head, remembering. "Yeah, we had no problems going into his house." After a pause, she said, "His shower stall was dry."

"What's that mean?"

"He'd told me he wanted to go home to shower and change. The shower was dry. He never used it."

She set her plate aside, stood, and walked over to sit next to Peter. "I want you to look at something."

"What?"

She took out her cell phone and found the pictures she'd taken in the forest. Before handing the phone to Peter, she said, "Are you all right to look at pictures of Jeff's body? It's not pleasant. His throat was ripped open and a chunk taken from his thigh, but I need you to tell me if he's wearing the same clothes he had on when you saw him last."

Her friend puffed out his cheeks and then released the breath in an audible huff. "Show me."

She handed him the phone, and he swiped through four photos showing Jeff's body in situ on the ground in the woods. He backtracked, swiping the photos in reverse and peering closely at the screen. Before she could take her phone from him, he swiped again, revealing a photo of the dead girl.

His face paled and he cursed.

"What?" Rachel asked, her stomach dropping.

"She's a friend of Jeff's."

"How do you know?"

"Check his social media profiles. I friended her because she's close to him and I wanted to interview her. She works at the university lab with him."

"What's her name?" She knew, but she had to hear him say it.

"Isabelle Marie Hodgkin."

"Oh, God, Peter, what the hell is going on here?" And whom should she tell about it? No one yet. The police would have identified Isabelle Marie by now, and they'd tie her death to Jeff's. Then they'd investigate both deaths as suspicious. All she had to do was wait for them to solve it.

"I don't know. Can I see the pictures with the grendels?"

She considered a moment. He was here to investigate grendels, but an open investigation was associated with these photos. She shouldn't show him, but then, he never should've seen the photo of the dead woman either.

For now, she'd keep the other photos to herself. The glimpse of Isabelle Marie's body had been an accident, fortuitous though it had been. If she showed him the grendel photos, she'd be consciously going against protocol—and revealing the photos to a journalist, no less.

"I'm sorry. I can't show you anything more. I only allowed you to see the photos of Jeff because you saw him before he died. So, was he wearing the clothes he had on when you left him after you bailed him out?"

"Yes. If he went home, he didn't change, and I guess based on what you found at the house, he didn't shower. You think he didn't go home?"

"Correct. Whatever happened, happened before he had the chance. What was he doing when you left him?"

"Talking on his phone, leaving a voicemail message. For Isabelle Marie."

"Then he didn't know she was already dead." Whoever had wanted Jeff dead had gone after his friend first, but why? What had the couple known that someone didn't want revealed, and was Peter somehow connected?

Rachel felt the reassuring touch of the gun holstered at her waist. She planned to keep it on her at all times even if she had to sleep with it.

CHAPTER 14

As she'd told Hound Dog she would, Rachel rose early the next morning after an uneventful night. She put coffee on and, after her morning run, started packing for the pending foray into the forests around Storm Lake. A few hours later, she was showered and dressed, and most of her gear was packed. Peter was awake by then, and they had breakfast together.

Hound Dog hadn't called, but he'd texted her a few times with questions and to let her know their other two teammates were on board. They planned to meet early the next morning at Rachel's place and head out in her SUV together, leaving Peter's car in her garage and the beater Code Master drove in her driveway.

As lunchtime drew near, the mail carrier's truck arrived at the community mailbox down the street. After it left, Rachel walked outside to get the mail since she hadn't picked it up the day before. She unlocked her mail compartment and peered inside. A thick, yellow envelope sat amidst the usual assortment of bills and flyers. She piled the rest of the mail together and checked the return address on the mysterious envelope. There wasn't one.

Curious, she stacked it on top of her other mail and locked the compartment. Hurrying back to her house, she rushed inside and dropped all the mail except the mystery envelope on her kitchen table. She pulled a jackknife from her pants' pocket and sliced open the envelope.

Inside, it contained a letter and a memory stick. She checked the postmark on the envelope. The stamp displayed the previous day's date. Rachel opened the letter and scanned to the bottom where she found Jeff's signature.

"Oh, my God."

Jeff had sent her what? Information? Data? She stuck the memory stick in her pocket so she wouldn't misplace it and read the letter. It was dated two months before:

Dear Rachel,

If you're reading this, something has happened to me. Yeah, sorry, it's one of those letters. I hate to involve you, but I don't know who else to trust. Not Dad, that's for sure. He's the one we need to keep all this from. Don't go to him for anything. We can't trust him.

Rachel paused her reading and looked up as Peter entered the room.

"Hey, what's going on?" he asked. "You look upset."

"I'll tell you in a minute."

He strolled to the coffeemaker. "I'm making another pot. You want?"

She shook her head. As he went to the cupboard to get the package of coffee, she moved to her home office and shut and locked the door. She sat at her desk and resumed reading.

I've been experimenting on grendels. I know that's not news to you because that's basically my job, but I mean I'm doing my own experiments. In secret. Rachel, these creatures didn't evolve here naturally.

No shit, she thought. She continued reading.

Again, I suppose that's not news to you, but I have proof. I've isolated and examined their DNA. It's fascinating. They're part monkey, part caterpillar, part hyena, part fucking human. Did you know they start out as larvae? Unbelievable, I know.

I can't explain everything in this letter. That's what the memory stick is for. Read through the reports on it. Take it to a scientist you trust if you have questions. I wish I could be there to help you, but obviously something has happened to me or you wouldn't be reading this.

A friend has this on hand and, if he did his job, he mailed it to you as soon as he knew I was gone.

Her throat constricted, and she gave a choked moan. He'd expected something like this. Her brother had feared for his life and hadn't told her about the danger. A spasm of anger made her want to crush the letter in her hand and throw it against the wall. She stifled the urge. No time for what-ifs. She'd gone through all those scenarios already. It hadn't helped her yesterday, and it wouldn't help her today. The anger she felt now was grief, she told herself. She wanted Jeff back and he'd never return.

She needed to focus on what he wanted her to do with the information he'd sent her. She hoped she could fulfil whatever mission he had in mind for her.

Peter contacted me for an interview. As of this writing, I haven't discussed anything with him. I'm waiting to get everything collated. He'll want to read these reports. He's wanted to investigate the origins of the grendels for a long time. This information should help him.

I'm sorry if this causes you trouble. I never meant to harm anyone. All I've ever wanted is to learn the truth, especially where it concerned our father and his company. He's a sociopath. I'm convinced of that. He's responsible for Mom's death. He and his company created these monsters. They mutated genes and these things developed from them. I'm disgusted by what he's done.

Why would he do this? Good question. Follow the money. Follow it to military and defence contracts. Imagine if the grendels could be controlled? Weaponized? What could they use them for? Their imaginations are the only limit and Dad makes money from it— ultimately, they're his pets. His company is working on a solution he can sell to people to protect them from the monsters he created.

Think that one through: he creates monsters and then develops a product people must buy from him to keep them at bay. I suspect he's got a repellent in the works, but I can't prove it. The grendels are a huge cash cow for Dad and his company—as long as people don't know he created them in the first place.

Follow the money. Follow where our family's money originates. The cottage? We all know Mom's family owned it. She inherited it when Grams and Gramps passed away. Twenty years ago, Dad started his business and focused on genetic research.

Don't know how much family history you know, but I dug into it despite Dad. He never told us much, and now I know why. Do you know our family name isn't originally Needham? It's Neumann, and our family comes from Germany. That's fine, as far as it goes, but I found out our ancestors rose up through the Nazi ranks and some of them became scientists doing genetic research for Hitler.

A sick sensation formed in Rachel's gut, and her mouth went dry. *That's impossible. Please, be impossible.*

She took a deep breath and continued reading.

Everything I found, all my sources, are documented in the files on the memory stick. Don't lose it. Make a copy and put it in a safe place. Do what I've done, and send it to someone you trust in case something happens to you. If Dad discovers you know all this, you'll end up as dead as I probably am.

If we haven't talked about this before, I'm sorry you had to find out this way. Help Peter investigate. Give him a copy of the files on the memory stick. People need to know what really happened. Dad made his money on the corpses of our friends and relatives. His company, the company he started with government and private funding, births evil. Trust no one at Dad's company. They're all in it.

Trust no one outside the company either. Dad has friends in high places, and I don't know which ones are in on his scheme. Politicians, for sure, from all levels of government. Our greatest hope is a journalist. Help Peter expose this. I've failed, so it's up to you.

I love you, sis. I hope we have many years together after I expose our father and his unethical, immoral company. But I don't count on it so this letter and this memory stick are my insurance. Take care, and go get 'em, Rache.

Love, Jeffy

The use of the diminutive burst the dam that had built inside her as she'd read. She let the tears flow unrestrained. Sobs wracked her body, and she gulped in air, unable to control herself. From a box on the desk, she grabbed a tissue and held it to her face. The sobs didn't let up until she heard pounding on the door and Peter's voice on the other side of it.

"Rachel? You all right? Let me in. Let me help you. Please."

"I'm fine," she cried out between gasps.

"You're not. I hear you crying. Did something else happen? You're worrying me."

She rose from her chair, the letter fluttering to the ground, stumbled to the door, and opened it. Peter stepped into the room and immediately took her in his arms. She buried her face in his shoulder.

"Shh. It's okay. Tell me what happened. Is it Jeff?"

Her breath hitched at the mention of her brother, and the anguished sobs renewed full force.

"What's that on the floor?" Peter asked. "What happened? Is it about Jeff?"

Her face still pressed into his shoulder, she nodded.

"May I read it?"

Again, she nodded, this time pulling away from him. Peter rested his hands on her shoulders, comforting her with his touch.

"Read it so I don't have to tell you what's in it. He wanted you to read it."

Gently, Peter walked her to the desk and eased her into the chair. He snatched the letter off the floor, slid a hip onto the edge of the desk, and read.

CHAPTER 15

By the time Peter finished reading Jeff's letter, Rachel had pulled herself together. Her sobs had ceased, and she'd used up another tissue drying her eyes and blowing her nose. Excusing herself, she went to the powder room off the front foyer to rinse her face. She returned to the office, feeling strangely calm.

Peter sat in the chair, the letter on the desk beside him, his head angled down as he stared at the floor.

"What do you think," Rachel asked.

He shook his head. "I'm still processing it. You believe it's true? What he says about your father?"

"In your investigations into the grendels, did you ever find anything to connect them to my dad's company?"

"No, but it's not as if they'd leave a tag on them."

"We won't know more until we read Jeff's files. Maybe we don't have to go to Storm Lake after all," she said, her voice hopeful. If Jeff had proof of what he claimed, Peter could use it to write his story. They wouldn't have to risk their lives and the lives of her team.

"Perhaps. But we need to find evidence. A gut feeling, sure, but that's where it all started. That little girl was the first human to fall victim to the grendels. After that, people fell like dominoes. The creatures got bigger, bolder. It was an invasion."

"I remember." Her heart throbbed as the memories flooded back. Spike. Mom. The little girl next door. The people at the marina. "Oh, God, so many people. They died so horribly."

She walked to the desk and leaned on it, facing Peter. "We need to fire up the computer and view these files."

He rose and waved her into the chair. "Do it."

***

Most of the reports were scientific and gibberish to Rachel and Peter. While Rachel understood more than Peter did, she couldn't draw any conclusions from what she found. Should they take this to the authorities or release it to the public in a news report? No. They'd need to do more research to follow through on either option. At the very least, they'd need to find someone to explain to them what they viewed.

They discovered a map of North America, shaded to show the spread of the grendels from initial discovery to major infestation. This made it obvious the area in and around Rachel's cottage was ground zero for the creatures.

"Storm Lake again. It always goes back to Storm Lake. Something's here, but we just don't see it," she said. "Jeff died over this."

"Probably."

"I'll make two more copies. You take one."

"Who will you trust with the other?" Before she could respond, he said, "Not Hound Dog."

When she opened her mouth to protest—that was exactly who she planned to give it to—he said, "He's too close to you. He's part of your team. Since you're often together, if something happens to you, something will likely happen to him. I'm going with the odds. Nothing personal to Hound Dog."

Rachel saw the logic in that.

"I'll mail it to my lawyer." She figured she could drop it

off today. "I'll make sure I'm not followed." The paranoia building inside her unnerved her. Had Jeff's life been like this for the last who knew how long? "God, what a mess. How did it get to this? My dad? Could he be responsible for these monsters?" Her eyes pleaded with him. "Who could be that stupid?"

"Money's always the motive when it comes to shady experiments. Or power. How does that fit?"

"I intend to find out. Jeff said not to tell my father, but he didn't say I shouldn't question him."

"Awfully risky, don't you think?"

"He's my father."

"Yes, and it's possible he murdered your brother—or had him murdered."

"My brother made a lot of mistakes. He was too vocal about ferreting out the people responsible for all this terror we've had to live with." She stopped speaking and her eyes grew wide. "Terror."

"What?" Peter asked.

"Would these creatures be used as weapons?"

"Too unpredictable and uncontrollable. Doesn't seem likely," he replied.

"Sure, the prototypes are. These might be the beta tests." She stood straight. "I'm paying my old man a visit."

When an expression of panic flickered across Peter's face and he leaned toward her in his chair, she said, "Relax. I won't ask him any direct questions. I'll scope the place out and discuss Jeff's funeral with him."

"Don't tell him we plan to visit Storm Lake."

"No, of course not, but I'll try to learn how it connects."

He threw her a dubious look but didn't press the point. Together, they left the office.

***

Stefan Needham's office was housed in the upper floor of the huge four-story building that made up his company's head offices and laboratories. Located on the outskirts of the city of Peterborough, Ontario, electrified fencing topped with barbed wire surrounded it. When Rachel pulled up to the front gate in her SUV, she noted the repairs had been done. The gates, the guardhouse, all of it looked as if nothing had happened.

As if Jeff were never here. As if her father wanted to erase her brother's existence—but that was ridiculous. Jeff's letter had made her irate and suspicious. She had to investigate it herself and make an informed decision. While she could believe her father's pursuit of money and power might cause him to hurt even those he loved, she doubted he'd kill them over it. He was their father. Of course they'd repaired the gate and the guard station. Anyone would. She shook off the fury so she wouldn't be tempted to do or say something stupid.

At the guard station, she pulled over and showed her driver's license for ID, keeping her protector badge in her jacket pocket. On this visit, she came as her father's daughter not as a protector.

The guard waved her through, providing her with a parking pass and visitor's badge. The badge had her name on it in gold lettering on a black background, identifying her as a VIP guest. This meant she could walk around on her own in the office hallways, but she wouldn't be permitted in the lab facilities without an escort who had clearance.

Familiar with the layout even though she hadn't visited in several years, she made her way to the corner office on the fourth floor. The plaque on the wall to the right of the office door read "Stefan Needham, CEO." The door stood propped open, allowing visitors to see the assistant at his desk in the reception area.

Rachel stepped through the threshold and greeted the young man who'd been her father's right hand for the last five years.

"Hi, Avery, how are you?"

"Fine, thank you, Miss Needham. I'm very sorry for your loss." His deep voice soothed, like the low rumble of percolating coffee. His dark brown skin was smooth and clear, his suit always perfectly tailored and impeccable. She'd always thought he could have been a male model. He carried himself with a grace she could never match if she practised for a decade.

"Thank you." She wondered if he was part of the conspiracy—if a conspiracy existed.

Avery had a family. Would he do anything Stefan Needham ordered even if it compromised his ethics as long as he was paid well for it? As an assistant, he'd see much of Stefan's business, be aware of his appointments. It might help her to ask him a few questions.

Rachel tilted her head at her father's closed office door. "He's in there?"

"Yes," Avery glanced at the multi-line phone. "On the phone. I'll watch for him to hang up and then announce you're here. Please, have a seat. May I get you a cup of coffee or tea?"

"Thank you. Coffee would be nice. Milk and sugar." She walked to the elegant couch across from the reception desk and sat down. Magazines fanned out on the coffee table before her, and as a distraction, she picked one up without looking at it. Avery left the desk and strode across the room to make her coffee.

She scanned the room, futilely searching for anything out of place. What could be in the reception area that would have bearing on Jeff's death?

Avery set the cup and saucer on the coffee table and gave Rachel a small bow. "Anything else you need, let me know."

"Thanks." She wondered what else she might need—other than to question him about Jeff. If she had time to kill, she should make use of it. She set the magazine down.

"Were you here when Jeff and his group protested outside this week?"

"Yes. I'm here all day every day unless I have an errand to run."

"Did you see what happened?"

"No. The front gate isn't visible from my windows." As if to prove his point, he glanced toward the windows and then turned back to his computer.

"You must have heard about it."

"Afterward, yes."

This was excruciating. Avery refused to elaborate on anything.

"Dad must've been furious with Jeff."

"I imagine so."

Rachel picked up the coffee cup and took a sip. It was rich and delicious. The aroma wafted up from the cup, and she almost moaned with pleasure. Avery always served excellent coffee here. Nothing but the best for her daddy.

His life was perfection. At least, on the outside. She supposed it had been perfection even on the inside, once, from his perspective. When Mom was alive. A loving wife. Two well-behaved children. The family had been his pride and joy. An emotional distance developed between them—he wasn't demonstrative or affectionate—but she'd always believed he was fair and that, in his own way, he loved them.

She'd also believed she loved him too. Mom had loved him. She'd depended on him. They'd each had their roles. Dad provided; Mom nurtured. While Rachel didn't understand the desire for traditional roles, she understood her mother had enjoyed being a stay-at-home mother.

They had money—lots of it, so Dad had wanted Mom to stay home and focus on raising the children. To be honest, they'd had nannies and housekeepers so Mom could also do the socialite thing with her other homemaker friends. The moms—yummy mummies, some called them, since they always dressed to kill even when taking their kiddies on a playdate—would shop, play tennis, and organize charity events and fundraisers for whatever causes they involved themselves in to keep busy and feel valued.

Rachel's mom had been involved in her children's schooling and active in the parents' association. The perfect mother. As far as Rachel knew, her mother had been the perfect wife, too.

She'd entertained Stefan's frequent business guests, planned parties and teas and dinners where million-dollar deals were made. Too bad Rachel hadn't had the wits to eavesdrop on these affairs, but then, she had no idea the future held such danger and intrigue.

"Rachel." Her father appeared at his office door, his black bangs drooping over his smooth forehead. She'd never noticed before how much he resembled Elvis Presley. He even had that quirky mouth. When she'd brought friends home as a teen, they'd swooned over him. A few of them had flirted blatantly with him.

It occurred to her she hadn't asked Stefan how Marne, his wife of two years, had taken Jeff's death. Rachel found it easy to forget Marne even existed, but dismissing the woman so easily wasn't fair. She'd never done anything hurtful or mean to the two kids.

Both Rachel and Jeff had moved out by the time their father had started seeing her. They'd met her only twice by the time Dad and Marne announced their engagement, and then Rachel and Jeff had attended the wedding. After that, Marne had been a minor character in Rachel's story. Jeff maintained the same distance from their stepmother.

Absorbed in her musings, she hadn't heard Avery announcing her to her father. Startled from her reveries by the sound of his voice, she said, "Dad."

"Come on in." He waved her in and returned to his desk. Over his shoulder, he said, "Close the door behind you."

Rachel set down the empty coffee cup—somehow, she'd finished the entire cup without remembering she'd done it. What a waste of such orgasmic coffee.

She rose, ready to beard father lion in his posh den.

CHAPTER 16

As ordered, she shut the door behind her. Rachel glanced at the lock and almost turned it but decided against it. Their interaction needed to appear informal—as informal as discussing a dead son and brother could get.

She arrived at the chair in front of his desk in two long strides and sat, her back straight, her feet together and tucked slightly under her chair. Her hands she folded in her lap. She got to business.

"Where's Jeff's body? When will they release him?"

"They already released it. It's at the funeral parlour."

"What?" She jumped to her feet. "Why didn't you tell me? You said you'd keep me in the loop, let me take charge of his funeral."

"Take it easy." Stefan leaned back in his chair, unperturbed. "The lab called and asked where I'd want the body sent. I gave them the name of the place where we held your mother's memorial."

The reminder of her mother's memorial scored a jab to her heart. Since they'd never found her mother's body, not even pieces of it, Rachel lacked emotional closure. Despite witnessing her mother's death, despite seeing the grendel swinging her mother's head by the hair in triumph after the kill, Rachel never felt as if her mother's life had ended. The memorial had brought her a tiny step closer to accepting it, but it hadn't provided the finality she needed.

She dropped back into her seat, calming her body with effort. She'd have called the same place anyway, and her father, not his assistant, had made the decision. That mattered most. She'd let him have this one.

"Okay," she said, "I'm sorry. I want it to be nice for Jeff."

"So do I, honey," he replied.

The kindness in his voice brought to mind the dad who'd spent afternoons teaching her how to skip stones on the lake at the cottage. For a moment, affection for him flooded through her, and she wondered if Jeff hadn't been following the wrong trail. Sure, Needham Scientific Research Facility explored genetic modification. Nothing wrong with that. A growing area of study, genetics provided hope for a better future. Mapping the genome had given them a huge leap forward. Naturally they'd take advantage of it if they had the resources.

And then Stefan glanced at his watch and said, "I'm rather busy, Rachel. Can we speed this along?"

The undercurrent of annoyance in his tone bubbled irritation through her blood. This was his son they discussed—his dead, barely into adulthood son—and that brought to mind how he'd let them go to Storm Lake without him the weekend the grendels appeared. If he'd known what awaited them in the trees, why had he allowed them to go there? Had he wanted his family dead? Or had he miscalculated? After all, he'd intended to join them the next day.

Unable yet again to reveal everything on her mind, she said instead, "Did you hear from Jeff after I called to tell you he was missing?"

"No. He never called me. We weren't on the best terms when he died."

"You could've reached out to him before all this happened."

"I tried. He refused to listen. Don't you think I wanted

him working in our lab? He was brilliant. We could have used his big brain on our side."

Interesting way to phrase it. Were there sides here? What were they?

"All you had to do was talk to him. He wanted to do what's right."

Stefan shook his head. "He bought into the conspiracy theories floating around about the company. I don't know why, but he believed we created the grendels."

"No truth to any of that?" she poked.

He chuckled. "None whatsoever. We do research. Provide intel on them to you protectors so you can enter the forests better equipped to fight them. We provide a necessary service. Beneficial research."

"What else do you do with the information?"

"What do you mean?"

"Do you experiment with it?"

"Of course. That's what labs do. We want to use this knowledge to create a better world through genetic engineering."

She tried a different avenue. "Are the grendels they brought in with Jeff's body still here?"

"Yes."

"May I see them?"

"We're working on them. It's not a good time."

"When will be a good time?"

"When my examiner and the examiner from the university are done with them."

No good. She'd be in the woods by then. "I'd like to see the results, then."

"I'm sorry, but those findings are classified." He paused, studying her. "What's your interest in this?"

"Are you serious? My brother is my interest in this." And the mysterious state of his body and the two grendels they'd found lounging against a tree. But intuition prevented her from vocalizing that. Perhaps he didn't have all the details on the state in which they'd found the creatures and Jeff; in which case, he wouldn't hear it from her.

She stayed quiet, watching his face as she considered the implications of what he'd said. It sounded logical. She just didn't accept that he did what he did for the good of humanity. Her dad wasn't a philanthropist. Whenever he got involved in charity work, it was strategically done: for PR, for tax breaks, for personal benefit.

"Have you been up to the cottage at all, Dad? You know, since it first happened."

He grimaced at her. "Why do you ask?"

She shrugged. "Jeff's death made me think about Mom. I wondered if you ever sent teams in after her."

"Once." He hung his head. "I sent them to where you and Jeff had said you'd seen her die, but they found only the boat. I had them pull it from the water, but we left it there."

"I wish you'd told me."

"Why?"

"I'd have gone along."

"Don't be ridiculous. You were barely fifteen then."

So, he'd waited two years. "What did they find? Anything helpful?"

"What do you mean?"

"About the grendels—where they came from."

"No," he said, quickly. "What's to find? The trees they'd grown in rotted away."

"Did you do any tests on them?"

"They examined them. Took samples." He squinted at her, frowning. "What is all this?"

"I'm curious. All this time and no one knows how they got here? Why they exist? Why they appeared where they did?"

He shrugged and glanced at his watch again.

"I know, Dad, you're busy," she said, a trace of resentment in her voice.

"I'm not trying to rush you out, but I have work to do."

"Yes, of course you do."

"That's not fair. You know I loved your brother."

She also knew he kept referring to Jeff in the past tense. "I still love my brother."

Stefan sighed in exasperation. "Rachel, please. What do we need to review regarding the funeral arrangements?"

She stood. "I guess your part's done. All you'll need to do is show up."

He rose, levelling his gaze at her. "You're upset, grieving. I understand. It's just you and me, kid. We have to stick together."

"Oh? Did you and Marne split up?"

He scowled. "Of course not. I meant our original family." He shook his head. "Take it however you will. Neither of you seemed to want to meet me halfway."

"Meet you halfway? What does that mean?"

"You should be running the business with me. You both should already be climbing the ladder here—Jeff in research, you in the business end."

"Me? Business?" She almost laughed. When his expression remained grim, she said, "You're serious?"

"I tried to interest both of you in what we're doing here. Neither of you wanted to work here—not part-time when you were in high school, not during summer vacations when you were in university. You showed no interest."

"That's not true, Daddy. You tried to force us into specific jobs. I wanted to work in law enforcement. You wouldn't even let me work on the security team here doing the smallest, most menial job. Even though you have your personal teams of protectors, you wouldn't let me join them. You wanted me in accounting. Jeff wanted to work in genetic research on grendels. You tried to place him in microbiology."

"I knew where you'd have best fit."

"No, you didn't. You wanted us where it suited you." To keep an eye on them?

"Which was best for you. I understood what you and the company needed. You were just kids. I had to decide for you. Who do you think I want to leave my business to? You're still named as my successor—Jeff too. Isn't it about time you

92

started acting like the future CEO of this company?"

"Not Marne? Or your investors?" He'd always made the investors a priority.

"Over my flesh and blood? No. I need you here, involved. I intend to live a long time, Rachel, but you need to be groomed for—" He bit off whatever else he wanted to say, snapping his mouth closed. After a second, he said, "Okay, you're angry. Why don't we wrap it up for today? Go arrange your brother's funeral. Let me know if you need help, and I'll get Avery to give you a hand."

"Avery. Sure. Got it," she said, her voice flat, cold.

He let that one slide.

"All right, then, sweetie." A smile lit his face. "Call me anytime, right?"

"Yeah. Thanks." She let him walk her out. As Stefan's door clicked shut behind her, she realized that not once during the time she'd spent with her father had they hugged or kissed.

***

On the way to her car, Rachel detoured to the laboratories. If her father didn't want her to see the bodies, she'd deke around him. Perhaps she could charm her way in. If she had to, she'd use her protector badge. Security doors manned by a guard stopped her before she could enter any part of that section of the building.

"Miss Needham," the guard said. "How may I help you?"

"My father said the grendels they brought in the other day are still here. I'd like to view the bodies."

"I'm sorry, but this section is off-limits to non-personnel."

"Didn't anyone call you to let you know I was coming down here?" she asked in a tone that betrayed utter puzzlement with a hint of frustration. Her heart thudded against her chest, but she'd played it pretty smoothly.

"No, but if you wait a moment, I can confirm it with the front desk."

"Confirm it with Avery—my father's assistant. He should've called down here when I left my dad. Oh, wait," she added as if it'd just occurred to her. "Here's my protector badge. I'm the one who brought the bodies in." She'd brought them in to Protector HQ, but the guard didn't need to know that.

The guard hesitated. Finally, he said, "I'll give Avery a quick call."

Rachel's heart sank, but she didn't give up all hope.

He placed a call to the CEO's office and Avery picked up immediately. Rachel listened to the guard's half of the conversation, plastering a bored expression on her face.

"I have Miss Needham here, Mister Bloom, requesting entrance to the laboratories where they brought the most recently captured grendel bodies. She says she has clearance?" His gaze met Rachel's as he listened to Avery's response. He frowned. "No, she said her father approved it. Said you were to call down?" After another pause, he said, "Yes, I'll hold."

Rachel knew she'd lost then. Avery would check with her father, and he'd tell them not to allow her in. Frustrated, she almost reached for the phone and demanded to speak to her father, but Avery must've returned because the guard said, "Yes, I understand. Thank you, Mister Bloom."

CHAPTER 17

Her father ordered her escorted from the building. He provided no option, refused to speak to her, and Avery hung up the phone after the guard assured him Rachel would leave. She went without struggling, in silence.

What would this do to her relationship with her father? Would he have her watched now? Had he had Jeff under surveillance? If so, then he'd known everything that had happened to Jeff. A ball of anxiety formed in the pit of her stomach. Her father had been concerned about what Jeff was involved in. However, Jeff had never indicated he worried anyone was following him. Perhaps the situation hadn't been that drastic. It's possible their father only knew what he heard from Jeff or from the media.

Somehow, she doubted that. Her father had always been the proactive type. His motto was strike first; strike hard. Had he struck Jeff into silence?

As Rachel drove home, she glanced frequently into the rear-view mirror.

***

The next morning, Rachel and her team left her house at five. Hound Dog drove, Rachel rode shotgun, and the other three squeezed into the back seat of the pickup truck. They had no issue from the sentries when they reached the gates out of the city. Hound Dog showed his protector badge and the woman on duty waved them through. She never even asked them to state their business.

When they'd left Rachel's, darkness still reigned as a crisp and clear early morning ushered them to the highway. Rachel wore a turtleneck under her down jacket. The woods would be chilly, but at least the trees would be shedding their leaves. Places for grendels to hide would be fewer and obvious enough that trained protectors could avoid them or hunt them down.

The creatures would be burrowing in for the long winter ahead. Based on what Rachel had learned over the years, grendels semi-hibernated through winter. They'd leave their nests to forage for food, stalking anything living. If the winter was particularly harsh, many of them would die before the spring thaw.

Yet more always burst from the trees come springtime.

In the intervening years since the grendels had first appeared, those who hunted them had learned to destroy trees that sported burls. Whether the bulge was just a burl or it gestated a grendel became irrelevant. Since they couldn't tell the difference, they'd chop down the tree and burn it.

Not environmentally friendly, and certainly not a solution for the long term, but if they didn't prevent new grendels from birthing, humans wouldn't be around to worry about the environment.

As they drove, Rachel kept her eye on the rear view. No one appeared to tail them, but she remained uneasy. At least the extra copy of the files from Jeff's memory stick would soon be in the lawyer's hands. Rachel had snail-mailed them—no return address on the envelope and with a note instructing the lawyer to store it in a safe deposit box until something happened to Rachel. She'd assured herself as she composed the letter that writing as if something would happen rather than that something might happen served only to highlight the seriousness of the situation. It didn't mean she'd eventually lose the battle.

While she'd been nervous trusting such valuable and dangerous information to snail mail, she worried hand-delivering it would endanger the recipient. If anyone her dad had sent to spy on her saw her acting suspiciously, all involved would be in immediate danger. At least this way, she could conceal mailing the files with a trip to the variety store to pick up milk.

"Our only entrance is from Storm Lake Road?" Hound Dog asked, breaking a silence that had lasted from the time they drove onto Highway 115 until they reached Highway 28 via Television Road—County Road 4 route.

"Correct," Rachel replied. "We have to pass through Ridley—whatever's left of it, anyway." She hadn't been up that way in twelve years. Every mission HQ posted that took a team out Ridley way she'd passed on. Pattenden understood and never pressed her to go. Missions out to Ridley had been few and far between anyway. Storm Lake missions had been rarer still—only one or two search and rescues in the years since the grendels had first appeared.

They had her father to thank for that. He always sent his teams in to clear out the area so he could get maintenance crews to the cottage. Or so he'd told everyone, including Captain Pattenden and HQ.

"Oh, my God," she whispered.

Hound Dog glanced at her. "What's up?"

"None of our teams from HQ ever go to Storm Lake because my dad's company has it covered."

"Yeah?"

"I'm just saying, if he's hiding something, covering up his role in this, it's the perfect smokescreen. He pretty much has his monsters guarding his secrets. We don't even know if he's actually clearing them or letting them proliferate to keep people out."

"A little dramatic, don't you think?" The speaker was Foot-Long.

"I hope so," she said. "Otherwise, we're in for a hairy time."

"No one goes into the woods anymore," he continued. "He'd have no reason to let grendels run loose. The threat of them is enough."

"I hope you're right, but stay alert out there. Don't assume anywhere is safe."

"At least we'll have indoor shelter, right?"

"Right," she said but wondered if they could expect even that much. What if the whole thing was a lie?

Any vehicles they passed on the mostly deserted roads belonged to protectors or the military. Unless someone had an excellent reason to venture beyond populated areas, people stayed within the confines of their towns or cities. Sometimes, people needed to drive from one town or city to another. In those instances, they either rented grendel-resistant vehicles, such as Humvees, or they hired protector escorts.

No one commuted to work in cars anymore. Heli transports or passenger trains carried people back and forth from big cities to outlying towns. Most people worked in the town or city where they lived, telecommuted, or, if they were wealthy or had high-ranking jobs, had protectors to escort or to drive them to work. Rachel had often received such assignments.

Their current route took them past small towns that no longer existed. Hound Dog sailed past decayed homes where grendels had ripped off the roofs to get at the people and pets inside. Rachel and her team occasionally flushed out grendels who'd taken over the ramshackle buildings and made them their nests.

As she stared out the window on the passenger side, she fell into her old habit of pretending to be outside the vehicle, running. She imagined the feeling of freedom running always gave her. In elementary school and high school, she'd joined the track team, loving the adrenaline rush she got from competing. Once, she'd contemplated running in the

Olympics, but that dream had died twelve years ago, replaced by the dream of vengeance against the grendels.

They drove over the bridge at Burleigh Falls. The rapids churned, and the control dam, built to regulate water flow on Lovesick Lake, remained, but nature had taken back the homes, motel, restaurants, stores, and campground that had bordered the road. Trees, weeds, and grasses had taken over. One large maple had toppled onto the inn's roof, smashing whatever the grendels had left intact after their initial frenzy.

Along Highway 28, they passed the now-defunct town of Ridley. As with other towns, the buildings were demolished, the lots they stood on overgrown. Rachel hadn't seen grendel activity along the way, but the creatures typically kept hidden until ready to attack.

They weren't stupid—she'd figured that out when they'd learned how to use tools to tear the roof from the marina store where she and Jeff had hidden twelve years ago. The same store where they'd first met Peter, who'd arrived to do a delivery and instead became saddled with two desperate children. The store would be the first stop on this journey.

Fifteen minutes after they passed Ridley, Hound Dog pulled the truck onto Storm Lake Road. Trees dominated the landscape on either side. The sun had risen, which made it safer even out in the forest, but some trees still had enough leaves on them to provide sufficient cover for lurking grendels.

Hound Dog maintained a speed of forty kilometres an hour, unconcerned he'd encounter oncoming traffic. Code Master had verified no teams headed here—not from HQ and not from the Needham research facility.

Within ten minutes, he pulled the truck into what had been the parking lot of a thriving marina. Rachel stepped from the vehicle into the bright sunshine of a crisp September day to confront her nightmare past.

CHAPTER 18

Birdsong and the rat-a-tat of a woodpecker floated from the forest around the large clearing in which the marina store and the house of the former owners sat. Normal sounds you'd usually hear in the woods. They reassured Rachel. Birds in the trees meant grendels weren't nearby.

"I'll check the store. Foot-Long, you and Code Master take the house."

"Wait a minute—" Hound Dog began as Peter said, "I'm coming with you."

Rachel, holding up a hand palm out, stared down Hound Dog, who still sat behind the wheel of the truck. Peter stayed in the middle seat in the back. The driver's door and left passenger door hung propped open. Foot-Long and Code Master had already vanished into the house, probably eager to escape the pending confrontation.

"Hold up, guys," she said to the two remaining men. "I need someone to remain with the vehicle in case we need to get out of here fast."

"You're leaving me on civilian protection." Hound Dog pressed his lips together. His voice was indignant. "I'm your second."

"I'm not doing this to punish you, Dog. You're my second, and I need Peter protected."

"And you're risking yourself by entering that store alone."

"He's right," Peter said. "I can protect myself. I'm not happy you want to leave me behind, but I can wait in the driver's seat. I've got a gun. I know how to shoot grendels, and I can tell the difference between a grendel and a human, so no accidents, I promise."

She almost laughed with delight at the knowledge they both knew her so well they'd guessed exactly where her logic fell. She grinned at them and relented.

"Okay. Dog, you're with me. Peter, hold the fort. The sun's up and we should be all right, but that can change in a moment if a storm rolls in."

Before she'd finished speaking, Hound Dog had jumped from the truck, rifle slung across his shoulder. Peter hopped out of the back and took his place behind the wheel.

"I'll want to explore the house and the store myself. I need to know what's happened since we were here last," Peter said.

"I understand. We're clearing them before we do any investigating. Don't want any surprises. If either building has a nest in it, we need to eliminate it."

In response, he flashed her a thumbs up.

Rachel took a step toward the store but stopped and turned back to Peter. "Where's your weapon?"

He patted a holster at his side.

"Take it out and have it ready."

He removed a baby Glock, resting it on the dash in front of him. It was smaller than Rachel would've liked, but if he had better aim with a chick gun, she wouldn't comment.

"Close your door," she said. Without waiting for him to do so, she headed in the direction of the store, her partner only steps behind her.

To reach the store, they had to walk down a set of fieldstone steps followed by a series of pressure-treated lumber stairs leading to a cedar porch. Carefully, they picked their way over any cracked and broken pieces up to the store's entrance.

The screen door Rachel remembered from her time here

101

hung askew on one hinge. The inner door remained in the frame, but it yawned open. Mud and leaves covered the porch and the floor inside, and a musty smell permeated the air.

Smashed shelving units and the remnants of the merchandise and packages of food lay scattered across Rachel's path. She picked her way carefully through the mess, her rifle slung across her shoulder, her gun held ready in her hand. Hound Dog moved quietly behind her, his faint inhale and exhale the only sound in the room.

The only footprints she saw belonged to bare feet too large to be human. Slowly, painstakingly, they made their way through the rubble. They opened closet doors, the bathroom door, and stepped through the open door to the back room. All were deserted. All were filthy. Their breaths puffed in the frigid air. Whatever sunlight filtered in through the shattered roof wasn't enough to warm the place.

"Funny how the grendels have five toes, isn't it?" Rachel commented when she confirmed the building was empty.

"I guess. Maybe it's nature's default for creatures that walk upright," Hound Dog answered. His tone held disinterest, as if he'd responded out of politeness and not because he cared about the answer.

Should she tell him about Jeff's discovery that grendels had human DNA? No, she'd spare him that for now.

"Could be," she said. "There's nothing here. Agreed?"

"Yeah. If anyone came here, they're long gone."

She pushed through the debris to what had been the front counter. The cash register lay open on its side, empty of any money it might have held.

"People came here since Jeff, Peter, and I left." She recalled the car that had almost run them off the road when they'd finally escaped from here in Peter's delivery van. What had become of the occupants?

She doubted they'd have come in here—the place had been crawling with grendels. Also, no vehicles sat in the parking lot aside from Hound Dog's pickup truck.

That thought brought with it another memory.

"The police cars are gone. My mother's car is gone."

"It's been twelve years." Hound Dog reached her side and kicked at the papers, leaves, and wrappers on the floor.

Using her most sardonic voice, she said, "And what? The grendels have learned how to drive and took off in them? If so, they also learned how to hotwire them or they picked the keys off the victims."

"You're a hoot, you know that, Frosty?" he replied, but his tone held humour rather than contempt. "Protectors have been here. Military personnel have too. They probably removed them."

"What for?"

Hound Dog shrugged. "Does it matter? Could've been cottagers escaping. I bet people ran for their lives then."

"They wouldn't have outrun the grendels." She considered. "But maybe when the grendels moved on ..." She tried to picture it but couldn't. Grendels didn't move on if food was available. No one on foot would get far with the creatures around.

So, perhaps, military or protector personnel had removed the vehicles. What other conclusion could they draw? The cars were gone.

"They took the money," she commented.

"It's not stealing if the owners are long dead." He shook his head. "Why didn't you kids take it?"

"It would've been stealing. I hoped everything would return to normal and the owners would come back." It would've seemed sacrilegious. Disrespectful. Dan and Enza, the marina's owners, could have relatives who might one day return.

A horn blast yanked her from her pondering. They raced for the door, weapons raised. Rachel went left, Hound Dog right. They peered through the broken screen door without touching it.

She heard a vehicle approaching. "People, not monsters. It's okay. Peter's just giving us a heads-up." She squinted, trying to see Peter through the windshield of the pickup truck.

He sat behind the steering wheel, his expression calm, his gun nowhere in sight.

"Let's go." She didn't wait for Hound Dog but pushed through the screen and walked back to the parking lot, her pace leisurely.

Two military vehicles pulled up beside Hound Dog's truck. Doors opened, and two personnel jumped from each Jeep. They carried assault rifles and had spare pistols and Bowie knives strapped to their belts. One man took the lead, striding purposefully toward the driver's side of the truck. The others, a man and two women, hung back, but they faced Rachel and Hound Dog, hands hovering over their weapons.

Rachel took charge before any of them could. "We're on a private mission. What's your business here?" As far as she knew, the army had no forays scheduled for Storm Lake, and when they did go into the woods on scavenging or hunting missions, they teamed up with protectors.

Unease settled around her, and she instinctively shuddered. Perhaps her father had sent them. She tried to shake it off. Paranoia. That's all.

The guy who'd been heading for Peter stopped and turned toward Rachel. "Search and rescue operation. A civilian went missing in this area."

He was a huge guy, taller and wider than Hound Dog. His jaw jutted out from a chiselled face. As the others did, he wore army fatigues, but none of their gear had identifying tags. If they were military, they kept it hidden.

More convinced than ever they worked for private industry, Rachel asked, "What would a lone person be doing out this way?"

"That's classified."

She shrugged that off and said, "Where are your protectors?"

"Didn't request any." He studied her for a moment. "What's your mission here?"

With a straight face, she said, "That's classified."

His brows furrowed, and he glanced from person to person, settling on Rachel. At the sound of approaching footsteps, they all turned to face Foot-Long and Code Master, who thudded across the home's wooden plank front porch and down the steps.

"House is clear, boss," Foot-Long said.

The group leader faced Rachel. "Who hired you?"

"I did," Peter hopped from the truck and stepped between Rachel and the group leader. "I'm Peter Sanderson." He held out his hand, and the man slowly extended his and they shook.

If the name Peter Sanderson meant anything to any of the newcomers, no one said or did anything to indicate it. When no other introductions appeared forthcoming, Rachel spoke up.

"We can keep an eye out for your missing guy. We're headed toward the lake."

"So are we," the leader said, his voice wary. "Why are you heading deeper into the woods? Leaving the main road?"

Rachel replied before Peter could answer the question. "Not your concern."

"Did you secure permission from your superiors, Protector?"

"Didn't need to. I'm off duty."

"Where's your pass to enter here?"

"Don't need one. We're heading to a property my family owns." She gave him nothing more. None of his business.

"Stay out of trouble. We're not here to rescue you and your civilian."

She laughed. "Right back at ya. And stay out of our way. We wouldn't want to mistake you or anyone in your team for a grendel and shoot you." She wasn't kidding. Her guys could evaluate a target in seconds, but she didn't know how twitchy Peter would get if he was terrified for his life.

Instead of replying, the leader gave a loud whistle and ordered his team back to their vehicle. Before they pulled away, he rolled down his window and called out to Rachel.

"You got flares?"

"Yes."

"You spot our man, send up a flare."

"You not expecting to find him alive?"

He frowned. "I don't know what to expect." He rolled up the window and, with a spin of his tires, raced from the parking lot.

CHAPTER 19

"I didn't know the army had anyone out here, boss," Code Master said. "I checked when we prepped for this trip, I swear."

"I believe you," she replied.

As Code Master was a thorough man, he'd have not only checked schedules but also would have set alerts up on his phone to let him know if something new came in after he'd reviewed the schedule. All civilians, protectors, or government teams foraying into the woods registered in a central database anyone could access. They'd posted their venture, identifying it as a civilian undertaking to salvage private property. This was a way of saying a former resident wanted to search for possessions or investigate property they'd lost to the grendels.

Often, civilians returned to the woods to search for lost loved ones years after the event when they finally had the money to pay protectors to take them in. Rachel had spun this outing as one such mission, using Peter's name as the hiring party. No one needed to know he went as an investigative reporter.

"I don't think they're army," Peter said.

"Agreed," Rachel replied.

"Then who are they?" Code Master asked. "No civilian

groups posted a search here either. Plus, they said this was a search-and-rescue operation. Who else but army or protectors would do one of those? Besides, they never posted it."

"They'd have known we were out here. We're on the schedule." She'd considered going covert, but that could put them at risk. Practical reasons existed for having the mission on the official schedules. They'd listed their expected date of return for three days out. If they didn't flag themselves as either returned or set a new return date, a search and rescue would begin.

"I never heard of a missing person report for this area," Code Master continued. "This is totally off the books."

"We'll have to be wary," Rachel said. "They must have their reasons for keeping this quiet, but I doubt they're ethical." She looked at Peter. "We might want to take the investigation in their direction later."

"Agreed." He tapped his lips with his index finger, then dropped his hand, and shook his head. "Mind if I go through the house and the store now?" He held up a digital camera. "I want to take pictures."

"Sure," Rachel said. "Coder, Foot-Long, you guys stand guard out here. Hound Dog and I will escort the civilian."

They started with the store. Now that Rachel could take her time rooting through the rubble, she found evidence of their last stay here. The note she'd left lay on the floor, torn and mud smeared. The sleeping bags they'd used were shredded, the blow-up pillows ripped to pieces.

"It's surreal," she commented.

"What is?" Hound Dog asked.

"All this. My last time here, I was a child." Before the weekend had turned horrific and violent, her biggest concern had been getting a taste of the red velvet cupcakes Enza expected in her next stock delivery.

Luckily, Peter had made the trip or she and Jeff would've died that weekend. After he rescued them and they made it to her father's in Peterborough, he'd offered them a box of the cupcakes as a parting gift. She and Jeff had eaten three each before their stomachs ached from the sugar overload. Rachel hadn't had a red velvet cupcake since.

"I want to walk down to the shore," she announced.

"Not a good idea." Hound Dog said it casually, but she heard the edge in his voice.

"You don't have to come with me."

"I'll come with you," Peter said.

"If you must do this, I'll go with you." Hound Dog squatted and pushed a broken piece of shelving aside, uncovering newspapers from the last known grendel-free day on Earth. He picked one up. "The civilian should hang back." He gave Peter a side-wise glance.

"I'm not hanging back," Peter shouted, scowling at Hound Dog. "And quit calling me 'the civilian.' You know my name. You're doing that to make me sound helpless and not part of your tough-guy group. I can look after myself, thanks. I've been on these missions before."

Hound Dog chuckled in reply. "Yeah, I am."

"Enough," Rachel said.

"This is my investigation. I'm paying you." Peter snapped a few final shots of the store and headed for the door. "You coming? House first, then we'll hit the docks."

"Peter," Rachel said, her tone compelling him to halt. "Yes, this is your party, but you're under my leadership. The second you put yourself or my team in danger, the party's over and we go home."

"Understood." He waited for her and Hound Dog to catch up. "How do we do this?"

She led the way, ordering Peter to fall in behind her, and Hound Dog took up the rear. Outside, the sky had clouded over, typical in this area. A bright sunny day often turned to rain, but the rain clouds frequently blew over as suddenly as they arrived.

As they entered the two-story house, Hound Dog sidled up to Rachel and said, "Those guys never searched the house or the store. Does that seem right to you?"

"I suppose it does if they had a known start location. They

might end up working their way back here, but if their starting point was a cottage along the lake, they'd head straight to it."

"Yeah, I guess that makes sense," he replied, sounding as if he didn't believe it but would accept it for now.

They toured the house, Rachel searching for signs of what might have happened to Enza and Dan. She found nothing. If they'd been killed in the house, she found no traces of them. Grendels wouldn't clean up a murder scene, so there would've been blood.

When they'd last been here, Rachel's mother had called to the marina's owners from the open front door and received no reply. The couple likely was already dead. They'd probably heard activity outside. Dan would've stepped outside with his shotgun to check for trespassers. The grendels would've got him then. If Enza followed him, they'd have caught her, too.

The roof on the house was intact, which also indicated the owners weren't hunted down indoors. The furniture still sat where Rachel remembered. Puffy pillows mouldered on the damp and muddy couch. An open book lay face down on the floor near a rocking chair by the fireplace as if a startled reader had dropped it there. Dishes sat untouched in the kitchen cupboards. A cup and plate sat in the dishrack next to the sink.

The mattresses on the beds and padding on couches and chairs gave off a dank, mouldy smell, and Rachel guessed from the rips and holes in them that mice nested inside. What had once been a homey, comfortable residence for a sweet old couple was now a decaying haven for rodents and God knew what else. If any grendels nested close to the house, they might scavenge here.

Rachel's eyes teared up at the thought of the kindly couple suffering such a gruesome fate, but she shook it off at the sound of approaching footfalls.

"I'm done here." Peter reached her side, Hound Dog close on his tail.

"Did you find what you wanted?" she asked.

"Not sure if it's what I wanted, but I found no evidence Enza and Dan had defended the place. No spent shells, nothing to indicate they'd holed up here at all."

"No, they disappeared before my brother and I got trapped in the store."

She led them from the house. On their way to the shore, she instructed Code Master and Foot-Long to remain on alert at their current posts.

The marina store overlooked a series of docks where boats once tethered. Only two of the four docks remained, the other two likely getting chopped up by ice over the years. Rachel started her search by stepping out on the dock closest to the western shore. The boat her mother had died in had floated between that shore and this dock.

As she scanned the weeds in the water and the rocks on the shore, fat drops of rain splatted onto her head, hands, and shoulders. Angry to have her quest interrupted, Rachel verified Peter's and Hound Dog's locations. Peter walked among the rocks and boulders on the shore. Hound Dog followed close behind him, on guard.

In the distance, a shot rang out followed quickly by another. A moment of silence reigned, and then more gunshot blasts punctuated the air.

Rachel blared out a two-fingered whistle to get Hound Dog's and Peter's attention. When they caught her eye, she waved them back toward the vehicle.

"They might flush grendels back out this way. Let's go."

They raced for the car. From the forest came the sound of leaves and branches rustling as something crashed through the underbrush toward them.

CHAPTER 20

Before they reached the safety of the vehicle, two figures burst into the clearing. Rachel raised her rifle but held back when she recognized the leader of the team they'd met earlier. Beside him lurched one woman from the group. The other two team members were nowhere in sight.

"Hold your fire," Rachel shouted at her team. "Friendlies."

"What the hell are they doing in there?" Peter asked. "They'd have had to trek through the deep woods to get out here."

"One of them's hurt." Rachel moved toward the pair. "Dog, cover us. No telling what might be following them."

She reached the pair and held an arm out for the woman to grasp.

"I'm okay. Just scrapes from the underbrush." Her breath came in ragged gasps. "He sprained his arm." She waved a hand in her partner's direction, where he stood cradling his left arm.

Rachel escorted them to the truck. "Where's your vehicle? What the hell were you doing in the forest?"

The leader answered. "We traced the civilian's GPS to the deep woods. The only way in was to hike it."

"Who sent you in here?" Rachel asked. "If we're going to

help you, I want to know what we're dealing with."

"A private corporation hired us. We're not free to discuss it. We've been given minimal, need-to-know information. The man we're searching for works for the company. They lost contact with him two days ago and put together this team to locate him."

Rachel thought of her father and his company, of Jeff's sudden death. "And your name is?"

"Chris Bowan." He suddenly looked very young, the weight of his circumstances pressing down on him. Still, Rachel guessed he wasn't any younger than she was.

She turned to the woman beside him. "And you?"

"Brenda Walsh." The woman held herself together well despite the fresh welts on her face that must sting like a bugger.

"What happened? Where are your teammates?"

"On the trail. We went in to locate Maddoc—the missing guy—and bring him out. The other two stayed to guard the trail. We walked smack into a grendel nest," Chris said.

Brenda continued the story. "The nest was empty, but we kept going. Our guy was nearby, according to the GPS tracker. We found two grendels and shot them. Another two appeared out of the trees, moving fast. We shot them and ran to where the GPS indicated Maddoc should be."

"Did you find him?" Rachel asked, assuming they'd probably stumbled across his body. No one could survive two days in the woods with a nest of grendels, especially not a civilian.

Chris and Brenda exchanged glances.

"What is it?" Rachel asked.

"We found his body. We need to contact the rest of our team and haul the body out," Chris replied.

"So call them," Rachel said.

"We can't." Chris tilted his head in Brenda's direction. "Her cell battery died, and I must've lost my phone when we ran through the forest."

"What training have you had for this?" Hound Dog broke

in, disgust clear in his voice.

"The company hired and trained us six weeks ago," Chris said.

Rachel gritted her teeth. *Amateurs.* This illustrated why private businesses and citizens needed to hire professional protectors. Too many big companies trained their own people, hoping to save a buck on search and rescues, retrievals, or expeditions into the woods. Professional protectors had survival training—which included wildcrafting and knowledge of plants used in first aid—advanced first aid training, and training in weapons and tracking.

"I suggest, Mister Bowan, you take the trail to where your teammates are waiting, get in your vehicle, and leave. Have your company hire a team of protectors to return for the body. Call it in when you get back to your vehicle."

She half-turned away from them, dismissing them. They had their own mission to accomplish. She refused to let a group of poorly trained civilians distract them. This wasn't any business of hers, and she had a deadline. She didn't want to keep her team in here any longer than planned.

Chris put a restraining hand on her shoulder. "Please, we can't leave him. We've eliminated the grendels. All we have to do is go back in, pick up the body, and return to the trail on the other side."

"We'll give you a lift to your vehicle—we're heading in the same direction anyway. From there, your team can call in what happened and get protectors out here to help you deal with the bodies. You know the grendel kills must be reported and their bodies collected."

"We understand, but the company wants to deal with the missing employee without involving Protector HQ. We'll call in the grendels. We want to take our coworker's body home first."

"I can't let you do that. We need to report this."

"Well, can you return to the site and see what you think?" Brenda asked. "Maybe you can tell us if a grendel attack killed him."

She could. Her experience as a team leader and former cop qualified and authorized her to assess a scene. But damn it, this isn't what they came here to do. Yet she couldn't ignore the situation.

"All right. Here's what we'll do: Hound Dog and I will follow you two into the woods," she told Brenda and Chris. "Peter, you go with Code Master and Foot-Long in the truck to find their vehicle and the other two members of their team. They must be getting antsy waiting for these two to return."

Code Master and Foot-Long exchanged glances but didn't protest. They understood the situation, and though the delay obviously frustrated them, they wouldn't disagree with the call she'd made. Peter scowled, but he too realized they'd have to take this detour. He perked up and his expression smoothed out.

"Might as well make the best of it. I can take pictures, right?" He looked at Rachel as he said this.

"Sure. If there's anything you can't legally photograph, I'll let you know." Perhaps he could get more than one story out of this trip. She'd be taking photos too.

Hound Dog waited patiently, his expression neutral. His gun, which he'd used while searching the house, was holstered, and he had his rifle at the ready.

"Peter's driving. He knows the area," Hound Dog said, sparing the three a discussion on the subject. He turned to Chris. "Tell him where to find your vehicle, and let's get moving."

The four who remained behind waited for Hound Dog's truck to disappear over the rise in the road.

Rachel told them she'd take the lead with Brenda at her side to guide her and had Hound Dog take the rear. She told Chris to fall in behind her and Brenda. The four made their way to the woods along the shore, climbing over rocks. As they passed the point where she'd seen her mother climb into the rowboat twelve years ago, Rachel halted the group and asked them to give her a moment.

She scanned the water. According to her father, his people had found the rowboat capsized in the water but hadn't recovered her mother's body. He'd had the boat dragged from the water and left on shore. She searched for a sign of it but found nothing to indicate there'd been a rowboat here at all.

"Sorry, guys. I had to check." She didn't explain to Chris and Brenda what she searched for, but she knew Hound Dog would understand. The lack of anything to signify her mother had even been there made her want to cry, but she squelched the tears and led her little group into the woods.

CHAPTER 21

Twigs snapped under Chris's and Brenda's boots, and Rachel whirled on them. "No wonder you two were attacked. Watch where you're stepping."

Rachel and Hound Dog passed among the trees like wraiths, neither giving even a hint of their location. The four grendels Chris and Brenda said they'd killed were probably the only nest in the area, but Rachel didn't trust the forest was clear of danger. These two incompetents certainly hadn't secured the site.

The rain fell more heavily, making the ground mucky and adding to the soggy mess they had to cross. Only a thin layer of soil covered solid rock. The entire area was part of the Canadian Shield, rock that made up the Earth's crust and near the surface in this part of North America. Even the trees here found it challenging to root themselves to the ground. Most of them, whether evergreen or deciduous, clung to the soil with roots spreading visibly across the ground. It made walking a trip hazard.

After ten minutes, Brenda sidled up to Rachel. "We're close to where we found Maddoc."

Rachel raised her hand, ordering them to halt. Rain pattered down through the trees. If birds or animals lived here, they kept still and silent. Wind tossed the treetops and made the air bone-chilling and damp.

"What are you waiting for?" Chris said.

Rachel turned a withering gaze on him, and he pressed his lips together with a scowl. She trained her ears on the environment. Had she heard movement just as Chris spoke? He hadn't even kept it to a whisper. Whoever had hired this team hadn't done a good job of vetting the crew. They were more than incompetent. They were reckless and stupid.

"Let's go." Chris moved the two steps needed to catch up to Brenda and Rachel. "We don't have all day."

"Shut up." Rachel kept her voice low, but her tone was as harsh as her words. She didn't have time for niceties. She needed silence.

"What?"

"Chris, if you insist on flapping your gums and ignoring my commands, I'm leaving you here to fend for yourself." She bluffed. Walking away from improperly trained civilians would be irresponsible. She just wanted to scare him silent. If he feared the protectors would withdraw their support, he'd have to call the company they worked for and admit their screw up. Likely, Chris's motive for dragging them in here was to have the protector team help clean up their mess.

The bluff worked. Chris fell silent.

A click alerted Rachel to a weapon somewhere outside their small group.

"Take cover!" she whispered.

Rachel and Hound Dog moved to melt into the trees, but before they could disappear, Chris and Brenda raised their weapons. Chris, whose left arm appeared fine, pointed his rifle at Rachel. Brenda had hers trained on Hound Dog.

"Freeze. You two aren't going anywhere," Chris said.

Four figures detached from the trees surrounding them, all holding rifles, all training their weapons on Rachel and Hound Dog.

"What the fuck is this?" Hound Dog said. His coarse words implied anger, but he spoke in a conversational tone, as if he were simply curious.

"You're coming with us," Chris said.

"We already were coming with you," Hound Dog replied amicably.

"Not here," came Brenda's response.

"Then where?" Rachel asked. "Was this even a search and rescue?"

Brenda and Chris grinned, and Chris replied, "In a way. We searched for you and your team, but it's not a rescue."

"Grendels never attacked you." Rachel contemplated shooting Chris. He and Brenda had tricked them into entering the woods. What about Peter? And Code Master and Foot-Long?

"The others. Where are they?" As she spoke, a crew member divested Rachel of her weapons while another confiscated Hound Dog's. Her heart sank as he thoroughly patted her down and found her ankle holster. He also took the Bowie knife from the sheath at her waist and her cell phone. But he didn't find the trinkets hidden on the inside of her belt—small items, such as a lock pick. They found all Hound Dog's concealed weapons and his cell phone.

Rachel gritted her teeth. They would find out her bare hands worked just as well—she looked forward to showing them all how well.

"You'll see them soon. This way." Chris waved his weapon in the direction they'd been headed. "Road's closer in this direction."

With a glance at Hound Dog, Rachel started walking.

They reached the road after a twenty-minute hike. Four military-type Jeeps sat in the roadway, a driver behind each one. Hound Dog and Rachel were escorted to different vehicles and ordered to sit in the back seat. Before she entered the vehicle, the woman guarding her cuffed her hands in front with zip ties.

As they drove, Rachel stared out the window, watching the vaguely familiar scenery scroll past. They headed in the direction of her family's cottage. Unease settled in the pit of her stomach. Did this involve her father? If he wanted to meet with her, he didn't need to do it at gunpoint.

She swallowed, futilely trying to clear the lump in her throat. The more time she had to think about things, the more convinced she became of her father's involvement in this kidnapping and in Jeff's death. But why?

Fervently, she wished Hound Dog were here with her instead of in the vehicle behind them. Of course, that was why they'd separated them. Individually, each of them made a deadly opponent; together, they'd be unstoppable.

Rachel leaned back in her seat, encouraging her body to relax. Worry and rage wouldn't help her. She needed calm so she could figure a way out when the opportunity presented itself. That the mercenaries hadn't killed Rachel and Hound Dog immediately gave her hope the person behind this—her father, insisted her brain—wanted them alive.

The rise leading to the cottage appeared. Instead of the dirt and gravel Rachel remembered from her childhood, the driveway was paved. Ten-metre-tall chain-link fencing led off in two directions, and the gate barring access to the cottage was no longer just a simple barrier to keep vandals out. Now, a large iron gate as high as the fence barred the way.

A man from the lead vehicle jumped out, unlocked it, and pushed it to the side. Instead of returning to his car, he continued into the fenced area on foot. The vehicles followed him in. She didn't see what happened after the last Jeep drove in through the entrance, but she assumed someone else took care of shutting and locking the gate behind them.

The vehicles halted, and a guard helped Rachel get out.

As she scanned their surroundings, she barely recognized the property that had once been her favourite place on Earth. For as far as she could see, the land, for at least four metres on either side of the fencing, was barren of trees. Barbed wire across the fence tops ensured that even if grendels made it to the fence on a cloudy day they would have a difficult time getting over it. Electrified, it resembled the ones surrounding her father's company's buildings. Even his home had electrified fencing.

The neighbour's cottage, formerly a simple wood cabin painted white she used to glimpse through the trees from the top of the driveway, was gone. In its place a much larger building, new, and gleaming with floor-to-ceiling glass, interrupted the landscape.

The view from inside must be phenomenal.

The sight of what had been their quaint chalet made her gasp and freeze in her tracks. A larger two-story building replaced the former cottage. The roof of this building, and the one on the neighbour's property, was metal. Nothing would get in that way again.

A prod in her back from her guard got her moving, but Rachel kept her pace slow. She hoped they wouldn't notice and Hound Dog would catch up to her. Even if the two couldn't speak to each other, his presence at her side would be a comfort.

The guard gripped her upper arm and quickened the pace, forcing her to lengthen her strides to keep up.

"This way," he said, voice grim.

"Where are we going?" She risked a glance back in Hound Dog's direction and panicked when she couldn't see him. "Where's Dog?"

"Don't worry about him. Your father wants a word with you." He directed her toward the front deck, a large, new structure made of composite boards. "This way."

She allowed him to lead her up the steps and in through the double doors of the entryway. Perhaps now, she'd get answers even if she wouldn't like what her father had to tell her.

CHAPTER 22

Rachel never saw where they took Hound Dog. Her guard led her into an office off the living area on the main floor of the new house. Her father sat behind a desk in a lushly padded leather chair. When she entered the room, escorted by the guard, Stefan had the man remove the zip tie from around her wrists and ordered him out.

"Close the door behind you," Stefan prompted as the guard stepped from the room.

As the door snicked shut, her father told Rachel to lock the door.

She did as he bid, wondering how she could take advantage of the situation. Everyone would leave them alone so long as her father refrained from calling them here. With the door locked, they couldn't enter at will. Unless a guard had a spare key, they'd have to break the door down to get in.

Without waiting for an invitation, she dropped into one of the two chairs across from her father.

"What have you done to Mom's cottage?" She kept her tone even, eliminating the distress from her voice with effort.

"Our cottage—your mother's and mine—even before she died. Now, it's mine."

"How could you build this monstrosity with grendels everywhere?"

"With enough money, you can accomplish anything. We set up the security first, tore down the old buildings, and put up the new ones."

"Buildings." She stressed the plural. "You bought the neighbour's property." What had happened was obvious, considering the security fencing included the other property.

"Of course. The Wilsons' relatives appreciated the money and wanted nothing more to do with the property where grendels wiped out an entire family."

Kelly Wilson, the little girl next door, had disappeared the day Jeff and Rachel had arrived at the lake with their mother. "Kelly's parents?"

"Dead—so we assume. Found a lot of blood in their cabin. The roof had been torn off. I did their relatives a favour by buying the place. I paid them a fair price."

"What's your interest in the properties here?"

"It's my private research facility."

Rachel rose and started pacing. She'd walked back and forth across the room three times before she realized she'd done it.

"What have you done with Jack? With Peter and my other two team members? Why were we brought here at gunpoint?"

"Don't play stupid, Rachel." He studied her for a moment, then said, "You hungry? Thirsty?"

"What?" she said, confused. "No. What's going on, Dad." Hopefully, the reminder of the familial relationship would bring him to his senses. Of course, if he was behind Jeff's murder, nothing she said would matter.

"I intercepted your message to the lawyer."

She sucked in a breath. "How?" No point in denying it.

"Oddly enough," he said, sarcasm dripping from every word, "broke variety store clerks are easy to bribe. You left the variety store, my guy went into the postal station there and paid the clerk to give him your letter."

He glared at her. "You think I didn't learn everything Jeff did? Everything he planned to do? I knew he had a contingency plan and he'd contact you. All I had to do was wait for it to show up at your door." He glared at her. "And to see what you'd do with it."

He shook his head. "You should've brought it to me, Rachel. We could've worked through this together. Instead, you took it to that boy. That virtual stranger." Stefan rose from his chair, glaring at her with a hatred in his eyes she'd never seen. "He's a reporter. A reporter!" He smashed a fist on his desk, rattling a ceramic mug filled with pencils and pens. Jeff had made the holder for him in art class one year. Seeing it on her father's desk, a sentimental token, seemed incongruous.

"What you're doing is illegal. Unethical. Immoral," she snapped.

"In your opinion. You obviously haven't thought this through and haven't bothered to learn my side of it."

"Your side. If everything Jeff had on the memory stick is correct, you're responsible for the grendels' existence. You brought this horror on us. You as good as murdered our mother yourself. I'm positive you murdered your son—my brother." Her voice rose too. For good measure, she kicked the chair she'd sat in, upending it.

"I've always wanted the best for our family. Your mother and I worked hard to get where we are."

"She's dead. That's where she got."

Anger flashed in his eyes. "She supported my work. We were a team. I dreamed about getting you on board. Do you have any idea where you'd be if you'd listened to me?"

"I dunno. Dead?" she sneered. "Jesus Christ, you sent us up here that May weekend knowing these monsters would be here? You're more monster than those creatures."

He stalked over and grabbed her by the upper arms. "Don't you mock me. Don't you *ever* mock me." He shook her until her teeth rattled.

When he released her, she staggered back a step.

"You're tough. I knew you'd survive. Shame your mother didn't make it, but you're more like me: a survivor, a realist."

His words burrowed into her. Once, she'd have felt proud of the comparison. Now? She loathed him. Any mention of similarities between them repulsed her.

"You and your brother betrayed me," he continued. "Now, you lose."

She swallowed, her throat clicking. "What now? Dad."

"You and your friends have arrived in time to participate in a little experiment. It hasn't been going well, and we needed new test subjects. Thank you for volunteering."

"What are you talking about?" She tried to quash the terror rising through her and failed. Her extremities grew cold and she shivered.

"Isabelle Marie didn't survive the injection, but we gave her a dose from an earlier batch. It worked to repel the grendels but killed the patient. The vaccine Jeff got didn't kill him, but rather than repel the creatures, it poisoned them when they ate him. What we want is a version that repels the beasts without killing the subject. We're sure we've nailed it this time."

She blanched and in a hoarse whisper said, "You bastard."

He grabbed her and, holding her at arm's length, looked her up and down. "You look great—fit, healthy. You'll do very well. Might even survive more than one outing."

"What do you mean?" Her voice had gone shrill, and she hated herself for the display of weakness. He'd love that, the psycho.

"You'll see." He grinned, and it was nasty and cruel.

He released her and unlocked the door. Rachel slumped, her shoulders drooping forward, dejection and failure making her want to drop to her knees. She'd failed. The opportunity to take advantage of the locked room had passed, and she'd never get another one. Whatever happened next, she was sure neither she nor her team would leave this place alive.

CHAPTER 23

As Rachel passed through the communal area that looked more like a family room than a corporate lounge, she glimpsed the stunning vista from the floor-to-ceiling windows. Tempered glass made up the entire lake-facing side of the building and afforded a panoramic view of the water.

If she wasn't certain this would be the last beautiful thing she'd ever see before she died, she'd have appreciated it more. Even in the pouring rain, the island across from the cottage sent waves of calm through her body. She paused and inhaled deeply, imagining the clean air from the lake filling her lungs.

The guard escorting her prodded her in the back, and she started walking. Rachel memorized the layout as they passed through the lounge, down a hallway, and into a large lab filled with tall cages. Each contained a small cot, camping toilet, a shelf with hand wipes, and, in some, a person. All four of her teammates were here.

Her eyes met each of theirs, and she gave a slight shake of her head, signalling them to remain silent. A man in a lab coat, obviously a scientist, opened a cage door and motioned for the guard to walk her over. Before she could enter the cage, two lab assistants appeared and restrained her, each grabbing one of her arms.

As she struggled, they removed her jacket and tossed it aside.

"Sleeve." The scientist nodded to the guard, who yanked up the sleeve of her turtleneck.

She felt rather than saw the needle go into her upper left arm and renewed her struggles. "What the hell? What have you done to me?"

"Relax. It's done."

He had them shove her into the cage and lock the door, and together they all disappeared.

The guard and the assistants left through the door she'd entered; the scientist went into an adjoining room. He shuffled around for a moment, and then everything fell silent.

Her hands shook, and Rachel wondered if it was from whatever they'd injected her with. In the cage to her left, Hound Dog stood as close to her side as he could get. A space of about a metre separated them. Peter was on the other side of Hound Dog. Foot-Long was on Rachel's right, and on his other side stood Code Master.

"What are these sick bastards doing?" Hound Dog asked. "Did your father tell you anything?"

That they all knew who was behind this didn't bode well. It meant her father wouldn't let any of them leave here alive.

"Did they inject all of you?"

"Yeah, before sticking us in these cages," Hound Dog said.

"They won't tell us anything." Foot-Long rattled the bars of his cage as soon as he'd spoken. His expression was more enraged than grief-stricken or defeated, which gave her hope. As long as they held it together, they might find a way out.

"Cameras?" Rachel asked.

Code Master replied, muttering to Foot-Long, who passed the information to Rachel.

"Two. One facing the cages, another above the cages, covering the other side of the room."

She frowned. "Motion-activated?"

Foot-Long consulted with Code Master and then replied,

"Yes, but we're in here, so the one across the room will film us continuously."

"Will it pick up conversation?"

"Coder says no, but we keep our voices low in case there're bugs we can't see. Thoughts, boss?"

"You figure they're monitoring the cameras?"

"We have to assume so," Hound Dog interjected.

She agreed. Her belt still held the tools she'd need to pick the locks on these cages, but that wouldn't do them any good if the cameras were monitored.

The lab door opened, and four guards entered the room, interrupting the conversation. The new arrivals strode purposefully to Foot-Long's and Code Master's cages. The scientist reappeared and crossed the room to join them.

One guard, the group leader, said, "These two, Doctor Janes?"

"Yes, please."

Both men in question backed away from the door of their cages as far from the guards as they could get. A guard opened Foot-Long's cage and indicated to him he should exit.

"Fuck you, asshole." Foot-Long lay down on his cot as if about to take a nap.

Rachel smiled, happy her men wouldn't make it easy for these thugs. She inched toward the door of her cage, quietly feeling for the credit-card-sized lock pick case inside her belt. With everyone's attention diverted to Foot-Long, including, hopefully, anyone monitoring the camera, she could unlock her door.

As the four guards descended on Foot-Long, Rachel slipped the case from her belt and removed the tool she needed. She edged to the door and leaned against the side with the lock. The tool palmed, she worked the lock as carefully and unobtrusively as she could while giving the guards and Janes surreptitious glances. When the tumbler clicked, she accomplished her task. As long as they didn't check her door, she could open it anytime.

She'd wait until they had Foot-Long and Coder free of

their cages. Then it would be three against five though she had no idea how long it would take whoever monitored them to raise the alarm.

Two guards had Foot-Long on his feet and escorted him from his cage. The other two opened Code Master's door and waved him out. His jaw set, Code Master stepped from the cage, his arms windmilling into the guards on either side of him. When Coder made his move, Foot-Long flung a leg out, knocking down a guard.

Rachel tossed her lock picking case into Hound Dog's cage. "Peter, too," she said, pointing at her friend. Without waiting to see what Hound Dog did, she attacked Janes first, grabbing his clipboard from his hands and cold-cocking him with it. He dropped like a lead weight and lay motionless.

The fracas between her team and the guards intensified, and she joined the fray. One guard was already down, leaving three, but as she reached the struggling group, the lab door burst open and two more guards rushed in.

One fired her gun into the ceiling, and everything stopped at once.

"You"—she waved a gun at Rachel—"back in your cage."

Rachel shuffled back inside, fury and helplessness overwhelming her. This had been their one chance. She'd watch for another opportunity, but the guards would be better prepared next time. As they slammed shut her cage door, she risked a glance at Hound Dog, hoping he'd concealed the lock picking kit.

He'd tried but failed. His gaze met hers as one guard found the kit while the other covered him with a gun. A team of four guards escorted Foot-Long and Code Master from the room.

"Where are you taking them?" Rachel demanded.

The guards didn't reply, but Janes, who stood rubbing his head near the cages, grinned at her. "The experiments will begin. They're the first. One's the control."

"Who's the control? What does that mean?" Terror filled her heart. *Oh, God, what will they do to my guys?* When no one answered her, she howled in rage and then shouted at Janes. "What are they doing to my men?"

"If you're good," Janes said, "I'll let you watch."

CHAPTER 24

Janes was as good as his word. He pressed a button, and a monitor descended from the ceiling. The screen faced the prisoners, as if it had been purposely set up for viewing from the cages. At first, Rachel had a vague idea that they kept prisoners entertained by watching television. Then, in dawning horror, she realized they wanted prisoners to watch what happened to those going before them.

The monitor activated, showing a forest scene. Trees grew close together, and a large shelter made of leaves and twigs nestled in the branches of a large maple. It resembled a giant squirrel nest, but Rachel recognized it for what it was: a grendel habitat.

None of the creatures were in it, but she spotted one in the nearby branches. Since the creatures typically hung out in pairs, she assumed the other one hid in the nest. If this was a group of three, then a third one would be close. If it was a group of four, another pair would be around somewhere.

Soon, Foot-Long and Code Master would appear on the screen. How much area did they have to work with? She recalled Isabelle Marie. Jeff. The grendels who'd behaved strangely.

What had Stefan said? A vaccine that repelled grendels without killing the subject. But to test it with live subjects?

131

She shuddered.

"Rachel," Peter called out.

She met his gaze across Hound Dog's cage.

"Yes?"

"We're in trouble." He gave her a rueful grin. "We have to leave. If no one else has reported this, we have to do it."

She returned the smile, remembering the first time he'd said those words to her. Then, as children, they didn't understand what they faced. Now, they were adults and trained to fight these creatures—at least, Rachel and Hound Dog were. If the three of them were tossed in the ring together, she and Hound Dog would have to protect Peter.

"Frosty!" Hound Dog said. "They're unarmed. Those bastards." He rattled the bars of his cage. "I'll kill them for this."

Rachel turned to face the monitor in time to see Code Master and Foot-Long spot the nest in the tree. Each held a thick stick, which she assumed they'd picked up en route to this destination once the guards had left.

"The girl we found"—Isabelle Marie—"was unmarked. But she was dead," Rachel said.

"What do you think that implies?" Hound Dog asked.

"My father said the dose she got killed her. Grendels prefer fresh kills so they left her alone." She paced her cage while watching the screen. "Maybe that was the problem. They wouldn't know if the grendels rejected her because they didn't take her down or because the vaccine worked."

"My God. They're testing a vaccine?" Hound Dog rattled the doors of his cage. His muscles bulged. Curses streamed from his lips.

"Dog!" Rachel shouted. "Not helping."

"I'll kill them, Frosty. I'll kill them."

"You and me both." Tears leaking from her eyes, she watched the screen in horror as the two grendels slipped from the trees and approached the men.

"Oh, God, what if they can't kill all four?" Rachel whispered.

"You think there are four?" Peter asked.

"There's at least three. Why would the experimenters separate the group? No, they're testing this under real-world conditions—that's why they didn't just tie the guys up and throw them in there. They want to see them fight. See if they can win if the vaccine repels the grendels." Then she realized what Janes had meant about the control.

"One of them isn't protected." Her gaze frantically scanned the lab, searching for Janes, or anyone else, to rail at. "One of them got a shot of the vaccine. The other got a placebo. He's the control."

"Then not all of us are vaccinated either," Peter said.

"Probably not."

The thought that their turn would come horrified her but not as much as the knowledge that, if their turn came, it meant either Coder or Foot-Long was dead. If the two men won against the grendels, would the experimenters consider the tests done? It wouldn't matter. They couldn't let any of them go, not after kidnapping them and using them as guinea pigs.

The only way out of here was in a body bag unless they fought their way out. Peter was right: they needed to escape and report it.

"Behind you!" Hound Dog shouted, and Rachel returned her attention to the video feed.

On the monitor, the screaming began.

***

Code Master's sweaty palms gripped the stick he held with trembling hands. Crude and flimsy, the stick was all he had for a weapon against the fangs and claws of the grendels. He'd never had to fight them hand to hand. They'd never found themselves in a situation where they weren't armed to the teeth and suited up with protective gear.

Four grendels to contend with. He'd spotted the two in the tree immediately, but he couldn't locate the other two.

The possibility existed there weren't another two, but Code Master doubted it. Pretending the odds were even could be fatal. He always assumed the worst, and so far, it had kept him alive.

Foot-Long stood wide-eyed and panting beside Coder. They'd positioned themselves where the trees left a small clearing, but, with the clouds and rain, the exercise was pointless. Only the sun breaking through could help them now.

"Get a grip, man. We'll take them. Together."

"I don't see the other two," Foot-Long replied. "How big is this place?"

"Can't tell. From the gate they sent us through, I saw fencing twenty metres out on one side. Didn't see how far the rest of it stretched. They'll be close."

Brush rustled behind them, and Code Master whipped around as the two missing grendels slipped from the foliage five metres away.

"Back to back!" Code Master shouted, and in seconds, the two men repositioned themselves. Foot-Long faced the new arrivals, Code Master the two from the tree.

The pair from the tree moved slowly toward Code Master, their nostrils sniffing the air. At Coder's back, Foot-Long panted with exertion even though he hadn't yet exerted himself.

"Calm down. Watch your breathing, Paul," Code Master said, hoping the use of Foot-Long's real name would help get him under control.

"We've only got sticks. We'll never kill them with sticks."

"We will. We have to. Don't think about it. They're just fugly humans. They bleed. Have hearts we can skewer. Remember that."

A scream tore from Foot-Long's throat, and he wrenched away from Code Master. Since the two from the trees didn't appear to want to lunge at him, Coder turned and shoved the tip of his stick through the eye of the nearest grendel, who had a grip on Foot-Long.

It shrieked and released the man, but the creature's partner had bitten into Foot-Long's thigh. Blood spurted from the wound. Code Master screamed in rage and, afraid trying to skewer the beasts anywhere else would snap the stick, speared that grendel in the eye as well. The eyes were the squishiest part of them, the rest of their bodies covered in a thick, leathery hide.

The two from the tree had joined the fight, and they also attacked Foot-Long, whose shrieks intensified as their claws raked his face and neck. Code Master hooked his arm around the nearest grendel's throat and wrenched the beast away from Foot-Long. The creature shrieked and squealed, trying to free itself from Coder's grip.

It struggled but didn't claw or bite at him. The noises it made grew more frantic as Code Master held on, squeezing and tightening on the creature's windpipe. Why didn't it claw him? Why didn't it try to bite him? It appeared as if the thing wanted to escape him rather than fight him, and it no longer slavered now that it wasn't attacking Foot-Long.

Sudden silence from Foot-Long drew Code Master's attention. The three grendels had ripped the young man to pieces and sat tearing meat from the bone and chewing on his remains. Code Master released the grendel, dropped to his knees, and threw up into the dirt.

CHAPTER 25

The moment Code Master released the grendel and fell to his knees, the fight was over. Foot-Long had been the control. Code Master repelled the creatures. The vaccine worked. Rachel stole a glance at Peter and Hound Dog.

Peter had collapsed on his cot, his face buried in the thin pillow. Hound Dog paced and snarled like a caged puma. Rachel turned back to the monitor. Would they get Code Master out now? Return him to his cage? She hoped they at least planned to do blood tests—any tests, so long as it kept him alive long enough for the rest of them to figure out an escape.

"What'll we do when we're out there, boss?"

On the screen, Code Master roared in rage and leaped to his feet. Grabbing his stick, he went after one of the wounded grendels. It sat clutching its broken eye and whimpering while its mates gorged on human flesh.

Coder rammed the stick into its other eye, and leaping onto the creature's chest, he yanked the stick out. He stabbed the monster with the stick, using all his strength to bore into the creature's head with the point. In moments, the thrashing ceased and the monster lay still. Coder rose and headed for the next grendel.

A shot rang out and Code Master dropped.

Rachel screamed. "Oh, God, they shot him in the head. Dog, they've killed Coder." She sobbed, not caring if it showed weakness. These guys were her partners, her friends.

The screen on the monitor went dark.

She ripped off her belt and tried to pick the lock with the buckle's tongue.

When the door to the lab swung open, Rachel stopped what she was doing and put her belt back on. Two guards entered carrying Code Master's body. Janes followed the procession. They set Coder's body on a slab near the sink on the other side of the room.

"You bastards. You didn't have to kill him," Rachel screamed at them. Her voice had grown hoarse and her throat hurt from the effort, but she disregarded it.

No one replied. No one acknowledged with a glance that she'd even spoken.

After Code Master's body was in place, the two guards left the room. Janes began stripping the corpse.

"At least have the decency not to work on him in front of us," Hound Dog called to Janes.

The doctor ignored him and continued disrobing their dead friend.

Peter rattled the bars of his cage. Thank God he was back on his feet. In a life-and-death situation, she needed everyone at full capacity. To escape, everyone needed to work together.

"Hey," Peter shouted. "At least tell us why they shot him."

Janes threw him an irritated look. "They shouldn't have." He spit the words out.

Rachel relaxed her shoulders and released the bars of her cage door. She hadn't even realized she'd been clasping them. If the doctor hadn't wanted Code Master killed after their test had verified the vaccine worked, then they might stand a chance. He'd have an argument about it with the guards' supervisor, and the scientist won these contests every time. His time and effort spelled money. The guards were only grunts, there to do his bidding. No more prisoners would be executed that way.

She moved across the cage to the side closest to Hound Dog. When he spotted her pressed up against the bars, he did the same.

"I have a few ideas," she said.

He listened and then relayed them to Peter. After that, they could only wait.

***

A long wait drew out the tension. Janes examined Code Master's body. While Rachel and the two men avoided watching him do it, they couldn't close their ears to the sounds of an autopsy performed nearby.

They spent most of the time discussing innocuous things, things that wouldn't matter to anyone listening, but kept them from losing their sanity. Peter told stories of his travels to other countries as a journalist. He talked about the spread of the grendel infestation and verified that, while it had started in Canada, it spread quickly to other parts of the world. The US became overrun within weeks. A month later, Europe had them bursting from the trees. From there, growth became exponential, until every part of the world had grendels.

The exceptions were hot, sunny climates and cold, barren climates. Deserts provided inadequate shelters and hunting grounds for the beasts, but some groups eked out an existence. Areas with palm trees had fewer grendel colonies, but they appeared even there. However, places where the sun shone often recorded fewer deaths by grendel. The Arctic Tundra remained free of them. The creatures needed trees around them and longer stretches of warm weather.

At last, the waiting came to an end. A group of four guards with guns swaggered into the lab. Rachel's father had not made an appearance since he'd caged her, but that didn't surprise her. He'd consider her a traitor and, as far as he was concerned, she was already dead to him.

A guard unlocked the cages, and Rachel and the men

stepped out into the lab. The three fell in line, Rachel leading, Peter in the middle, and Hound Dog taking up the rear. On her way out the door, Rachel snatched up the jacket they'd tossed aside when they'd brought her in and she put it on. As they walked, she scoped out each guard and verified what weapons he or she carried.

In her belt, she still had hidden matches and other tools, among them a thin penknife. She planned to give the knife to whoever turned out to be the control subject. That person would obviously need it the most.

The guards led them through a tunnel that ended at a set of double steel doors. Every so often, along the corridor, she spotted a surveillance camera. The last camera hung above the exit doors. One guard led the way, the second walked beside Rachel, and the last two brought up the rear. They passed the second-last camera. Rachel slowed her pace, the guard next to her automatically easing up to match her reduced strides.

As they neared the double doors, she braced herself. When the lead guard pulled out a set of keys to unlock the doors, she smashed against the guard beside her and knocked the woman into the wall. The second Rachel moved out of his way, Peter lunged forward and hurled himself onto the lead guard's back. Hound Dog, meanwhile, busily smashed the heads of the last two guards together.

One went down, but the other slugged Dog in the jaw, snapping his head back. Rachel's guard recovered just as quickly and manoeuvred her handgun up and ready. In such close quarters the advantage was Rachel's. She gripped the barrel of the gun and twisted it from the guard's hands. Raising it high above her head, she smashed the grip on the guard's head. As soon as the guard went down, Rachel shot out the camera mounted above the doors.

"Run!" Rachel bellowed it as she heard multiple footsteps headed their way.

She clocked the guy Peter continued to struggle with, stole the handgun from his holster, extra ammo from his magazine carrier, and the keys from his ring. She pushed through the doors, and Peter stumbled out behind her. Hound Dog ran out only seconds behind them, a rifle in his hands.

"I couldn't get a gun," Peter said, his voice apologetic.

Rachel shoved the handgun at him. "Never mind. Take this." She kept the rifle she'd swiped for herself.

"After me." She didn't wait to see if they followed. The plan was to have Peter in the middle, and she trusted Hound Dog to ensure it happened. Anytime they spotted a camera, they shot it, removing surveillance. As they ran, she listened for pursuit and movement in the trees around them. The creatures could be anywhere, and she didn't assume they'd stuck her group in with the already wounded monsters.

Her enemies weren't stupid. They'd have killed the first group and replaced them with a new one. That's what probably took them so long to bring Rachel and her friends out here. In almost no time, they reached the small clearing she recognized from the video. The grendel habitat was still there, and in the tree surrounding it perched four creatures.

She whistled at them, and they immediately swung down and charged at the newcomers. The three friends stood, a metre apart, weapons raised, and let them come. Breath held, Rachel waited to see who repelled them and who would be their target.

All four ran at Rachel.

Her first thought was relief, but she didn't have time for a second thought. She turned and ran back toward the building and the doors they'd come through. An excellent runner, she spent much of her exercise time on the track and running through whatever neighbourhood she lived in. Of the three of them, she was the best suited to do this.

Hound Dog and Peter kept pace with the grendels as they loped along behind her. While she was breaking a sweat, the creatures ran with ease and grace. Before she reached the double doors, one of them pulled her to the ground. She spun around in its slippery grasp and wrestled with it, trying to keep her throat out of its reach.

Its head blew off, and she was free. Not sure if Hound Dog or Peter had made the kill, she ignored it and unlocked the doors. As she flung them open into Peter's waiting grasp, two guards met her. She dove between them, hoping the three grendels on her tail were close enough to get through the doors.

The shrieks of the guards told her they'd succeeded. She ran back down the hallway, rifle ready. Two pairs of boots pursued her, but she knew the footsteps belonged to Peter and Hound Dog. As they ran, Peter's handgun fired at regular intervals, blinding the cameras.

No more guards appeared. Perhaps, Rachel and her crew had defeated them all. Her father was probably scrambling to call in reinforcements. The trio stumbled from the corridor into the deserted lounge area.

"Where to?" Hound Dog asked.

"I want to say we take down my father, but we need to get the hell out of here. We'll get back to HQ and go public with what we've found." She looked at Peter. "You ready to write the story of your life?"

CHAPTER 26

Rachel led them outside. The rain had stopped, but the wind had picked up, making it a chilly ten Celsius. At least it was above freezing, but it was cold for September. They walked to the gate as if they belonged there. The guard at the guardhouse didn't notice they weren't his people until they barged in on him. By the time he'd realized his mistake, Hound Dog had a rifle pointed at his head.

"Open the gate," Hound Dog said and relieved the guard of his rifle.

When the guard hesitated, Hound Dog prepared to fire. "Have it your way."

"No, wait. I'll open it." The guard flung his hands up, palms out. In an instant, he had the gate unlocked and rolled back.

"Where's my truck?" Hound Dog scanned the area.

The guard shrugged. "I didn't see a truck."

"They might have left it on the road," Peter suggested.

"Why?"

"No time for this," Rachel said. "Tie this guy up, Dog. Peter, step out and find us a vehicle—any vehicle."

"But we don't have keys."

Rachel gave him a you-must-be-kidding look. "Just locate one. We'll take care of the details."

"Okay, boss." He grinned and slipped from the guardroom.

While Hound Dog finished immobilizing the guard, Rachel rooted around the room and scooped up a backpack containing bottles of water and what looked like someone's lunch. She assumed it belonged to the guard.

"Sorry, man," she said to the guard, "I don't know where we're going or how long it'll take to get there, and they stole our packs." While she was at it, she took the knife from his belt and another gun and extra ammunition she found in a drawer below the control console.

"Have a nice day." Hound Dog saluted the guard, who lay tied up on the floor, and stepped outside. "Coming, Frosty?"

"Right behind you. Let's find Peter."

Janes and her father still lived—unless they'd run across the grendels. She didn't know if any guards remained, but anyone left in the building would have to watch for the creatures. That bought her small group time but not a lot.

Rachel scanned the area for Peter, Hound Dog sticking so close to her side she bumped into him.

"Gimme space, will you?" she said, a touch of irritation in her voice.

"Relax. Don't forget, you're not immune to the grendels."

"Right. But you don't have to be on top of me."

"Ah," he sighed, "that's a nice picture."

"Knock it off." Her lips quirked into a tiny smile. He'd taken the edge off the fact that she couldn't see Peter anywhere.

"I should've sent you with him," she muttered.

"You talking to me?"

"Yeah."

"Never travel alone, Rachel. I won't let you forget that."

"All right, then I should've gone with him. Or we shouldn't have split up. I forget he's a civilian. Wouldn't automatically—" She spotted Peter. "Oh, thank God."

Hound Dog and Rachel jogged up to meet the journalist.

"Found a vehicle?" she asked him.

"Yeah, took some time. They're corralled over there." He waved a hand toward the south end of the compound. "No one's around. There are only four. None of them are your truck, Hound Dog." Peter sounded apologetic.

"Never mind. If we find it on the road, we're in luck."

"I still have your key in my pocket," Peter said. "Maybe that's why the truck's not here."

"Thank goodness for lazy guards. Let's go," Rachel said.

They followed Peter to the vehicles and hot-wired one of the military-type trucks. Hound Dog drove, Rachel riding shotgun. Peter had slid into the back. They drove through the gate without incident. To Rachel, it all seemed a little too easy.

***

Inside the building, Stefan hid in his office while the two remaining guards from the lab hunted down the grendels his daughter had so inconveniently set loose. Lucky for her, none of the personnel in this compound had been vaccinated—something to be rectified now they'd verified this batch of the vaccine worked. Before they could go after Rachel and her friends, they'd have to neutralize the grendels.

Stefan changed the view on the monitor to the lab. Doctor Janes huddled inside, the door shut tight to keep out the grendels. The view on the monitor changed as Stefan searched for his guards and their quarry. One corridor showed a grendel body. The guard in the guardhouse who'd been left bound and gagged had freed himself, but Stefan had ordered him to stay there. Grendels or no, he needed someone watching the gates. The monitor showed the man standing, gun in hand, flipping through the camera views. Stefan could almost smell the man's tension through the screen.

The whole thing was taking too long. Rachel and her posse might be long gone in the vehicle they stole—provided they made no pit stops. If they found Hound Dog's vehicle, it would solve all Stefan's problems, but he couldn't count on that. He picked up the phone and made a call.

***

Hound Dog kept to the centre of the muddy road and drove at a steady forty clicks.

"Watch ahead." Rachel scanned the path in front of them, uneasiness intensifying with each kilometre they put between themselves and her former cottage.

"Relax. We're away." He braked. "And there, ladies and gentlemen, is my truck. Come ta Papa, baby."

"No, let's keep going."

"I'm not leaving my truck."

She put a hand on his arm. "Why'd they leave it here?"

"They didn't have the keys. Let's ditch this thing and get my truck. Okay?" At first when he looked at her, he scowled and his words had been laced with annoyance. But when their gazes met, his face softened. "It's okay. It'll be much better driving my truck. It's certainly in better shape than this piece of crap." He slapped the dashboard, the thud reverberating through the vehicle.

"I agree with Hound Dog." Peter leaned forward so his face stuck out between the two in the front. "We can jump out. Check it out. It'll only take a moment."

"That's what worries me," Rachel replied. "We don't know how many people they had on-site, but they won't want to let us go. They won't want us to make it back alive. Not with what we know."

"We're out," Hound Dog insisted.

Rachel stared at him, her expression bland. "We're not out of the woods yet."

"Oh, Frosty, you didn't just say that." He took her hand in both of his. "I don't want to argue. I'm getting my truck and we're leaving."

She capitulated. If it were hers, she'd want it back too, and everything seemed fine. "All right. I'll go with you. Peter can wait in the vehicle we know works."

Hound Dog gave her a funny look. "What do you think ... never mind. Let's get this done."

She hopped onto the road. Daylight was fading fast, and she wanted to be on the highway soon. Her ears tuned in to the forest sounds: crickets, a crow's caw, and the breeze wafting through the trees. Birch trees had a distinctive, almost musical sound when the wind blew through them. Water trickled somewhere—a tiny stream she knew flowed nearby.

If anyone or anything else moved through the forest, she couldn't hear it. She allowed herself to release tension she held inside with a deep breath in and a drop of her shoulders.

Hound Dog crept up to the vehicle. Both of them had weapons ready. Dog carried a handgun, and Rachel bore a rifle. Peter had handed over the key to Hound Dog and switched to the driver's seat of the stolen vehicle without Rachel asking him. In the fading light, Hound Dog opened the driver's door of the truck and peered in.

He poked his head back out and signalled to Rachel all was well. She stepped forward and opened the front passenger door, waving at Peter to join them. The Jeep's door opened, and Peter's footsteps alerted her to his approach.

Hound Dog climbed into the driver's seat and turned the key in the ignition. It clicked but didn't start. Rachel's heart went cold. Before she could say anything, Hound Dog tried again to start the vehicle. She heard another click as the engine started.

Jumping from the vehicle, she screamed, "Get out. Bomb."

She sensed more than saw Hound Dog leap from the truck. As she ran, she grabbed Peter by the arm and dragged him after her. They had to get at least two hundred fifty metres from the truck. Up ahead the road had a culvert on either side for the stream to pass underneath. She raced to it and dragged Peter down with her just as the truck blew.

CHAPTER 27

Debris rained down around them. Twilight grew daylight bright as fire consumed the truck.

"Oh, God, Hound Dog. I don't know if he made it." Rachel's voice choked. Her heart thudded painfully in her chest. She raised her head to see past the fire's fury.

"Stay down." Peter pressed a hand to the top of her head.

She complied, ducking and covering her head with her arms as pieces of truck and burning detritus peppered the area. The crackle of fire drowned out the forest sounds, and gas fumes, smoke, and an aroma of burning leaves assaulted her nostrils. At least it had rained all day. Even so, she feared this would cause a forest fire.

"We've got to find Jack." Her breath hitched as she spoke. "I won't leave him, Peter." She was close to tears, close to hysteria. Hound Dog would need her to stay calm and think things through. If he'd survived the blast, he'd be on the other side of the road.

But evening's darkness deepened with each passing minute. They needed to get away from the fire, and if grendels lurked, they'd come after her. At least Peter and Hound Dog were safe as far as the creatures went.

She rested her forehead on her hands for a moment and let the despair take her. When she raised her head, her eyes were dry and her jaw set.

"You hurt?" she asked Peter.

"I'm okay. You?"

"Fine. My ears are ringing." She took a quick inventory. "My arm hurts. I wrenched it when we landed in the ditch. I can walk, though." They were both soaked and muddy, too, but that wasn't worth mentioning.

She stood and he did the same. They climbed from the culvert and tried to figure out where everything had landed. The Jeep they'd stolen had flipped onto its side and lay engulfed in flames. Hound Dog's truck, of course, was blown apart. The fire continued to burn, which at least gave them some light to see by, and it didn't seem to be spreading.

But they needed to get more distance from it before the Jeep's tank blew. Part of her hoped the fire would take off and burn down her father's torture compound with him inside.

"What were the odds of us getting out of there?" she asked, but she talked more to herself than to Peter.

He replied anyway. "Pretty small, I guess."

"It seemed too easy." She shook her head. "Not getting past the guards and away from the grendels—that was fucking hard and took everything we had. But leaving the place. No one was in the lounge. One guard manned the station, and he didn't even know we'd escaped." She fell silent.

Her father had done this. He'd ordered them to booby trap the truck. *Why?*

"You think they let us go figuring we'd go for the truck?" Peter asked.

"Maybe they intended to dispose of our bodies in it after they finished with us. If we'd blown up with it, it would destroy all the evidence. We're physical, living proof of what he's doing, especially you and Hound Dog. Traces of whatever they injected you with will be in your blood. Who knows what it's done to your cells or DNA or whatever."

"Oh, great, thanks. I hadn't considered any of that."

She put a hand on his shoulder. "We'd better book before they send out a party to verify we're dead."

They picked their way over the rubble and through burning patches. As they went, they stamped out what flames they could. The main conflagration would be too much for them to put out, and they couldn't risk going near the burning Jeep.

Rachel guided Peter around and behind the remnants of their means of escape, and they began the search for Hound Dog—or his body. The prospect of finding him dead almost paralyzed her, but it would be better to know. If he was dead, she needed to see it for herself. She wouldn't leave the woods without finding him. If he was injured, she refused to leave him behind.

Even if the grendels left him alone, her father's people would hunt down any survivors in the woods. Hound Dog would be a precious find for them, especially wounded and unable to fight back.

Worry and building panic made her speed up her pace. They started as close to the driver's side of the truck as the fire would allow them to get. Each metre out gave her hope he was alive even if injured.

She tried to hurry. Every moment they stayed here increased the odds they'd be recaptured. Even so, she scoured the area carefully, checking behind every bush, around every tree, in each ditch and depression.

Peter spotted him first.

"Over here!"

Her heart flew into her throat at his words, and fear sent a wave of numbness through her body. She ran to where Peter crouched and dropped beside Hound Dog, who lay face down in the mud. A finger to his throat verified he had a pulse.

His shoulders and head had taken the worst of the blast. He'd made it a safe enough distance from the primary blast, but he'd sustained secondary blast injuries from flying junk. While it helped he'd been dressed for a cold fall day, which had afforded him padding, it hadn't shielded him from all the shrapnel. Blood covered the back of his head, and a piece of metal lodged in his left shoulder.

"We need to remove this piece of metal. Hopefully, it's not too deep. First, I want to bandage his head." Rachel removed her jacket and stripped off her turtleneck. She tore it into strips and bandaged Hound Dog's head.

Peter watched her, helping where he could. "What do you want me to do next?" he asked once she'd tied off the makeshift bandage. "How will we pull the metal piece out without killing him?"

"It's embedded in the muscle, but it doesn't look too deep. I hope, anyway. We'll find out. We need to find a silver birch tree with fungus growing on it." She looked Peter in the eyes. "I'll have to do it. You stay with him."

"Rachel," he said, his tone a warning.

"I have to. You don't know what to look for." She stood, unable to waste more time arguing. "I have a handgun." She scanned Peter up and down. "You left yours behind?" She kept accusation out of her voice. It wasn't his fault. For her, for Hound Dog, keeping a weapon handy was second nature. Not so for Peter.

She removed the gun from Hound Dog's holster and handed it to Peter.

"Take this. Keep it ready, and don't set it down for any reason. If you see a grendel or a person who isn't me, shoot first and ask questions later. They'll search for us soon." She considered. "Hopefully not until daybreak. They'd have heard the blast and assumed we'd gone up in it. They won't want to come out at night and risk getting caught by any creatures in the woods. Grendels are most active at night." That was both a blessing and a curse for them—for her, anyway. Peter and Hound Dog were okay as long as the vaccine remained potent, but as always, she didn't want to assume anything.

Rachel pressed strips of her shirt around the wound in Hound Dog's shoulder. He never stirred as she worked, which worried her. The head wound could be fatal if he didn't get help soon. She put her jacket back on and searched the trees, jogging from one to the next, focusing on the birches. After a while, she found one that had the fungus growing from it.

The growth looked like a large, white platter. Using the Swiss army knife from inside her belt, she cut the chunk from the tree. She considered searching for another one as a backup but decided against it. This would have to do. She raced back to where she'd left Peter and Hound Dog. Dog stirred and opened his eyes when she dropped next to him and gently removed the wad of cloth she'd left on his wound.

Damn. This part would hurt. She'd have preferred it if he'd been unconscious. She'd also have preferred having bottles of water with them, but she'd have to make do with what she had here. In other words, almost nothing.

"Peter." She waited for him to raise his head and meet her gaze. "You'll have to pull out the metal piece."

When he blanched, she said, "You have to. I've got to patch the wound. Before we do this, I'll prepare the fungus. In the meantime, I'll need your shirt. Tear it into strips. It'll have to wrap around his shoulder." She indicated with her index finger the direction they'd wind the bandage around the shoulder and tie it on.

"All right." He set his gun down and did as she'd asked while Rachel trimmed the fungus using the knife. This wouldn't be the most sanitary dressing, but they'd have to live with it until they could get Hound Dog to a doctor. He moaned just as Rachel finished her job on the fungus.

"Shh, it's okay," she whispered in his ear. "Can you hear me, Jack?"

"Rachel?" He croaked out the word and fell quiet.

"Jack? I'm here. Can you hear me?" She waited for him to speak again. When he didn't respond, she pressed her finger to his throat to check his pulse. To her relief, it felt strong and steady.

She looked up at Peter. "Time to pull this thing out."

CHAPTER 28

They did it on the count of three, Rachel counting and Peter gripping the top of the metal shard. When she hit "three," he yanked it out, and Rachel pressed the prepped piece of fungus over the wound. Together, they wrapped the strips of shirt over and around the shoulder to hold the fungus in place.

"Fuck." The curse came from Hound Dog.

Tears of relief dripped from Rachel's eyes, and she brushed them aside.

"Dog, you okay?"

"No, I'm fucking dying. What happened?" His voice was stronger than when he'd first awoken, and she wanted to shout out the victory. Instead, she stroked his cheek with her finger.

"We had to fix your shoulder." She leaned in close to his face. "I hate to do this to you, but you need to get up and moving."

He groaned in response. "Leave me here."

"You know I won't." She'd sounded irritated and mentally kicked herself for letting him hear it.

"Don't worry, Frosty. I'm kidding. I'll be ready to go when you say. Jump right up and run after you. We'll hike to the highway. Catch a lift."

"Is he delirious?" Peter asked, frowning with concern.

She shook her head. "He's being Hound Dog." Another couple of tears slid down her face. "We've got you, Jack. We're not letting you lounge around any longer, you lazy ass." She stood and Peter followed suit, picking his handgun up as he rose.

"You take the right side; I'll take the left," she said.

Peter's brows pulled together again, his lips turning down. "This'll hurt."

"We can't help that." Annoyed he pointed out the obvious when they had no alternative, she bit her lip to keep from snapping at him. "On three. We do this together. He's got to be awake to help us. We won't get far if we have to drag him the whole way."

Subdued, Peter said, "Understood."

Grateful he said nothing else to raise her ire, Rachel counted and together they eased Hound Dog to his feet. He let out a roar as he tried to straighten up, and he collapsed on them, nearly dragging them all back to the ground.

"Quiet!" Peter said in a loud whisper.

"Sorry," Hound Dog replied through gritted teeth. "My shoulder's on fire. My head's on fire. And it felt like you guys just poured kerosene on them both." He let out a string of curses that made Peter flush in the glow of the nearby blaze.

The fire had died down a little, but it would continue to burn for a while. It hadn't spread beyond the vehicles on the road. Since no trees grew close to the road—her father had his crews keep the roads relatively grendel-free by cutting the foliage back on either side—it was more difficult for the fire to spread.

They maintained a slow pace since Hound Dog kept passing out, and after dragging him for a few paces, they had to stop and rest. Rachel's back ached. Her throat and lungs burned, probably from inhaling smoke. She tried to ignore it but couldn't shake the gritty scratchiness in her throat and the pressure in her lungs. Peter, when he spoke, sounded as hoarse and uncomfortable as she did.

Hound Dog's throat and lungs seemed to fare better probably because he'd been lying on the ground below the smoke for the worst of it. They'd worked their way beyond it, away from the direction the wind blew it. The rain picked up again, a slow, chilly drizzle that seeped into their bones.

Every so often, while they rested, Rachel tilted her head up and tried to ease her parched throat with rainwater. They needed to find water soon, and her stomach had already alerted her to its hunger. Peter's stomach also growled out its desire for food. Hound Dog's remained silent, his preoccupation pain in the upper body.

The next time they took a forced rest when Hound Dog drifted into unconsciousness, Peter suggested they try to sleep. They huddled in a clearing, the rain soaking them, but they couldn't risk going under the trees. Hound Dog lay on his front, his upper body draped across Rachel's thighs so his head could rest on her lap.

"We must've walked ten kilometres," Peter said.

She hated to tell him but had to. "We've walked three, and they'll catch up to us in minutes once they pick up our trail."

Peter moaned. "How is that possible? How do you know?"

"I know how to estimate distance covered based on our walking pace, which has been slower than a turtle's." Her words and tone trumpeted her frustration. "I can't go any faster."

"*We* can't go any faster," Peter replied.

From Rachel's lap came Hound Dog's voice. "Leave me. I'll catch up. I'm slowing you down. You'd be at the highway if it weren't for me."

"I swear, if you suggest that one more time ..." She couldn't finish the threat. She could do nothing to him that was worse than what he already endured.

"What?" he said and panted a little from the exertion of speaking.

"I'll"—she had a sudden idea—"set fire ants on you again."

He gave a wheezy chuckle and coughed. "Then I'll have to sic spiders on you again, Frosty."

"Deal. You don't ever suggest we leave you, and neither one of us will have to retaliate."

His hand moved to her leg, and he squeezed her kneecap. "I'm awake. Let's walk."

"Are you sure?" Peter asked. "You look like hell."

Hound Dog made that chuckling sound again. "You'd better be talking to Frosty, big guy." He coughed. "Get me up. You two are slowing me down. Do I have to take the lead here?"

Rachel opened her mouth to respond when, from deep in the underbrush, came the rustling of movement. Whatever was in there headed straight toward them.

***

All Hound Dog wanted to do was pass out and never wake up, but when the rustling of leaves and brush to the west of them reached his ears, he tried to raise his head. It throbbed and pounded and felt as if someone had thrust a sword through it.

Peter, already on his feet, brandished a handgun. Rachel gently extricated herself from under Hound Dog, resting his face on the ground. He forgave her—she only did what was necessary to protect them.

With effort, he raised his head, then his torso, until he rested on his hands and knees. Next to him, Rachel swapped a rifle for Peter's gun and set the handgun on the ground in front of Hound Dog.

"If you can, we need all hands," she said.

He rose to his knees, clutching the gun in his right hand. "I'm with ya." The effort to say that while hoisting the gun almost brought his face back down into the dirt, but he rode out the wave of pain and stayed on his knees.

Who'd have thought the day would come when he'd be grateful for simply staying on his knees? He turned his face up to the rain and let it trickle down his face and into his open mouth. Not exactly Evian, but it would have to do.

"There's more than one." Rachel spoke calmly, but when Hound Dog checked her out, he could see her shaking. Might be the cold, but he doubted it. Her nerves were frayed.

They had to get out of here. Dog gritted his teeth and staggered to his feet. He refused to greet death on his knees. They'd eliminate whatever burst through the trees, and then they'd hit the road. It had to be close, but close was a relative term, wasn't it? What before would've taken him two minutes to walk now took him twenty, and he could only manage it if Peter and Rachel supported him.

He'd never been so helpless, and it sucked. Someone would pay for doing this to him if he could only remember what had happened. In a moment of terror, Hound Dog's memory faltered, and he couldn't recall why they were here or how he'd been hurt. He almost asked his companions but then realized it would only frighten them more if they discovered he'd lost his mind.

The brush ceased rustling, and something—some things—paused, panting and hidden from view. Chills ran up Hound Dog's spine.

"Get behind me, Frosty." He wanted to call her Rachel because maybe this would be the last time he'd get to say her name. But he didn't want to scare her, so he stuck to her nickname, but when he said it, even he heard the affection in it.

"No." She moved in front of him, shielding him.

Irritated, he said, "Damn it, get behind me. It's grendels."

"Sure," she agreed. "If so, I'll step aside and let you have them if I miss them. If it's my father's thugs, I'll take them out with my rifle.' She threw a haughty glance in his direction. "But I won't miss."

When the creatures burst into the clearing, Rachel fired first.

CHAPTER 29

One dropped from a bullet to the head.

"All right, you had your shot," Hound Dog hollered. "Step aside."

The three other creatures moved fast, descending on Rachel as she struggled to line up another shot.

Hound Dog knocked her aside with his left arm and took his shot with the handgun in his right. Another grendel dropped, followed immediately by the third as Peter squeezed off a shot that hit true.

The fourth leaped on Rachel, sinking its teeth into her thigh. She screamed, the sound chilling Hound Dog and sending his blood and adrenaline pumping. He dropped on it, dug his fingers into its eyes, and when it opened its mouth, he hauled it off Rachel. Since he didn't know where he'd dropped his gun, he yanked a knife from the sheath at his belt and sliced its throat open.

While the beast twitched its last, Hound Dog hurled himself beside Rachel. Peter already pressed on the wound with his hands.

"Oh, God, I'm sorry. I'm sorry," Rachel stuttered out between sobs. "He didn't get the artery. I moved, Dog. I moved in time, and he didn't get the femoral artery."

"Okay, Rache, it's okay. We'll fix it." His head swam, and

he gritted his teeth and focused all his effort on not passing out on top of her.

They were two team members down. The only one unhurt was a civilian.

"I'm sorry," she said again. "I should've done what you said."

"Can't argue with that, sweetheart." He patted her cheek. "This'll kill me, but my shirt must be sacrificed to the cause."

He met Peter's gaze over Rachel's head. "I'll need your help."

"Okay, anything," Peter replied.

Hound Dog directed Rachel to put pressure on her leg while Peter helped remove Hound Dog's jacket and T-shirt. Peter then tore the shirt into strips, and they bandaged Rachel's wound. They needed to get to a doctor for Rachel's sake as well as Hound Dog's. A grendel's bite didn't contain poison, but it could cause an infection.

The pain came rushing back into Hound Dog's head and shoulder as the adrenaline rush diminished. His vision greyed and he dropped onto his butt, drawing his knees up and putting his head between them. Nausea threatened, and he focused on his breathing, trying to quash the queasiness.

"How can we possibly keep going?" Rachel's voice held despair, and she dropped her chin so her hair hung in her face.

"Don't quit on me, Frosty. You're the only thing keeping me going."

Peter leaned into Hound Dog's face, making him lurch back. He let out an involuntary yelp of pain followed by a string of curses.

"What?" He glared at Peter.

"Sorry. We should get moving."

Hound Dog checked his watch. Eleven o'clock. Dawn was hours away. They hadn't reached the marina yet, and he doubted they should head that way. The place could be another trap. With nowhere else to go, it would be the perfect place for an ambush.

"A boat." Hound Dog's voice danced with excitement. "Either of you know where an old cottage around here might have a boat?"

Rachel slowly raised her head, and the look of hope on her face warmed Hound Dog's innards.

"It's a long shot, I know," he said.

Peter considered. "The closest cottage is the one on the point."

"Yes," Rachel agreed. "They had watercrafts, and the cottage is located before we'd get to the marina, if we alter our route a little. We'll have to backtrack, but that might help us. My father would expect us to try to make it to the marina, not head to a place that's totalled and a dead end." She fell silent a moment before she continued. "But if any of the boats are there, we could strike out into the lake, go around the island, and cut back to the highway through the creek that feeds from the lake. Or we could cut across the lake and take a different road altogether. We'd lose any pursuit that way."

"Unless they anticipate it and have motorboats," Peter said quietly.

She sighed. "I don't know what else to do. If we follow the road, they'll find us. If we stay in the woods, more grendels will attack us—and then my father's people will find us."

Peter helped Rachel to stand and then assisted Hound Dog to his feet. Hound Dog's vision wavered again, and he closed his eyes, biting back a groan. He placed his left arm around Rachel's shoulders and his right one around Peter's.

"Can you walk with me hanging off you, Frosty?" Her wound was fresh. He'd had time to get accustomed to his. At least, that was how he saw it. The bite on her leg, when he'd examined it, hadn't looked deep, but the creature had shredded the tissue. She'd have a wicked scar for the rest of her life—which would hopefully go beyond tonight.

"Yes, as long as you stay conscious. Try not to pass out or we'll all go down." No annoyance tinged her voice; she simply stated a fact.

"I'll do my best," he replied, and as one, they started moving.

The pace was excruciatingly slow topped with painfully slow and with a delightful cream filling of hideously slow. To make matters worse, Hound Dog kept losing his train of thought and caught himself regularly wondering what someone had just said.

Twice, he must have nodded off because he suddenly came to lying on the ground, his head in Peter's lap. He was beyond caring how it looked, but he missed the intimacy of resting on Rachel. That he always referred to her in his head as Rachel and not Frostbite wasn't lost on him. He chalked it up to the direness of their situation and that he perhaps wanted his last night on Earth to be spent touching a woman rather than a man.

But he figured he preferred the man over the cold, wet ground.

At this point, he remembered they needed to keep moving. One more grendel attack might do them in. He alerted the other two to his readiness to continue the hike, and they started the cycle over.

In this way, they made it at last to the cottage on the point Peter and Rachel had discussed. Hound Dog first glimpsed the building through a foggy haze. He had to squint into the moon-dim night where he discerned the outline of a small bungalow-type structure. The roof was gone, of course, and, more to the point, a tree had fallen on it and shoved most of it off its foundation and into the lake.

"I guess we're not going in," Peter commented.

"Not tonight," Rachel answered. "Help me and Hound Dog find a place to sit, and then you search for boats. They had an aluminum fishing boat. If we can find that and the oars, we'll be okay."

Peter agreed and helped them hobble over to what remained of the back porch. It had detached when the rest of the cottage slid away, but the cedar boards were in good shape, and a built-in bench spanned the perimeter. When the two wounded had settled in, Peter started walking away.

Rachel stopped him. "Peter."

He halted and turned to face her, his expression puzzled.

"Let's see that gun at the ready."

"Right." He held it up and walked away.

Rachel turned to Hound Dog, her brown eyes sparkling black in the moonlight. "How's the shoulder and the head?"

He shrugged. "It won't kill me tonight, I suppose. How's the leg?"

She smiled, making his heart beat faster. "It won't kill me tonight, I suppose."

To lighten the mood and get under her skin, he said, "Damn, Frosty, I wanted to be the first one to bite you there."

"Shut up, Dog," she said, but she didn't sound angry or even unhappy.

Suddenly, Hound Dog wanted like hell to get home and start over with her. If they died here, she'd never know how much she meant to him.

"Listen," he said, "I have to tell you something."

"Sounds serious." Her expression grew grim, and she leaned toward him. "Is it your head?"

"No." As soon as he said it, his shoulder and head both kicked up the throbbing and burning. "I mean, yes, that's always an issue, but something else."

"Okay, shoot."

"If I don't make it—"

She cut him off. "Don't start." Tears sprang to her eyes, and he found that touching enough he figured they didn't need to have the conversation after all.

"All right. How about this: when we get home, we make a new start. Forget I dosed you with spiders, and I'll forget you put ants in my pants."

She closed her eyes for a moment. When she opened them, she said, "Interesting. A clean slate. You going to suddenly turn into a gentleman?"

"A gentleman?" He scoffed at the idea. "You won't get

any mamby-pamby romance crap from me. No, you've got to hold your own with me, sweetheart."

She laughed, the sound deep and from the belly. "Oh, thank God. I thought you were going soft on me."

From below them came a splash and a shout. They both jumped to their feet, each letting out a groan of pain.

"What now?" Hound Dog said.

CHAPTER 30

Rachel picked her way down toward the water where they'd heard the cry. The voice was Peter's. On the positive side, he hadn't sounded frightened or hurt, so she hoped it meant he'd found the boat. But he should've known better than to blast out their position like that.

She kept her pace steady so she didn't lose Hound Dog, partly for his safety and partly for her own. If grendels lurked, she needed him to cover her. She'd never make such a mistake of arrogance again. Her refusal to accept she might be injured in a grendel attack had cost them the full use of her left leg.

Up ahead, she spotted movement by the water. A man wrestled with an aluminum boat, and when she squinted, she verified the man was Peter. The boat was half in the water, as was Peter, up to his knees. He struggled to drag the boat back up the rocks, but it kept sliding back in.

Behind her, Hound Dog dropped to his knees. She turned back to help him and spotted the camera.

"Dog." She pointed to a metal pole looming above the roof of the cottage.

He raised his head and faced the direction she pointed. "Shit." He slowly regained his feet. "Do you think they're monitoring it?"

"If they are, they already know we're here, assuming the camera belongs to my father. It's probably motion-activated."

She reached him and offered her arm. When he took it, she let him lean on her and guided him down to the water.

"Stay on shore and watch for grendels while I help Peter," she ordered.

"I'll do better than that. Hand me your rifle."

She knew what he wanted to do and preferred that option to providing her father and his people an unobstructed view of their activities. Rachel handed over the rifle and said, "Have at it."

"Here." He held the handgun out to her. "I don't want you unarmed. Ever."

She accepted the gun without comment and then made her way down to the rowboat. She peered into it. "No oars?"

Behind them, the rifle blasted and the camera smashed. Bullseye.

"No," Peter replied. "The boat was half in the water. I had to empty it and drag it back onto the shore."

"We'll have to search for oars. We need a way to manoeuvre."

"I got it. Let me look in that shed they have next to where the cabin used to be."

"Watch yourself. They probably have more than one camera out here. You got your gun?" she asked even though she could see it hanging at his side in his hand.

He gave her a sheepish look and raised it, holding it out in front of him as he made his way back up the rocky slope to the shed.

"They saw him messing with this boat." Rachel lifted Hound Dog's arm and draped it around her shoulders.

"I can stand," he said, his voice flat, but he didn't remove the arm. "What can we do about it? Now they know where we are and that we're trying to leave by boat."

"They don't know if we've found the oars." She gave him a side-wise glance. "I have an idea."

Peter found oars and returned with them, but when he

heard Rachel's plan, he balked.

"No way. Not a chance. Not on your life."

Hound Dog laughed. "Tell us what you really think, civilian."

"Don't call me that."

Dog laughed again and then slapped Peter on the back. "It's a term of endearment."

"Great. Thanks." His voice dripped sarcasm, but Hound Dog didn't seem to notice.

"Look, we've got to do this. They'll come here first. If we're still here, they'll deal with us. They may never even realize you escaped."

Rachel stayed out of it, preferring to allow the two guys to let off steam. But she couldn't give them too much time. By dawn, the place would be crawling with her father's guards. He may not even wait until sunup.

"But they'll have you," Peter protested.

"They won't have us. How many can they send? We dealt with most of them."

"No, we dealt with whoever we dealt with. They expected us to fall into their booby trap—and we did." Peter's face turned red with rage and strain. "We're lucky to be alive." He pointed at Rachel and continued the rant. "She's not protected against the monsters. What if grendels show up? She's already been bitten."

Rachel had heard enough. "Okay, time."

The two turned and stared at her.

"You're going, Peter. You can move fast. If you aren't moving fast enough, Hound Dog and I will slow down the pursuit."

Peter snorted. "That's fine for me, but how will you two get out of here?"

She replied, speaking to Peter but looking at Hound Dog, "We'll find a way."

***

VAL TOBIN

It took more convincing, but when they refused to change their minds, he relented. He gave Rachel a kiss on the cheek and a hug that lasted long enough for Hound Dog to throw him a dirty look and then hopped into the boat. They'd ensured its water worthiness and had set the oars into the oarlocks. He took a handgun, leaving one gun and two rifles with Rachel and Hound Dog.

After telling him to get the story into the paper as soon as possible and to trust only Captain Pattenden with what had happened, Rachel pushed the boat out into the water. Peter glanced back repeatedly as he rowed farther and farther away from shore. He'd paddle across the lake, skirting the small islands that broke the surface.

Most of them would be infested with grendels, he assumed, so he would draw close to them. If Stefan Needham's people overtook him, he'd greet them with grendel backup. If the guards weren't vaccinated, he could use the creatures as monster shields and pick off whoever followed him onto an island.

Rachel had made sure his gun was fully loaded before he left, and he hoped to never have to use his weapon, but if he needed it, he could put a good dent in any pursuit. The lake at this time of night—which he'd established as just after twelve thirty—was mirror calm. He heard no sounds, not even of loons, which made him sad.

At this time of year, he should hear them calling to one another in their strange, melancholy voices. Their absence left an aching void in his heart for things long past. He tried to shake off grief by focusing on rowing. His muscles already ached, but he ignored the pain, reminding himself Rachel and Hound Dog had it worse.

If—when—he made it to the road, he'd have to hike to the highway and find his way to Bancroft, the nearest still-functioning town. Peter turned his face up to the sky as he pulled back on the oars. The clouds obscured the stars, for the most part, but enough of the rain clouds had passed that the moon peeked out at frequent intervals.

A desire to scream into the silence overwhelmed him, but he reined it in. There'd be no rest nor release for him soon. In the distance, a motor roared to life. He froze and listened.

Out on the lake, the noise seemed to come from multiple directions, but he knew that was just a trick of the sound across the water. Sweat that had bloomed on his back and under his arms from the exertion of rowing turned icy, and he shivered.

Was it getting louder? Was it headed in this direction?

Peter gritted his teeth, redoubled his efforts, and skimmed across the surface of the lake.

CHAPTER 31

Hound Dog and Rachel heard the motor at the same time Peter did, but they knew exactly from where it came: the direction of the Needham buildings on the south-west side of the point. The breath caught in Rachel's throat. If the boat headed to the cottage behind which Rachel and Hound Dog hid, their plan might work. If the boat headed after Peter, they'd failed in the worst way.

"I should've gone to look for the boat," Hound Dog said.

"That wasn't up to you, and you weren't in any shape to do anything physical," Rachel replied.

"We should've told him to watch for cameras."

"I'm to blame on that score," Rachel said. "I didn't think of it. Why would they bother to put a camera here?"

"Maybe the camera didn't belong to your dad." Hound Dog sounded as dubious as Rachel felt.

"Those cameras were new."

They'd taken out two more cameras. Hopefully, her father would believe they remained up the lake without a paddle. It explained why he'd sent a boat out on the water when the pursuers were as likely to run into grendels if they put into shore as they were to locate three people who wanted to disappear.

"The racket they're making sure gives us a heads-up, don't

it?" Hound Dog commented.

"What are you getting at?"

"Why would they let us know they're on their way?"

She shrugged. "What can we do about it?"

"We can leave a trail for them to follow."

She stared at him. "Let's do it." She paused. "But they know we found a boat. If they don't see one abandoned here, they'll think we're all on the lake."

"Search for another one. Quick. We'll leave it here and a trail for them to follow."

Rachel hesitated. All kinds of issues with this suggestion came to mind, but she couldn't think of anything better. And, like Hound Dog, she always functioned better when taking action. She didn't want to go out sitting around waiting to be shot at even if they could turn it into a final blaze of glory.

"Okay."

They searched the grounds but couldn't find a rowboat similar to the one Peter had taken. A kayak and a canoe were the only crafts available. Since the canoe resembled a rowboat more than a kayak did, they dragged it to the shore and submerged it halfway in the location where Peter had found the rowboat.

Since they didn't need to locate paddles for it, Rachel and Hound Dog turned from the shore and, without their usual caution and care, walked through the mud and up the slope. They headed toward the old marina. Neither cared any longer if an ambush awaited them at the end as long as Peter escaped.

Behind her, Hound Dog huffed and panted. She slowed her pace, and when he caught up, she had him put his arm around her shoulders.

After another few minutes of limping along, he said, "I've got to rest or I'll fall."

She stopped and they sank to the ground. Above them, tree branches swayed in the wind. The clouds had parted, and a dense spackle of stars covered the sky. The night noises had ceased.

"Shouldn't we hear crickets at least?" Rachel asked.

"Don't ask me," Hound Dog said. "I don't know what's normal anymore."

"None of us do." Normal had left the building twelve years ago. No matter how many hunts they went on, the grendel herds never seemed to thin out enough. The wildlife hadn't bounced back, but she'd have expected crickets to proliferate since grendels didn't eat insects. Some cricket species survived well into October even in the north, and the calendar still said September.

Around them, the bushes rustled. Both heaved to their feet in unison, guns at the ready. They stood back to back as Code Master and Foot-Long had done when facing the grendels back at the lab.

"Pick them off. Can you get off two shots okay?"

Used to Hound Dog's non-stop comments and questions when he was nervous, Rachel simply said, "Yeah."

But it wasn't grendels that stepped from the shadows. Three figures detached from the trees in front of Rachel, and they were human.

Rachel held her fire when she realized she faced Captain Pattenden.

"Oh, thank God, Captain. What are you doing here?"

"The schedule said you'd be here until tomorrow, but when I tried to reach you, I got no response. I found two volunteers and came after you." She took a step toward them, her two teammates standing their ground.

Hound Dog relaxed against Rachel's body and then turned around to face his captain and her team. When he recognized them, his body went rigid, and his grip tightened on his weapon.

"Hi, Cap. Good to see you." His voice sounded casual, but Rachel knew him well enough to hear the suspicion colouring it. "A night-time foray's risky."

"I was worried." She nodded at Rachel. "Your father is too. He asked me to let him know when you returned. Said grendels attacked you, and you lost Coder and Foot-Long. Is that true?"

Rachel froze at the mention of her father.

"You talked to my father?" She raised her rifle. "How'd you locate us?"

The captain frowned. "Surveillance."

"The cameras." Her suspicion that Pattenden had thrown in with Stefan Needham deepened.

Too late, she heard the *phtt, phtt* of shots fired from a silencer, and something stung her butt cheek. She cried out even as Hound Dog did the same. The three people in front of them ducked as Rachel and Hound Dog fired their weapons, but they both missed.

Everything went dark.

***

Rachel woke to a pounding head and relief at the realization she wasn't dead. She lay on a bed and had the sinking feeling she'd awakened back in her father's lab. If so, everything they'd suffered through over the last number of hours was for nothing. Neither she nor Hound Dog would be injured if they'd stayed there. Then again, Peter would still be with them. As long as he was free, they had a hope of stopping her father even if she and Hound Dog never lived to see that day.

She kept her breathing even and steady so any observers wouldn't know she was awake. All the while, she listened and tried to get a fix on where she was and who might be with her.

Hound Dog better be nearby and not dead. If they'd hurt him, she'd make sure they paid for it. She already owed them payback for what they'd done to Code Master and Foot-Long.

Voices and footsteps approached. She recognized Captain Pattenden but not her male companion. They made small talk—nothing helpful. They arrived at Rachel's bed without the clank of a cage door opening, which told her she wasn't back in her father's lab after all.

Rage at the situation overwhelmed Rachel. She'd trusted the captain with her life—with the lives of her team—and she'd betrayed that trust by working with Stefan. How much had he paid the bitch to betray the protectors? With a sinking sensation, she remembered telling Peter to trust no one but Pattenden. Rachel had an urge to leap up and lunge at Pattenden's throat but controlled it with massive effort. Instead, she opened her eyes to face the enemy.

CHAPTER 32

She was in what appeared to be a hospital room. In the bed next to her rested Hound Dog. The bandage around his head looked professionally wrapped, and she assumed his shoulder was also. She raised the blanket to check her thigh and found it tended to as well. And her clothes were gone. She wore a hospital gown. No panties.

"Rachel, I'm so glad to see you awake." The captain sat on the end of Rachel's bed.

Fighting an urge to kick the woman, Rachel instead said, "Where are we? How'd I get here?"

"You're in the HQ infirmary."

"My dad?" Rachel hit the button to raise the head of the bed so she could sit up.

"Don't worry. I've notified him you're safe."

Was Pattenden really pretending her father was on their side? After what Rachel and Hound Dog had endured at Stefan's hands, was there any use in continuing the charade?

"Drop the act, Captain. Quit pretending he's not a sociopath who wants to hunt me, Hound Dog, and Peter down."

The captain's face registered shock. "What do you mean?"

"You work for my father. You know exactly what I mean."

"I called your father's office yesterday when you didn't return my call—none of you. I tried Dog, Coder, and Foot-Long before I tried him. Since he has property on Storm Lake, I called him to ask if you'd contacted him." She paused. "Where's the reporter?"

Rachel ignored the question. She refused to provide any information to Pattenden until she made sure it wouldn't be fed to her father. The captain's words told her they hadn't found Peter, and Rachel intended to keep it that way.

"How'd you track us? You said you used the surveillance cameras. They're my father's."

"No, they're not. Protectors installed them."

"When? Why?" The idea was a good one, but why hadn't she known about them?

"Two years ago, we started putting cameras in places where our hunters were likely to revisit—mostly around places where residences or cottages stood. Campsites. Resorts. People want their properties back. The government funds the effort. The goal is to increase vigilance, provide better safety for our hunters, and potentially reclaim these sites for the rightful owners. We haven't finished installing the cameras—it's not an easy task—but we determined that if we're sending teams in, casualties are lower if we can assess the area first."

"Don't the grendels rip them down?"

"That's what we all assumed at first, which is why we hadn't done this before. Research has shown they don't climb metal poles very well—nor do they want to. They don't care about inanimate objects. They want food. Anytime they've ripped apart anything, they did it to get to food."

Rachel nodded. The captain verified what Rachel had suspected.

"What now?" The question came from Hound Dog. His bedsheets rustled, and the motor on the bed hummed as he raised the upper half to a sitting position.

Rachel studied his face. His expression remained calm, pain-free, and his movements were smooth and methodical.

No one brought up the question of why Pattenden had had them shot with a tranquillizer dart to bring them here. If she was on their side, all she'd have had to do was ask. Rachel gave the room a quick scan but didn't see any cameras. If she could get the captain to leave, she could discuss with Hound Dog what to do to find Peter.

The motorboat they'd heard came to mind then. She hoped whoever drove it hadn't realized Peter was out on the water virtually unprotected. At that reminder, the panic built. She had to get Pattenden out of the room.

***

Despite the grendels scurrying in the shadows, Peter dragged his boat onto shore on an island in the middle of the lake where the remains of a cottage stood. The main building had a missing roof, and natural forces had completed the demolition. Two trees had smashed in the main structure, and the elements had taken care of the rest. The grendels, staring at him with beady eyes, squatted in or under the trees surrounding him.

Peter didn't even try to enter the mess that used to be a family's summer retreat. The boathouse interested him more. If he could find a working motor, he'd have a chance of outrunning whoever hunted him.

That whoever was out there might not be searching for Peter Sanderson specifically kept him from having a full-blown panic attack. Even so, the adrenaline rush he always got when facing danger energized him. He wished he hadn't lost all his reporting tools back at the lab and longed for his digital recorder, his cell phone, and his tablet.

Instead, he had to settle for committing everything that happened to memory. He mentally narrated his movements as he broke the padlock on the boathouse with an axe he'd found in a shed. The voice-over in his head sounded a little like Kiefer Sutherland, and Peter imagined himself the hero in the movie they'd one day make of this. If it wasn't too far in the future, Matt Damon could play him.

Movements in his periphery made him look up, but it was only the grendels. They hovered around him, probably confused as hell that what looked so edible from a distance repelled them when they ventured close. Peter mentally thanked the vaccine's formulator. It worked beautifully.

Perhaps, he should return to the lab and help them finish the testing. This vaccine could work wonders for humanity. They'd once more be the top of the food chain. Heck, they'd be able to leave an infant among the creatures, and it would be as safe as if resting in its mother's arms.

But no matter how he tried to spin it in his mind that Coder's and Foot-Long's deaths were an accident, he couldn't buy into it. They'd been murdered. Stefan had tried to kill his daughter by blowing up Hound Dog's truck. Stefan Needham did nothing for altruistic reasons, and that would never change. Anyone associated with him had better watch him carefully. He'd betray and murder his family to accomplish his goals.

Inside the boathouse, Peter found it in relatively decent shape. The roof hadn't been ripped off—probably because whoever had owned the cottage hadn't been inside the boathouse when the creatures attacked. The grendels had sensed food only in the cottage, so they'd had no reason to break into the outbuildings.

Two speedboats sat docked in the water. They'd been shielded in here from the elements, but that didn't mean they worked. If they'd sat here for twelve years, the engines would've seized and the gas in them would be old. Their batteries would need changing, especially since, in this neck of the woods, the temperature could drop to minus forty Celsius in the winter.

He searched the boathouse for the keys, all the while listening for the approach of the boat he'd heard before. At first, he heard nothing but the movements of the creatures outside. Despite the noise Peter made rooting around in cabinets and cupboards, the grendels made no move to get into the boathouse. They understood the person prowling around in there wasn't edible. To Peter, that meant they knew who he was. They'd observed him from the time he left his boat to the moment he stepped into the boathouse.

They're intelligent enough not to be fooled by peek-a-boo. An interesting thought.

Jeff's notes had mentioned the grendels' ability to recognize faces. Peter still had the memory stick Rachel had given him for safekeeping. He'd locked it in a safe deposit box in the bank and hid the key to it in his vehicle. When he returned, he'd ensure legitimate scientists doing serious grendel research to benefit all humanity had access to those notes.

He located the keys to the boats. If he turned them on, he'd probably make enough racket to give away his presence, but hopefully, he'd be long gone by the time the bad guys arrived. He went to one boat and tried the keys until one of them fit. When he turned it in the ignition, the motor never even sputtered.

Of course, it wouldn't work, but he'd had to at least try. Peter left the key in the ignition and ran back to the fishing boat. In the dark, the grendels resembled skinny apes. Three of them huddled nearby. They kept a distance of at least three metres from him.

He scanned the lake in the direction from which he'd come. Everything was calm and quiet. The motor in the distance had quieted. A cold sweat broke out on his neck, and he shivered. What if they'd reached the island while he'd been screwing around in the boathouse? Quickly, he determined which way was closest to his target—Storm Lake Boat Launch, located two kilometres to the north-east of the island.

Peter made a move to slip the boat quietly back into the water when he changed his mind. Perhaps, he could get himself a motorboat after all. He smiled in the darkness as he headed for the crushed cottage.

CHAPTER 33

A woman from the cafeteria appeared with trays of food for Rachel and Hound Dog, and Captain Pattenden took the excuse to leave. As soon as the door closed behind the food server and the captain, Rachel climbed from her bed and, holding the back of her gown closed, searched the room for their clothes.

Hound Dog broke a packet of crackers into the bowl of chicken soup and tucked in, blowing on each spoonful before shovelling it into his mouth.

"Eat, Frosty. Whatever else we do, we have to eat first. Take food when you have the chance."

He was right, but her stomach was in knots, and she didn't know if she could handle even a bite. She didn't find their clothes but held panic at bay with the hope it was because they'd been too soiled and torn to keep. At least they could've let them have their underwear. For a moment, she allowed herself to be distracted by the question of whether Hound Dog wore boxers or briefs. But only for a moment. Peter needed them to get moving.

"Our clothes are gone," she told Hound Dog.

"Are you surprised? I had pants and underwear left. Your pants were shredded where the grendel bit you. You'd already torn your shirt into pieces. I guess they could've salvaged

178

your panties and bra." He grinned. "I'd have paid money to see you wearing just those."

"I thought you were going to grow up," she said.

His expression sobered. "Old habits. Sorry."

She gave him a contemplative stare. "It's disrespectful because I'm your team leader."

"I said I was sorry. It's nothing personal."

"It's personal to all women, Jack."

He fell silent. The room became too quiet until her stomach growled, breaking the awkward silence. She returned to her bed to eat her meal. If nothing else, she needed nourishment. She'd need all her energy for whatever came next.

After she'd filled the hole in her belly with soup, crackers, and half the tuna sandwich they'd provided, she said, "Why drug us and bring us here?" She opened the bottle of water and took a swig.

"I wondered that myself. If Cap told us the truth, they only had to explain it to us. We'd have walked out with them."

She considered. "Would we have? I wouldn't have left Peter. He needs us. With a team, we could've followed him …"

He understood why she'd trailed off. "Yeah. Followed him where? How? Find a boat while your father's people are searching for us? While the team and you are grendel bait? And there's no telling where Peter went ashore. If he went ashore."

"At least my father's people will have the same problem." She didn't vocalize her fear that, by now, all her father's people had been vaccinated. Surely, they wouldn't want to inject themselves without further tests. She was no scientist, but she believed whatever they learned from Code Master's body wouldn't be as helpful as if they could run more tests on a living person.

"We need to get out of here and find Peter. We shouldn't have left him."

"It was the best decision at the time. We slowed him down. He needed the chance to escape."

"I understand all the reasons we did what we did, but he could be here with us now."

"Sure," he said. "Caught with us if Pattenden is on your father's side."

She reached under the covers and pressed on the bandage covering her wound. She winced at the stab of pain. "They patched us up."

"Yeah. For what? To turn us both over to your dad?"

"You done eating?" She pushed the tray table aside and got out of bed again. "Let me see your bandages."

He shoved his empty dishes away and let her examine his head and his shoulder.

"It all looks good. How do you feel? Can you move?"

"It's fine."

"You know what's funny?"

"What?"

"They never brought a doctor in to talk to us. I'd like to verify you don't have a concussion."

"We can't wait around for that."

"I know." She sighed. "Let's go. We'll get spare clothes from our lockers and slip out."

"That's gonna be a trick. We've got no vehicle."

"I'd settle for clean clothes. One thing at a time."

They both used the facilities first, not only to wash up and use the toilet but to scope out their environment. They couldn't use searching for a bathroom as an excuse to leave the room.

They crept to the door and opened it. To Rachel's dismay, a guard stood on the other side.

He said, "Can I help you?"

She spoke boldly, as if she had no idea he was there to prevent them from leaving. "No, thanks. We're heading out."

"I'm sorry." He looked genuinely regretful. "Captain Pattenden assigned me to guard this room and allow no one in or out she hasn't authorized."

"Why?" Rachel replied.

"Didn't say. I'm just following orders."

"She's got no right to keep us here," Hound Dog cut in.

"I'm sure she has her reasons. Should I send someone to track her down?"

"Yeah, you do that," Rachel said. She gave the guard a dirty look even though it wasn't his fault they were stuck here.

"Close the door, please, ma'am, and I'll call her."

Without responding, Rachel slammed the door in his face.

"Now what?" she asked Hound Dog. "Do we wait for her or jump the guy in the hallway? I'm good either way."

"I think," Hound Dog said, grinning, "we wait. Why jump him when we can jump two for the same price."

Rachel couldn't stop a laugh from bursting out. "Works for me," she said but immediately sobered. "We're not strong enough to take this guy on. We can't go two against two."

"We may not have to. Hear me out."

"All right," she said. "What've you got?"

CHAPTER 34

Peter kicked in the cabin's front door, hoping the trees on the roof wouldn't crash down on him when the cottage shook. The place smelled mouldy and damp. He stood for a moment in the foyer to let his eyes adjust to the inkier black inside.

Too bad the roof hadn't been completely ripped off. Starlight and moonlight would've helped. After standing still and scanning the area around him, he figured out the kitchen was on his left. With luck, the family who owned the place stored candles and matches in there. If not, he'd have to expand his search to the living area and then the bedrooms.

He'd have preferred a flashlight, but the batteries in those would've crapped out a long time ago. Candles and matches would work best—especially the matches. He primarily came for those.

As he worked, he was aware of time passing and the sound of the motorboat starting up again. Did that mean they'd hunted down his friends and now came after him? Had they interrogated the two protectors, torturing them to tell what they knew about Peter and where he might have gone? He pushed the visions of torture and pain from his mind. If he didn't, he'd freeze and they'd find him curled up in a little ball on the musty couch.

It didn't take him long to stumble across a drawer with

emergency candles and boxes of matches. Relieved, he struggled with the stale matches and lit a candle, then he pocketed as many as he could carry. With that bit of light, he found a holder for the candle, one with a wide base and a rounded glass cover to shield the flame from the breeze outside.

Peter scanned the cottage in the semidarkness, for the first time seeing it as a place where a family once gathered to have fun and spend time together. It would've been quaint in its time. Rather than a television, a wood-burning stove was the living room's focal point. A couch, love seat, and armchair surrounded it. In the corner of the room, a dollhouse as demolished as the cottage stood next to a large chest that probably held toys and games.

The sight of items indicating the presence of children hurt his heart. While he hoped the family hadn't been here that fateful weekend the grendels first appeared, he doubted it. The family members were all probably dead these past twelve years.

He picked his way through the debris back outside, the weight of tragedy stooping his shoulders. As he worked to execute his plan, he questioned the sanity of it. The odds were fifty-fifty his pursuers would catch him before he could escape, but if he didn't try, he'd spend the rest of the night paddling on the lake, and they'd still catch him. At least this way, he could feel as if he had a measure of control over his fate.

As quickly as possible, he collected the driest wood he could find, as well as small twigs and sticks to use as kindling. The cottagers had a woodshed stocked with nicely seasoned hardwood—very well seasoned, considering the number of years it had sat untouched.

He found a large fire pit in the centre of an expansive clearing outside the back door. He cleaned the pit out as best he could and stacked his kindling and small logs beside it. Since he'd always enjoyed camping and often did it when in pursuit of a story, his fire-making skills were sharp. He had a blaze going after a few minutes of struggling with the old matches. He stoked the flames up enough for someone to think a dumb city slicker had built it for warmth even though pursuit was close.

When he considered it perfect, he walked the island's perimeter to verify the fire could be seen flickering through the trees surrounding it. He wanted it to look as if he camped there for the night and had built a small fire for warmth. Hopefully, it wasn't so obvious they'd suspect a trap.

The grendels kept their distance from the fire. Most people knew grendels hated fire, which might make whoever chased him believe he had valid reasons for the blaze.

By the time he returned to his campfire, he was confident it burned bright enough but not too bright. He only had to wait for his prey to appear. Peter sat on a log at the edge of the forest and scanned the horizon.

Come and get me.

***

The wait, for Peter, felt like hours. In actuality, it was only forty-five minutes. The boat chugged its way closer to the island and then veered directly at it when whoever was in it spotted the bonfire.

Peter's palms grew clammy. Now it was happening, he had a momentary regret he'd started all this. He could've paddled far in forty-five minutes. What had he been thinking? The panic escalated, and he almost ran from his hiding spot to the other side of the island where he'd hidden the fishing boat.

Calm down. This'll work. Then I'll be speeding away from here, and they'll be trapped—with the grendels.

He waited and watched, his breathing shallow and rapid.

Two men pulled up to the shore, and both stepped from the boat. So far, so good. He hoped like hell one didn't hang back to guard the damn thing. If that happened, Peter might have to shoot him, and Peter had never killed anyone in his life—had never even wanted to until this excursion to Stefan

Needham's resort from hell.

The thought of Rachel's father brought Rachel to mind. What had happened to her and Hound Dog? He hoped they'd made it out of the woods and found a ride back to HQ and safety. Maybe they were on their way back for him already with a search party.

The two men stood on the rocks at the edge of the shoreline and conferred in low voices—probably discussing strategy. Separate and risk attack from the grendels— assuming the two men hadn't been vaccinated—or stick together and risk Peter finding the boat before they found Peter. The smart money was on them splitting up. Each had a rifle and probably other weapons Peter couldn't see in the dark. He fervently hoped they assumed him too stupid to consider pursuit by boat.

His hopes were dashed when only one man made his way up the slope toward the woods and the fire. The other left the boat but only climbed partway up the rocks. Instantly, the grendels swung down from the trees, loping toward the men, who reacted quickly and efficiently.

The rifles blasted, but Peter didn't waste time checking to see if they'd hit the targets. He crept toward the boat, staying close to the water's edge where he could use the rocky shoreline as cover. The two men continued their assault on the grendels. Peter reached the boat and climbed into it while shoving it off the shore and into the water.

He didn't get far before he heard a shout of discovery and a bullet whizzed over his head. Hunched over, Peter tried to pull-start the motor. The first tug failed. A glance at the shore showed one man approaching. Should he use his gun or try the motor again? Peter tugged at the starter, but the attempt was feeble, and the motor sputtered and coughed.

Damn it, the gun.

The man, almost on him, waved and shouted at Peter to surrender. Another bullet sailed over his head, and beyond the first man, the second one approached, rifle raised.

Heart despairing, Peter held up his hands in surrender.

CHAPTER 35

They agreed they needn't physically attack the captain. What they did would depend on how she responded to their desire to walk out of here. Neither Rachel nor Hound Dog had heard from a doctor, and Rachel's main concern was Hound Dog's head wound.

Voices floated in from outside the door: the captain greeting the guard and the guard responding in kind.

Rachel sat on the edge of her bed. Hound Dog stood next to his, one hand clutching the back of his gown closed.

After a quick tap on the door, the captain opened it and stepped into the room.

"Everything all right with you two? My man outside tells me you want to leave." She glanced first at Hound Dog and then settled her gaze on Rachel.

"Your man would be correct," Hound Dog replied.

Captain Pattenden shot him a look, displaying her displeasure at his tone. "You aren't ready to leave yet. You're both too injured, and you haven't told me where Dalton Morin, Paul Fraser, and Peter Sanderson have disappeared to. You left as a team. Only you two returned."

"Really?" Rachel laced her response with surprise. "Didn't my dad tell you anything?"

"He said grendels attacked you and you lost two of our

men. Lost as in dead." Her voice rose a decibel. "Where's the reporter? How did you lose two men as solid as Morin and Fraser? I find it difficult to believe mere grendels could take them down."

"What did you tell my father?"

"What do you mean?"

"Did you tell him Hound Dog and I are here?

"Yes, of course I did. He's worried about you. He asked me to keep you here until he could come and see you."

"I'll bet he did." Rachel risked a glance at Hound Dog, who'd shifted to stand behind the captain. They'd have to be quick. Any racket from Pattenden would bring the guard into the room, something Rachel and Hound Dog counted on. They needed uniforms and weapons. After that, they'd worry about how to get back to Storm Lake to find Peter.

"What's going on with you, Needham? What happened to the others? What aren't you telling me?"

Hound Dog crept closer to the captain, but just as he poised to move, the door opened and he held back.

"Rachel, I'm so glad I finally caught up to you." Stefan Needham stepped into the room, an aura of command and arrogance wafting off him.

Two guards, wearing uniforms sporting Needham Scientific Research Facility labels on the breast pocket, followed close behind. They moved quickly to intercept Hound Dog and block him in.

"What the hell is this?" Hound Dog, understandably infuriated, took a step backward and bumped into his bed.

"We're cooperating with the research facility," Captain Pattenden replied. "I've given the go-ahead for the two of you to participate in whatever work they're doing there."

"Participate!" Hound Dog roared. "You want to know what happened to Coder and Foot-Long? They're dead, all right." He waved his hand in Stefan's direction. "That fucking guy killed them with his experiments. I'm not going along with this. What the hell is wrong with you?"

Rachel hoped to see shock or horror in her superior's

expression. Part of her continued to hope Pattenden remained somehow innocent in all this. One glance at the captain, however, removed all doubt: Pattenden had betrayed them.

"When did he buy you, Captain?" Rachel spit out the accusation, her expression filled with revulsion. "I hope he paid you well, you traitor. You told him our location. You spied on us using the cameras after he called you to tell you we'd escaped."

Her boss, who Rachel would've considered a good friend only a few days before, fixed Rachel with a cold stare. "I'm sorry. It's nothing personal." She said nothing more. No explanations followed, no justifications.

At least she didn't give me that old bullshit about how it's just business. Rachel's hands curled into fists. She and Hound Dog were outnumbered four against two, and Hound Dog might have a concussion. At the very least, his weakened state meant he couldn't afford to reopen either of his wounds. Even so, if they left this room with Stefan and his men, they'd probably never live to see freedom again.

Stefan had come in unarmed. Pattenden carried a gun in a holster at her waist and nothing else, but the two guards were armed to the tits. They each carried a rifle and had handguns in the holsters on their belts. Each also had a knife in a sheath strapped to his leg. They'd have to neutralize the two guards first, but she couldn't forget the sentry outside the door.

"Take the male to the Peterborough lab." Stefan ignored his daughter for the moment.

"I don't think so." Hound Dog readied himself to fight.

"You'll find your buddy there," Stefan said, as if offering a tantalizing tidbit.

"What does that mean?"

"It means Rachel's reporter friend is already on his way to the lab, where he'll enjoy our hospitality. You'll have his company. For as long as you're there."

A chill raced up Rachel's spine. Hound Dog's face contorted in a grimace, but when he spoke, he only said,

"Fuck you."

Stefan motioned to the captain, who pulled her gun and pointed it at Rachel.

"We want you, not her," Stefan said. "You want her to live, you come with us. Otherwise, the captain shoots her in the head and we take you with us anyway."

Hound Dog went corpse pale. Rachel edged her way closer to the captain. Pattenden spotted the movement.

"Freeze, Rachel." The captain took a step back, the gun levelled on Rachel's chest.

The two guards stood well away from Hound Dog, so he couldn't make a grab for a weapon either.

"I'll make it easy for you, boy," Stefan said. He called out, "Doc, can you come in here?"

The door opened, the sentry on duty holding it, and a man in a lab coat entered the room, pushing a wheelchair. Stefan indicated he should push the chair to Hound Dog.

"Take a seat, son."

Hound Dog turned his gaze onto Rachel. She could only stare into his eyes, pleading silently for him to stay safe. Without a word, he sat in the chair. Immediately, a guard strapped his arms and legs to the chair. The doctor stepped in and plunged a needle into Hound Dog's arm.

"What the hell are you doing?" He struggled but slowly wound down and slumped forward.

"Get him to transport," Stefan told the doctor.

One guard held the door as the doctor pushed the wheelchair through it. Rachel stood, helpless, and watched her closest friend disappear from her life.

***

The realization Hound Dog had been her closest friend for the last two years struck Rachel like a hammer blow to the solar plexus. They'd had each other's backs for so long she'd taken him for granted—as he'd taken her for granted. It was the way of things, acceptable, because if you didn't trust your partner, in this line of work, you were injured or dead.

She had to find a way to rescue him before they hurt him. That she intended to get him back wasn't even a question. Sooner or later, she'd find her opportunity or they'd kill her first.

Her father approached her and waved the guard and Captain Pattenden from the room. Rachel chuckled mentally. She might get her chance sooner than she expected.

As the door swung closed behind the departing pair, Stefan turned to face his daughter.

"I'm disappointed in you."

She smirked. "Aww, you sad I'm not evil like my father? Imagine how I feel. My father is asshole of the decade. You literally brought monsters into the world."

"I'm tired of this. I'm tired of you."

"What do you want from me? I won't help you. What'll you do to Hound Dog?"

"Tests. Then he'll be turned over to the Dark Market."

She wanted to scream in rage but choked on the attempt. The Dark Market had come into existence at the turn of the twenty-first century. A covert economy, part of the dark web, everything done there was illegal, immoral, and despicable. Those who worked in it were destined to die in it as slaves. None of them chose to be there. Those who ran it would kill to continue the sordid activities.

The police busted a small percentage of the criminals running the Dark Market, but when one mastermind went down, two more inevitably popped up and carried on, business as usual.

"Why?" Her voice quivered as she spoke. The thought of Hound Dog turned over to that foul community for—what? She shuddered.

"A guy who can fight grendels? He's valuable."

"The grendels don't attack him." She forgot her terror for a moment, unable to comprehend what her father might get from this.

"Not now."

"What do you mean?" She shouted that last bit, frustrated with his piecemeal parcelling of information.

"Oh, this vaccine will wear off. If you don't get a follow-up booster, the protection from the first shot will weaken after a few weeks. If we put him in a cage with one, it'll attack him." Stefan beamed a grin at her, his eyes shining with excitement. "You should see it. Man against monster—or woman against monster." He scanned her up and down. "You, my pet, will beat him there. You can go straightaway since you never received the first shot. I'll even put money on you to win."

She charged him then, shoving him against the wall, grabbing for his throat. Her fingers found purchase, and she squeezed, but he shoved his arms between her forearms and pushed down until her grip eased. His head thudded the wall and then bounced off. He cried out in surprise and shock, roaring when she continued her ferocious attack by stomping on his instep.

Since she was barefoot, it didn't hurt as much as she would've liked, but it caused enough pain to distract him. Before she could stick her thumbs in his eyes, arms snaked around her waist and hauled her off him.

"I'll kill you," she shrieked at her father.

Another pair of arms restrained her, and two more guards entered the room. Behind them, she glimpsed a doctor with another wheelchair. She kicked with fury and fear, but she'd lost this battle before it'd even begun.

CHAPTER 36

Days blended into weeks for Rachel until she lost track of time. Each morning, she ate, she trained, and she bided her time. The week after training ended, they sent her to the death matches once a week in the afternoon or evening. In the ring, she fought a cage match against a grendel. So far, she'd won each event. Her reward for doing so was continuing to live. She'd seen more than one fighter lose a match, and the grendel's reward for winning was to feed on its opponent.

Young, strong, and agile, Rachel had always fought well and was an excellent martial arts fighter. Often, an instructor had invited her to compete, and she'd been proud to do so, but her heart had always been in hunting monsters not in competitive sports. Now, she was grateful she'd participated in those events. In an environment where she had to win or die, she needed every advantage. Experience made these matches easier for her to survive.

So far, she hadn't seen Hound Dog at any of the competitions, and she didn't know if that made her relieved or terrified. He'd been a good fighter, and she expected he'd last long in this horrifying circuit, but only if he stayed focused and determined. His tendency to let his opponent psych him out made him vulnerable. Of course, a grendel couldn't taunt him or use any psychological tricks, but it wasn't the grendels she worried about—it was the grendel trainers.

The trainers wanted their creatures to win, and they used sabotage against the human opponent as part of their strategy. Often, Rachel battled a grendel whose trainer stood on the periphery hurling insults and distractions at her. It violated the rules—the assholes who ran the events wanted a clean fight, and no, they didn't see the irony in that—but the trainers did anything they could to win.

A winning grendel could make hundreds of thousands of dollars for its owner and trainer. With money like that at stake, cage fighters had to understand they fought two opponents, not one. Her coach made thousands from her fights, and he'd taught her enough tricks to keep her on top. He also ran interference if the grendel's trainer blatantly broke the rules, but mostly, once the portcullis rose and the grendel entered the ring, she was on her own.

When she'd first arrived, she'd tried to learn as much as she could about her surroundings and those she met in the fighting world. Each fighter had an owner, and in Rachel's case, her father owned her and won money from her fights. Unfortunately, handlers kept the fighters isolated from one another. The owners probably worried the fighters might escape if they mingled—a reasonable assumption. She'd have personally led the rebellion.

As things stood, the only human contact she had was with her coach and her sparring partners. Management swapped out the sparring partners regularly so she couldn't get close to them, and her coach had all the warmth and compassion of a honey badger.

Tonight, the tension in the arena reached higher than usual. Rachel sensed it the moment she stepped into the ring. Her long, black hair hung in a braid—they forced her to keep her hair long since the audience grew frenzied with excitement when a grendel grabbed her by the hair and went for her throat. Even the male fighters wore their hair long.

As for clothing, she wore a white T-shirt and cargo pants, but her feet were bare. Her fights had become boring, she'd been told, because she won too quickly when she wore combat boots. Tonight was her first barefoot show.

The crowd's roar thundered, vibrating the floor, the steel-mesh-enclosed main ring, and the metal bars of the cage inside the ring. Music added to the ruckus. It blasted from speakers high in the rafters above.

Tony, her coach, slapped her on the back. "Stay alert, Frostbite."

They'd kept her nickname and used it as her stage name. Lights shone onto the stage, making it difficult for her to see much of the audience except the ones in the first three or four rows. They all sported Frostbite T-shirts, hoodies, or jackets. Images with her face or ones including her whole body in fighting stance and her name in neon emblazoned the shirts.

Some audience members wore T-shirts with grendel names and images. She recognized the names of grendels she'd killed in the cage and smiled. Those shirts weren't worth much now unless they had her face on them as well and the date of the fateful fight.

This circus, illegal as it was, raked in money. She assumed the organizers had paid big bribes to allow it to continue here night after night, week after week, and month after month. Beyond that, it might stretch into years, and she didn't plan to find out how long she could keep it up before a grendel punched her ticket.

She ignored Tony—she spoke as little to him as she could. If he cared at all about her as a person, he'd help her escape this life of slavery, and so far, he'd shown no inclination to do so. At least, she wasn't a sex slave. In the Dark Market, youth was a commodity, and when slaves weren't streamed onto the fighting circuit, they went into the sex trade.

Rachel wished she could do something about that. Instead of hunting grendels as monsters, she should've hunted the monsters in the Dark Market. These exploiters were more evil than the grendels ever could be. She promised herself that if she ever returned to the real world she'd become a cop again and destroy the slave trade.

Something pinged off her face. She pressed a hand to her cheek while Tony, seeing what had happened, scanned the crowd to find the culprit. Rachel followed Tony's gaze to a young boy with a cardboard barrel of popcorn in his lap and a giant soft drink in the cup holder in his chair.

"Relax, Tony. It's just popcorn," Rachel said.

Some of these fans, like that kid, were jerks. Probably picked up the behaviour from his old man. Abuse hurled at the fighters was tolerated, even encouraged, up to a point. As long as it excited the fans, making them spend more money on souvenirs and food or larger bets, the coaches and trainers ignored it. If it caused problems or threatened to injure a fighter, security would intervene. However, when that happened, most of the people in the stands hated it and took it out on the fighters. The last thing Rachel needed going into a fight was animosity from the audience.

Tony scowled, an expression he favoured so much he sported a permanent resting bastard face. "I'll give him one more chance. Little prick."

"He's a kid. Leave him be."

"Not if he distracts you."

"You're distracting me more than he is. Leave me be."

Tony's scowl smoothed into his natural frown, and he hocked a giant loogie onto the cement directly in front of Rachel's feet. She ignored it, used to his disgusting behaviour. The whole guy disgusted her. He looked like a pig, and he acted like one. One day, she hoped to smash his pig nose into his pig face on her way out of here. She grinned inside. A girl had to have her dreams.

The roar of the crowd intensified as the announcer stepped in front of the cage door.

"Ladies and gentlemen," he enthused, "welcome to tonight's main event."

The crowd roared a response, and another popcorn kernel

bounced off Rachel's face. She curled her hands into fists but kept her face impassive, refusing to give the kid the satisfaction of acknowledging the transgression. A glance in Tony's direction confirmed he'd missed it. She rolled her shoulders, easing the tension in her neck. If she didn't relax, it would cost her in the cage.

The announcer introduced Rachel and Thunder, her opponent. Thunder snorted and grunted beyond the darkened entrance of the portcullis.

As each name boomed across the arena, a spotlight glared down first on Rachel and then at the portcullis. The bright light sent Thunder into a frenzy, spittle raining in all directions from his frothing maw. He grasped the bars of the gate and rattled them while he roared his fury.

Screams and cheers from the audience shook the rafters, increasing Thunder's rage. "Thunderstruck" began to play at eardrum-shattering decibels, and the crowd chanted and clapped and stamped to the music. The vibrations on the floor intensified, and the air thrummed with energy.

Rachel swallowed her terror. Fear had no place in the ring. She gathered a large glob of spit into her mouth and, careful not to hit anyone, launched it toward the crowd.

Fans in the front rows noticed the show of defiance and arrogance and jumped to their feet. A chorus of voices screamed "Frostbite!" over and over. Below it, other voices shouted "Thunder!" Still others chanted "Kill the bitch!"

She was the bitch.

The cage door she faced opened, and Tony nudged her forward. She stormed through the gate and into the centre, rubbing her hands together as if in eager anticipation, but mostly for show.

The ring's door slammed closed behind her, and immediately, the portcullis keeping the grendel secured rose. Before it had opened fully, the creature lunged at her.

CHAPTER 37

Rachel ducked, and the creature flew over her back and slammed into the cage's bars. It continued to snarl and drool, ready to taste her flesh if she made even a small mistake. The floor under her feet was smooth stone, as if they'd polished it to make it more slippery and treacherous. Furious it hadn't occurred to her that if she won too quickly they'd up the ante, she planted her feet and adjusted her centre of gravity to brace herself.

For tonight, her goal was to win. After she'd done this a few times, she'd drag it out so they wouldn't have an excuse to change anything else. Ultimately, if she didn't escape she'd die in the cage one day, but she refused to let it happen today.

The creature picked itself off the floor and lunged again. Sloppy but fierce in their attacks, the creatures weren't trained to fight—they were conditioned to fight. Their trainers made them beefy walls of muscle, quick on their feet, and with lethal teeth filed to sharper points than they sported in the wild. Rachel had cut herself on those teeth at least twice, and those were her closest calls. The sight and scent of blood threw grendels into a frenzy of insatiable hunger and made them almost invincible.

She blocked the second and third attacks, always throwing the beast hard into the bars to hurt it. If she could break bones, especially ribs, it would slow down. Once she knew she had hurt it enough and could draw close without getting bitten, she'd move in for the kill. In the meantime, she had to keep it busy. And stay on her feet. She planted her feet a stable hip-distance apart, one foot back a step, her knees slightly bent, toes spread.

On the next lunge, she cracked an elbow to its head, intending to send it sailing into the bars again, but as she spun to the side, its fingers found purchase on her arm. Instantly, she changed her motion and threw her body into its torso, destabilizing it. But she lost her footing on the slippery floor, and before she could hurl the grendel's body away, she hit the ground. The creature twisted and bit into her arm.

Rachel screamed, more in anger than in pain, but the crowd went insane, their roar increasing when drops of her blood flicked into the air. While she wore her hair long, the grendel sported a bald head, what little hair it grew shorn off before every fight. Human fighters weren't given the option to grab hold of their opponent's head by a braided leash. But that didn't mean she had nothing to latch onto.

While the creature sawed into her arm, Rachel used her fingers to stab it in the eyes. It howled and parted its teeth long enough to allow her to slip from its grasp. Ignoring the warm blood streaming in thin rivers down her arm, she tackled it before it could catch its breath.

She imagined sliding her fingers into a bowling ball for grip. With one hand, she burrowed two fingers up its nose while two others dug into its eyes. That gave her a firm grasp, but it wasn't over by far.

Its claws raked across her chest, shredding through her tank top. A second passed before she felt the sting, but she'd been expecting it. Rather than loosen her hold, she tightened it and slammed Thunder's head against the floor.

Its claws raked across her arms, her chest. They barely missed her face.

"Die." She grunted the word out under her breath. While she fought because she had to, she always kept her vocalizations to a minimum. The crowd loved it when fighters swore, cursed, screamed, or cried. She refused to satisfy their every lust.

Thunder's head hit the floor, and its arms lost strength. Even with her blood dripping onto it, it couldn't rally the strength required to pitch her off. She dragged its head back again, and with a final furious whack, cracked the creature's skull open. Its arms dropped, and its body went limp.

Rachel tossed the corpse aside and stood. Her breasts flashed the audience, but she ignored it, refusing to give anyone satisfaction by revealing her humiliation. She stood straight, a neutral expression on her face. Blood continued to stream down her arm and chest. The pain built, and she welcomed it. An injury meant a respite from the fighting to heal.

The cage door clanked, and Tony and the announcer stepped inside. Tony wrapped a towel around her shoulders as the announcer raised her bloody arm into the air and declared her the winner.

The crowd screamed its appreciation.

***

The roar of the crowd assured Hound Dog Rachel had won. She'd become a huge draw, and the fans loved her. If she'd lost, they'd be lamenting. He opened his eyes, which he'd closed when she and the grendel had hit the ground, in time to see her stand.

Fury made the blood rush to his face when he saw her tank top hanging in strands and her breasts visible. One nipple thrust through the tatters. Men jeered and catcalled, shouting at her to take it all off. If only he could leave his seat at the back of the arena and rip their heads off …

After weeks in Stefan Needham's labs, giving blood, stool, and whatever samples they wanted from him, Hound Dog had found himself tossed into the grendel-fighting circuit. He'd yet to enter the ring for a real fight himself, but they'd started training him for it.

At first, he'd taken the news he would fight grendels barehanded as a joke. The creatures found him repulsive. They'd be easy prey for him. Then his captors demonstrated that the vaccine's potency had worn off. Now when he entered a grendel's vicinity, it salivated and tried to attack him. Once in the cage with a creature, he'd be in as much danger as anyone else who'd never been vaccinated.

They'd brought him to the show, chaining him into a crappy seat in the back row. Albert, his coach, sat beside Hound Dog, providing a play-by-play even when his eyes were open and he saw for himself what happened.

His wounds had healed—at least, the physical ones had. Inside, he was an emotional wreck. Losing control of his entire life made him crazy. He clung to rationality by a wispy grendel hair. The only thing keeping him from either killing himself or going berserk and forcing them to kill him was the knowledge he might reunite with Rachel. Somehow, he had to either alert her to his presence so they could organize an escape or escape himself and rescue her.

Neither option seemed likely. They kept him chained all the time, even when he trained. He tried to view that as flattering rather than humiliating. They feared him, he told himself. Time to show them they had good reason.

The shackles holding him secure were the type used to restrain convicts. He had a pair of cuffs on his ankles, which linked by chain to cuffs on his wrists. They used two different keys, but that didn't concern Hound Dog. A hairpin or wire or something similar would work. He'd kept his eyes open for anything he could use to pick the locks, but, so far, had found nothing.

What if he never crossed paths with Rachel again? She'd been injured—hopefully not severely. Her coach had escorted her from the cage without having to call for a stretcher, and she walked without leaning on anyone. Even so, they'd give her time off to heal before putting her back in the ring. If he didn't act now, he might lose his one chance to get to Rachel.

He slanted a gaze in Albert's direction.

The coach, his expression impassive, met Hound Dog's gaze.

"Get up." The fight over, the arena clearing, Albert rose, preparing to escort his prisoner back to the cell. He never got the chance.

CHAPTER 38

When the stadium's lights came on, she spotted him at the back as Tony guided her toward the exit, and her heart skipped a beat. Hound Dog. Beyond all odds, Hound Dog was here in the arena. He'd watched her fight. They were training him for his turn in the ring. They'd made her watch the fights when they first brought her here, so Rachel knew exactly what her partner's presence here signified.

Instantly, she forgot the searing throb of her wounds and the slim chance of escape. She vowed not to leave without him even if she had to kill to do it.

Too bad she'd killed the grendel. If Thunder were still alive, injured or not, she could have set him loose in the crowd. Probably just as well. She could bring herself to kill her captors to save her and Hound Dog's lives, but she didn't want to have innocent people as collateral damage on her conscience.

Tony had taken time to wrap bandages around her wounds and drape a fresh towel around her shoulders. He hadn't put her shackles back on, probably assuming her injuries and exhaustion made her less of a flight risk. Perhaps, he was showing kindness toward her or trying to make her feel grateful for the small favour. Whatever the reason, she planned to take advantage of the synchronicities falling into place, including the fact an armed guard manned each exit.

Most of the seats had emptied by the time Rachel left the ring. A few stragglers made their way toward the other exits. Tony led her to the one used mainly by staff and fighters. When they arrived, he paused and waved her through the propped-open door. The guard stood inside, to the left of the doorway, where he could view those still in the arena and those who exited.

Rachel glanced once in Hound Dog's direction to verify his location. He shuffled toward the exit at the north end of the building. In one fluid motion, Rachel snatched the gun from the guard, launched herself backward onto the ground, and shot Tony and the guard before anyone else could react.

From there, she belly-crawled along the filthy floor, barely acknowledging the wetness and stickiness pulling at her fresh bandages. The screams and the feet pounding toward the exits registered on her radar, but the remaining guards, all armed, concerned her more. She pressed to the ground, using seats and any people between her and her enemies as shields.

A bullet whizzed past her head, not too close a call. The trajectory was way off. She squinted, focused on the guard, and pulled the trigger. The shot missed and ricocheted off the wall.

Someone screamed, a male voice, and it echoed and then ended in a thud. A man had fallen from the upper deck. *It didn't sound like Hound Dog*, she insisted. More shots fired, but not in her direction. Rachel smiled. Hound Dog had a gun.

***

At the first shot's pop, Hound Dog dropped into a crouch.

"Get up. We're moving out." Albert shoved his prisoner, which pitched Hound Dog onto his hands and knees.

When Albert grabbed Hound Dog by the arm to lift him up, he jabbed the coach with an elbow to the teeth. This time, Albert went down, and as the surrounding confusion escalated, Hound Dog jumped on the other man.

The coach was older than his fighter and not as fit, but Hound Dog had the shackles to contend with. He kept his position of dominance for only a moment before Albert kneed him off. Hound Dog snarled and lunged again, ramming his head into the other man's chest. They'd trained him to fight dirty when facing a grendel, and he used that training to beat down his coach.

He smashed the base of his hand into Albert's nose, hearing a rewarding crunch. Albert's head snapped back and hit the concrete floor knocking him out. Hound Dog searched Albert's pockets for the shackle keys. When he found them, he freed himself from his chains and reoriented.

Where was Rachel? The guards?

One guard huddled by the door at the top of the arena. Another one, closer to Hound Dog's location, crouched behind seats just inside the east exit. They seemed to be all that remained of the security detail, and they focused entirely on Rachel.

After another scan of the arena, he spotted her crawling across the floor, shielding herself from the gunshots. She wouldn't last much longer if someone had called for reinforcements. No one would've called the cops. If anyone involved the police, they'd shut down the whole thing. Bribes were paid to a select few on the force, but most cops were honest and ethical. They'd arrest the guards—and probably himself and Rachel—but those who ran this slave circus would lose money if that happened. No, the owners would handle it internally.

So, he had more time than he otherwise would have if this were a legal enterprise, but not much more. He crawled toward the closest guard.

It was almost too easy.

With the guy distracted and shooting at Rachel, Hound Dog came at his quarry from below and tackled him. The hard part was knocking the man unconscious—he had a serious instinct to win the fight and Hound Dog still had sensitive areas from previous wounds. In the end, Dog came out on top—literally—and wrested the gun from the guard's limp hands.

He leaped to his feet and shot at the remaining guards. *Pop, pop, pop.* Three blasts from the gun, but they all missed. He snarled in frustration and ducked when the guy spun around to return fire.

Another guard went down under fire from Rachel.

Hound Dog scoured the room for her and spotted her near the ring. Too far from the last guard. It would be up to him.

"I got you covered, sweetheart," he muttered.

How he'd missed their partnership. He'd kill to save her—had killed already if Albert died from his head injury. The only kills he'd ever wanted to make were grendels. Now, he supposed he'd committed murder. He tamped down the horror at what he'd done. After all, he didn't know for sure he'd killed the coach. No doubt, though, about what would be the result if he shot the guard.

Hound Dog held his breath, aimed, and fired.

CHAPTER 39

The last guard dropped to the ground, dead. Hound Dog pushed the reality that he'd killed from his mind and raced to meet Rachel, who half-sprinted, half-trudged up the stairs.

Her expression betrayed weariness, but every time they locked eyes, she quickened her pace.

"Don't hurt yourself getting here, baby," he said with a grin. Inside, he ached to see her so worn down.

"Oh, Dog." She choked on the next word and almost tripped.

Her oily hair stuck out in spikes and spindles wherever it had escaped the braid. Blood-smeared bandages covered her chest. She'd dropped the towel she'd worn draped over her now bare shoulders. A gun dangled loosely from her hand, and the glaze in her eyes told him pain wracked her body.

"You're doing all right so far, Frosty. Hold it together a while longer."

She brightened at his words and, after drawing in a deep breath, she said, "No problem. I'll get you out of here."

He threw a glance at each of the exits. Which way should they go? Two upper, two side exits. Each led to freedom, but which one offered the easiest out?

The pounding of footsteps on concrete interrupted them. Pursuit approached from all the exits.

Her face fell, but she held her head high and waved to him, signalling he should come to her. He settled on the eastern side exit and jumped two steps at a time until he reached her side. When he grabbed her arm to lead her to his preferred destination, she gasped out, "No, down."

He allowed her to lead. She knew the arena better than he did, and he trusted her. Down they went.

***

As footsteps pounded into the stadium, Rachel urged Hound Dog through a hidden door under the stage, closing it softly behind them. With luck, their pursuers not only hadn't spotted them but they also didn't know the trapdoor existed. If she were the praying type, she'd be doing it, but she hadn't been the praying type since her mother had lost her head to the grendels.

Beside her, she heard Hound Dog's soft inhales and exhales. She slowed and quieted her breathing. The racket outside meant the guards hunting for them wouldn't hear their breathing, but she didn't dare speak. Dim light under the stage filtered in from cracks in the wood frame and the trapdoors on each of three of the four sides. The fourth side was her destination and the darkest. That portion of the platform on which the stage rested led into a corridor and a possible way out.

She took Hound Dog's hand and together they crept into the darkness. The pandemonium outside their shelter told them they were surrounded. No way out but one, and she had no idea if the way would be open when they arrived at the end.

Slowly, her eyes adjusted to the dimness. Echoes of footfalls ahead announced the approach of guards. Panicked, she scanned the walls, the ceiling, the floor.

"Nowhere to hide," she muttered, more to herself than to Hound Dog.

"So, we charge them," Hound Dog replied.

"What?" It came out a half-gasp.

"The best defence is an offence. We charge. By the time they realize we're not guards, we'll be on them."

She gave a nod and, as one, they sprinted headlong toward whatever awaited them.

***

All remained quiet behind them. If anyone had followed them into the passageway under the stage, Rachel couldn't hear it. Ahead, however, was another matter. Distinctly she heard the tread of boots on concrete and the rustle of movement.

"Ambush?" she whispered.

"Here?" Hound Dog responded in a hushed tone.

She squeezed his hand in the affirmative. "Up. I'm down."

He returned the squeeze, acknowledging he understood. She felt a slight breeze as he hoisted himself up to cling to the overhead pipes between the rafters. With luck, they'd bear his weight and his strength would hold out. He wasn't as tired as she was, but he'd find it a challenge even so.

The footfalls headed in their direction. No lights reflected on the walls, making her uneasy. The guards probably wore night-vision goggles.

She caught herself before she looked up at Hound Dog to see how high above her he dangled. Too low and they'd spot him. She crept behind his location by about four metres, lay flat on the floor, and aimed her gun toward the middle of the tunnel.

A faint swish above her made her glance up, a scowl on her face. She kept quiet but Hound Dog hissed for attention so she leaped to her feet.

"A vent. Get up here."

She welcomed the news but needed to reach it before the guards arrived. Soundlessly, she handed him her weapon and hauled herself up to meet him. As she pulled herself through the opening, her arms quivered, ready to give out. Thankfully, he pulled her the rest of the way. Once she climbed all the way in, he handed her the grill he'd removed, and she pressed it in place.

In silence they slithered through the ductwork, Hound Dog leading the way, pausing only when they heard footfalls below them. When the heavy tread of booted steps faded away, they continued to crawl forward. Sweat drenched Rachel, and she had to pause for a moment to curb a bout of dizziness.

Hound Dog must have sensed she no longer kept up because his quiet slithering fell silent. He made no comment, just waited, and when she resumed her forward motion, he carried on. They crawled past several opportunities to climb out of the ductwork and stopped frequently to listen for movement below. Twice, they heard the tramp of heavy boots as teams of guards rechecked the tunnels, but no one checked the vents. What a relief Hound Dog had discovered them. Her desire to hide outweighed any desire to kick butt or get revenge.

At last, he signalled her they should leave the passage. Rachel inched forward and skimmed metal grating under her hands.

"End of the line," Hound Dog whispered. "It curves up ahead. We need to find a way out of here or they'll find us."

He picked at the grate and lifted it out. When she tried to move into the opening, he stopped her. "Me first."

She wanted to argue—craved to argue—but let him take the lead. It made sense. Her whole body throbbed, and her bandages were torn and leaking blood. Between the two of them, he was the more agile and energetic.

She squeezed his hand, and he handed her his gun and climbed down. When she heard his feet touch the ground, she passed both weapons down to him and then slipped into the opening. Hound Dog grabbed her waist and eased her to the floor.

They stood silently for a moment, getting their bearings in the pitch-dark corridor. Rachel found the wall on either side and faced what should be the direction they needed to head. A faint tracing of artificial light, probably from streetlamps, showed beneath the wall up ahead. A door? It had to be. This corridor, she knew, led from the arena to the parking lot behind it. Guards likely stood sentry outside.

"This way," she whispered. "I'll open the door. You go high. I'll go low."

"Got it."

They crept to the door and Rachel tested it. It was locked, but from the inside, so she unlatched it. On the count of three, she cracked it open and peered out into the fading daylight.

CHAPTER 40

The intercom buzzed. Stefan punched the button harder than he meant to and barked out a "What?" more gruffly than his assistant deserved.

"Captain Pattenden here to see you, sir." Avery's voice came across calm and even.

Stefan exhaled coffee breath and reached for a mint, his nerves soothed by his assistant's mild manner. "Thank you. Send her in. And you can head home."

"Yes, sir, have a good night."

She entered the room and strolled to the chair across from his desk. Her manner displayed the same calm Avery had shown. Stefan's nerves sparked again, making him scowl. Was he the only one taking this seriously?

Rachel and Hound Dog were loose. Not only did that cost him revenues, but they'd also taken out some of his best guards.

"Thank you for seeing me." She smoothed a strand of hair off her forehead, and as she did, her hand trembled.

Good. She should be afraid. Her life hangs by a thread.

"We've sent protectors to hunt for them."

He already knew that, so he scowled at her and remained silent.

Her throat bobbed as she swallowed. "I didn't alert the

police. We don't want to attract attention to the arena until it's been sanitized of any trace of grendels."

"How far along on that are they?"

"Almost done. Then we can file a missing person report on Rachel." She didn't mention Hound Dog. His family had filed a missing person report on him with the police weeks ago.

The police already searched for Peter, but he was safely ensconced in the lab right here in Peterborough. Stefan had reported him trespassing on restricted property. He'd provided video footage of the reporter prowling around on his Storm Lake property

He'd neglected to mention Peter had been forced there by Stefan's guards. If all went as planned, once his daughter and her pal were in custody, they'd be turned over to a police station loyal to Stefan. Before long, this nightmare should end, and Rachel and her irritating companion would be back in the lab.

Shame. She made a killing for me fighting grendels. He'd glowed with pride every time she'd won. Tough for a woman. A killer. Too bad she lacked loyalty to her family. To her father. He'd punish her severely for that. Did family mean nothing to her? He'd have given her everything.

At one time, he'd envisioned letting his kids take the company reins while he went into politics. Together, they'd have been unstoppable. Ungrateful kids. He'd worked hard to instil in them his values: ambition, drive, determination. Where had he failed?

Perhaps she needed time in the sex trade. Maybe then, she'd learn to appreciate all he'd done for her, all he'd given her, and that gratitude would translate into the loyalty he demanded. He'd made her life too easy, giving her whatever she wanted. Allowing her to choose her career path. He'd always opposed her decision to become a protector, but buying Pattenden's loyalty afterward made up for it. His lips curled into a sneer.

"Sir?" Pattenden said, fear in her voice.

Stefan blinked at her and returned his awareness to the moment. He rose and she jumped to her feet.

"Find them, Captain. You get paid for results. If I don't see them in the lab in two days, you're cut off."

She met his gaze and held it, no trace of the fear he'd detected a moment ago. "Maybe we've been going at this all wrong."

His brows rose. "I'm listening."

"What do they want?"

"Rachel?"

"All three of them." She pressed her hands on the desk and leaned forward. Her lips were full, enticing. Stefan couldn't take his gaze off them. He hadn't slept with her—had avoided any hint he'd want to. She was a paid lackey, nothing more. The last thing he wanted was to have an affair, but she tempted him.

"I don't know," he replied. "What do they want?"

"You, sir. They want to break you. Now Rachel and Dog are out, they'll want to catch up to Sanderson, and he wants his story. Why don't we let them have it?"

"You want to use my facility as bait?" He dropped back into his chair.

"It already is."

"How so?"

"They'll head here."

"They wanted to get to Storm Lake."

"And they found it—more than they wanted, actually. Right?" She stood straight and spread her arms, palms turned toward him. "But they didn't get files or photos. Peter will want that."

"If they reconnect with Peter." He saw where her logic led, but, at best, she only guessed. Rachel and Hound Dog could simply disappear. Both were clever enough to survive anywhere—in the bush if they had to, vaccinated against grendels or not.

Stefan's cell phone sounded, and he picked it up. The call display showed his wife.

Through gritted teeth, he said, "Yeah?"

"Stefan?" Marne's voice bleated in his ear.

"What is it?" He had no time for her, but he kept his tone even.

"Will you be home soon?"

If she asked him to stop for milk on the way home, he might lose it. "No. Too much going on. You carry on with your evening."

"But we were supposed to have dinner together."

"You ought to be used to this. Invite a friend over. I'll call you when I'm on my way." He disconnected and invited Pattenden to sit. Maybe she had something, a germ of a plan, that would get them Rachel and Hound Dog without too much trouble. When the phone sounded again with his wife's ringtone, he declined the call, sending it to voicemail.

***

Through the crack in the door, Rachel made out the shapes of two men pacing about ten metres from the exit. They patrolled this section of the parking lot, empty of all but one vehicle, a panel van. She closed the door.

Hound Dog leaned in and whispered in her ear. "How many?"

"Two," she whispered back.

"We go out guns blazing, it'll bring on the rest of the troops."

"If we don't get out of here, they'll find us eventually."

"Isn't there another way out? What about up?"

"We already tried up. It ends here." At least, she assumed it ended here. The corridor was simple, its purpose to get grendels in and out of the arena. A hint of grendel stench lingered in the air, but she was so used to it, she barely noticed.

"Why aren't they storming this passageway?"

She considered. "They've been through more than once already. Now, they're watching the exits in case they missed us and we want to escape this way. Not a bad plan, considering we're trapped here like rats."

"Rats with guns," he replied.

"I've got an idea." Quickly, she explained what she wanted to do.

"You're out of your mind." He leaned against the wall, and for a moment, she worried he might be too exhausted to help her. Her own reserves were tapped, and she functioned on adrenaline and grit alone.

"What else can we do?" she asked. "At least this way, we're not sitting here waiting for the cleaners to reach us— and if you don't think they'll come down here to sanitize the stink from this corridor before calling in the cops, you'd better think again."

He drew himself up to his full height and raised his weapon. "I guess we have no choice then. Back up. When I open the door, we're going to win or lose. If we lose, it'll be in a hail of bullets. Ready?"

Rachel backed up into the passageway's darkness. "Ready."

Hound Dog flung open the door, banging it against the outside wall. "You two," he screamed at the two guards, waving his rifle in a come-hither motion. "Get your asses over here. I've got 'em trapped and need backup." He ducked back inside, letting the door slam shut.

Rachel hugged one wall and Dog the other, and they waited for the guards to appear.

CHAPTER 41

Accustomed to taking orders, the two guards stampeded into the passageway. The first one went down with a blow to the head from Rachel's rifle before he'd taken three steps into the darkness. She shoved his body aside and waited for Hound Dog to take down his man.

By the time the second man had stepped inside, they'd lost the element of surprise. Before the protector could take him out, the man drove an elbow into Hound Dog's gut. Breathless, Hound Dog dropped to one knee but didn't allow the guard to swing his arm up again. Dog flung forward, using his head as a battering ram.

The guard didn't have much chance to regain his advantage—Rachel recognized grendel-fighting tactics in the moves Hound Dog made. Within two minutes, the tussle ended, and Hound Dog hadn't pulled out all the tricks from his grendel-fighting bag.

"You done playing?" Rachel asked when the guard lay prone on the ground and Hound Dog braced himself against the wall with one hand, his breath still heaving.

"I gotta say I'm glad they finished my training before I went up against this guy. He's smaller than me, but he's quick."

"Never mind. Move it out before the real reinforcements

come." She paused long enough to rifle through their pockets and steal whatever cash the unconscious men carried. Neither she nor Hound Dog had any money. The eighty-plus dollars she scavenged would help them at least buy food later. As a bonus, she snagged the keys to the van from the guy she'd taken down.

They burst from the passageway, prepared to blast away, but that, as Rachel expected, turned out to be unnecessary. The two sentries they'd taken down had been the only ones tasked with watching this exit. After all, how many guards should it take to watch one door after a patrol had already cleared the corridor? They took their time approaching the van and verified no one waited in ambush inside it before she settled into the driver's seat.

"Head to ..." Hound Dog trailed off. "Where the hell are we?"

"You kidding me?"

"No. They brought me here in a van without windows. I guess it's near Peterborough. Didn't seem like a long drive."

"I've been here long enough to figure out which way we need to go. Buckle up and hang on. We're hitting the country roads."

Without a word, he slid his seat belt on as Rachel peeled out of the parking lot.

***

She hadn't been kidding when she'd advised him to hang on. The woman drove like a maniac.

"You'll get us pulled over. Slow down," Hound Dog complained.

The pothole-riddled dirt road they drove on hungered for a fresh load of gravel, and the way Rachel tore along it, the dust they spewed in their wake would certainly attract attention. When she ignored him, Hound Dog leaned in, squinting to get a better look at her face in the dim light from the dashboard.

Her eyes focused on the road ahead with manic intensity, and her upper teeth gripped her bottom lip. Sweat beaded her brow. When he glanced at her hands on the wheel, they white-knuckled it at ten and two.

"Frosty."

The van sped up.

"Frosty." Louder this time.

She leaned forward and the van accelerated.

"Rachel!" he barked.

"What?" she threw him a distracted glance, but at least when she faced front, she eased up on the gas.

"We're away," he said, his voice gentle. "We got away."

She hiccoughed, and he realized she was close to tears.

"You're all right, got it? We're all right."

Who knew what hell she'd survived the weeks she'd been in the fighting circuit. If he could pummel someone for what they'd done to her, for what they'd done to him, he'd happily beat them bloody. For now, he could only offer feeble attempts at consolation. At least he could distract her with practicalities. "We'll have to ditch this van soon, eh?"

The van slowed a little more, and when he glanced at the speedometer, it registered at the speed limit. He let out a tiny breath of relief.

"Yes. Sure. I'll find somewhere to pull in."

"No." He shook his head for emphasis.

"What? Why?"

"They'll have this van on an all-points bulletin soon. I don't want to stop anywhere populated."

"I'm sure they have an APB out already." She ran a shaking hand across the side of her face, briefly closing her eyes as she did.

The van remained steady despite Hound Dog's trip-hammering heart. He fisted his hands but kept them at his side so she wouldn't notice. "We should go into the woods. Find an abandoned vehicle. Switch it out. Or if we find a van, steal its plates."

She groaned and said, "We have nothing. A few dollars.

What'll we do?"

"Steady, boss."

She must be overtired. He'd never seen Rachel Needham so shaken. It unnerved him. Up ahead, the dirt road they drove on crossed another road. A red flashing light indicated a stop sign. When she pulled up to the intersection, he said, "Turn right."

She hesitated. "You want me to head to Trestlenorth?"

"We'll find something there. Trust me."

After another moment's hesitation, she turned right.

They found in Trestlenorth what he'd expected they'd find: ruined homes, abandoned vehicles, and no humans in sight. As the van rolled along the deserted road, it occurred to him they'd been lucky the arena was outside Peterborough city limits and in a secluded area. That meant they didn't need to cross any patrolled or guarded sections of the highway or pass through any manned gates or checkpoints. However, it also meant they had to watch for grendels.

It took them two hours, but at last, they found a vehicle and the keys to it—and, most important, it had no blood on the upholstery. A family car, they found it in the garage of an abandoned house, the family who owned it probably dead. Since the car worked when they tried it, Hound Dog guessed it hadn't been sitting too long. They didn't give the house much attention beyond making sure nothing and no one lurked inside and searching for the car keys there. The roof had been ripped off, and nature had reclaimed much of the interior. If the family had died inside the home, they found no evidence of it, but they didn't search too diligently for blood spatter.

Hound Dog took over the driving at that point. One, he wanted to let Rachel rest and recover from her ordeal in the ring and what came after, and two, he'd had enough of her speed-demon recklessness. Admittedly, this behaviour was new to him. She was normally the most cautious person he knew. If he'd become the careful one in this relationship, they were in trouble.

He spared her a glance as they drove through the night's darkness. Her eyes closed, she rested her head against the passenger door. Beyond the car's high beams, the dirt road stretched, straight but hilly. Trees, rocks, and bogs filled with grasses and bulrushes whizzed past though he kept their speed under the eighty kilometre per hour limit.

"Frosty?" He whispered in case she slept.

Her eyes popped open.

"Mind if I turn on the radio? We should get a handle on what's in the news—about the arena."

Without replying, she flipped on the radio and adjusted the dial. Rock music blared out.

"I wanted news."

"We wait long enough, we'll get news," she said.

"All right." No need to argue—they weren't in any immediate danger. She probably needed the respite. The clock on the dashboard read seven forty-eight. They'd get the news on the hour so just a twelve-minute wait. He could live with that. They needed to talk, anyway. After weeks apart, he wanted to know how she'd coped, how she'd survived. Frankly, he wanted to know if she'd thought about him at all, but he wouldn't let her know that.

He opened the conversation with the practical. "We should stop soon. Catch some sleep."

As if his words triggered it, she yawned. "Oh, God, Hound Dog, I'm sorry. I almost dozed off and left you to do the driving when you must be wiped."

"We're both wiped. Ideas?"

They discussed it, and as they agreed to pull off the road at the next uninhabited property they spotted, the news interrupted them.

The top story was the gunfight at what the DJ reported was an abandoned arena outside Peterborough, with two dead and four wounded, and Rachel Needham and Jack Ainsworth wanted for questioning. Rachel switched off the radio.

"We're in trouble, Dog," she said.

CHAPTER 42

"You mean more trouble than we were already in," Hound Dog corrected.

"Sure."

When he said nothing more, she put her hand on his and gave it a squeeze. "I've been thinking."

He kept his eyes on the road. "Shoot."

"Exactly."

He shifted his gaze to hers, slowing the car as he did. "What?" He faced the road but kept his speed down.

"We've got to go after my father."

He had an uneasy feeling he understood what she'd meant by "shoot" now. "Not guns blazing, Frosty. We're already suspected of killing two people and injuring four others."

"It was self-defence. They can't think we wanted to hurt anyone. Those guards were the bad guys, not us."

"I'm sure that's how Bonnie and Clive saw it too."

"Who?"

"The gangsters."

She chuckled, her insides warming as she released stress. "Bonnie and Clyde."

He grinned. "Yeah, them."

"They really were the bad guys. We're not." She slid her hand from his.

221

"We're gonna be if we go after your father and blast our way in. Those guards we killed probably have families."

"Those guards made sure we stayed in the ring and would've shot us dead if we hadn't killed them first." She kept the details to herself, but they'd tried to do more than that. If she hadn't had the mad fighting skills she did, a few of them would've raped her too.

More than one young grendel fighter—males and females—had been abused sexually by the guards. Some disappeared, and Rachel didn't know whether they'd been murdered or forced into the sex trade. Often, those who vanished had only average fighting skills but above average looks. She'd had to be quick, clever, and vicious to keep the guards off her.

"They were pigs, Jack, all of them. Every fucking one." Her voice contained an edge of hysteria, but she couldn't help it.

"Okay," he replied. "I'm sorry for whatever you endured."

Silence blanketed them until Hound Dog broke it. "You don't have to tell me about it, Rachel, but if you want to, you can."

She studied his face and saw only compassion.

"Another time." To her ears, she'd sounded bitter, but his expression didn't change. As it always did, hearing him use her given name made something inside her flutter. She relaxed her hunched shoulders and inhaled. In a more gentle voice, she said, "Another time."

Hound Dog slowed the car. "Up ahead."

When Rachel squinted past the car's high beams, she saw movement on the road. She could only make out humanoid shadows. Grendels? They'd better be certain. If grendels, then speeding up and mowing them down would be best. If humans …

What would people be doing out here in the night with grendels about? They had to be grendels. The figures scurried across the road, seemingly unconcerned about the car bearing down on them. She opened her mouth to tell Hound Dog to punch it when one figure raised a weapon and pointed it at them.

At the same moment, Hound Dog slammed on the breaks. "Hold on!"

Rachel did as he suggested and grabbed the handle above the door. Tires squealed and a cloud of dust obliterated everything outside the vehicle, which spun. The rear dipped as if it had lost the road.

"Christ, we're going into the ditch," Rachel hollered.

Hound Dog shifted gears even though the car was an automatic. He frowned, his face taking on a look of intensity. "We're fucking not. They're not getting us."

A shotgun blasted behind them—they'd turned around and headed back the way they'd come.

"Go!" Her nerves ratcheted up a notch, the adrenaline flowing. She focused on Hound Dog's face.

He concentrated, tongue between his teeth, the tip sticking out from between his lips. After glancing into the rear-view mirror, he grimaced. "Fuckers are chasing us. What the hell are they doing out here? An ambush? How'd they know?"

The questions were rhetorical, so she didn't bother to reply. Good questions though. How had they known to wait for them here?

"No sirens," she shouted, cutting off Hound Dog's mutterings.

"Not cops then," he yelled. "They're from your dad."

"Then he knew where we'd go. How?"

The shouted conversation continued, more as a distraction than as any attempt at a solution. Both clammed up when their pursuers closed in. Hound Dog tromped on the gas, pushing the needle on the speedometer higher until it hit one hundred forty kilometres. Then higher. A turn forced him to slow, but he careened around it at a hundred clicks. Behind them came a crash, and a horn wailed and cut out.

"One down." He hit the gas again.

Rachel kept her eyes on the road behind them. One car remained, not getting any nearer but not dropping behind either.

"Twenty-eight ahead," Hound Dog said.

"Take it. Toward Bancroft."

"We won't make it far on that highway."

"I'm not trying to."

"Then what?"

"Burleigh Falls."

"What's at the falls? We're not going to Thelma and Louise into the chute."

She guffawed. "No. Get to Thirty-six. We'll lose them on the fire routes."

"I hope you know where you're going, because those dirt roads dead end."

"Why do you think we haven't seen any grendels?"

He replied immediately. "They expected us to head that way and cleared it. Did you figure out how?"

"I was stupid, Dog. It might still get us caught. We headed away from the arena by the most logical route."

"He'll have roadblocks in other areas. And if he doesn't, the cops will."

"The cops weren't on the lookout for us until well after my dad set this up. Trust me. He had everything in place before he called it in. They let us get outside any perimeter the police would set up."

Without another word, he hit the gas again, and they roared on into the night.

***

After an hour of dodging and deking, Hound Dog lost the tail on the fire routes and the two headed for Bobcaygeon.

"We can't hit the town," Hound Dog said, a warning in his voice.

"Have you seen it since the grendels arrived?"

"Once. Destroyed like all the other small towns."

"Then you saw it before they rebuilt. Tough townsfolk. They pulled it back from the brink."

"Then we really can't go there. Someone'll recognize us and turn us in."

"Only if they catch us. We have to sleep. Find a place we can hide."

He did as she suggested, and they found an empty barn to shelter in. People inhabited the homes within the town proper, but the surrounding farms were deserted. This barn, strong and sturdy, was intact while the house on the same property had been destroyed.

The people in the house had attracted the grendels more than whatever they'd stored in the barn. With treeless fields stretching away from it on all sides, the property offered grendels nowhere to hide except within the barn or the demolished house. When they opened the barn doors, they found stacks of hay and empty horse stalls.

She said, "The horses were out in the paddocks when the grendels attacked."

"How do you know?" Hound Dog asked.

"The stalls are empty." If they searched, they'd probably find the bones in the fields. They wouldn't search, but they retraced their steps, and after killing a nest of three grendels, they scavenged the house for supplies: bandages, bottles of water, and unexpired packaged or canned food. They collected a small stash in plastic bags and headed for the barn. They scoured it once more for traces of grendels and found nothing.

They pushed the barn doors open as wide as they would go so they could get the car inside and then turned it to face the exit in case they had to leave in a hurry. When done, Rachel headed for the loft.

"You want me to take the first watch?" Hound Dog asked.

"Go to sleep, Dog. I'll watch for vehicles from up there." She pointed at the loft as she headed toward the ladder with the grocery bag containing the water, bandages, and first aid kit.

They'd probably be fine, but it wouldn't hurt to keep her eyes and ears open. By the time she climbed to the top of the loft and settled herself near the door overlooking the fields facing the road, the wounds she'd ignored since she'd escaped the arena throbbed. Blood seeped through the bandage around her torso when she peeked under the T-shirt she'd swiped from the house.

She sat out of view near the loft, peeled off her shirt, and removed the bandage. Uncapping a bottle of water, she washed her wound. The disinfectant made it sting, and she gritted her teeth until the pain dwindled to a throb.

After she applied a fresh bandage to the wound, she checked the bag for snacks. She'd left most of the food they found in the bag she'd left below with Hound Dog, but she'd thrown a few chocolate bars into this one. Her stomach rumbled, and its emptiness gnawed her innards, but the prospect of figuring out how and where to cook food exhausted her too much. For now, the chocolate would have to do. She unwrapped a bar and nibbled.

CHAPTER 43

In the quiet of the early morning, a cock crowed in the distance. It comforted Rachel to know Bobcaygeon, at least, had cleared out the grendels enough to keep farm animals alive. This farm might have lost the battle, but others nearby had life that refused to be chased away.

From below, Hound Dog's gentle snores drifted up, making her smile as she recalled other times she'd heard him. They'd camped together as a team on grendel raids, and Dog always made sounds in his sleep. Coder and Foot-Long slept like coma patients and never noticed.

After struggling to fall asleep despite the annoying racket, Rachel always caved in and crawled from her cocoon to nudge him through his sleeping bag. The memory of her two lost friends brought tears to her eyes and thoughts of Peter followed. What was he enduring at her father's hands? Was he still alive?

Rage bubbled up in her then, and she had to restrain herself before she woke Hound Dog and stormed her father's lab right now. She wiped the tears away and took deep breaths of the fresh country air to settle herself. The sun shone brightly over the fields that stretched out to the road in the distance, heralding a glorious fall morning that would quickly melt the frost that had gathered overnight.

She hadn't seen a car since she'd sat down to her watch four hours ago. Hound Dog would rise soon. His internal body clock would signal to him to wake up and take his turn as sentry so she could sleep.

As if on cue, she heard him stirring, shifting. The barn door groaned as he slid it to the side, probably to go take a piss outside. Before long, his head poked up through the opening, and he shoved a bag onto the floor ahead of him.

"I'm starving. You eat while I was out?" he asked.

"Chocolate."

When he saw her face, his expression changed from slight boredom to concern. "Everything okay? You were crying."

Figured he'd notice though she'd done her best to wipe away the evidence. "Emotional, I guess."

He climbed into the loft and went to her but kept his distance. He dropped to the floor across from her and sat cross-legged. "We've had no time to cut loose since we escaped. I'm not surprised it backed up on you. Wanna talk about it?"

She shook her head. His expression flashed hurt, but he stifled it. Annoyed he took it personally, and, worse, tried to pretend she hadn't just wounded him, she snapped at him without meaning to.

"What I've been through doesn't matter. I can handle it." She relaxed. "I was thinking about Coder and Foot-Long. Jack, they didn't deserve to die that way. I miss them." The tears welled up again. "And Peter. They're hurting him right now if they haven't already killed him."

Hound Dog moved closer and wiped the tears from her cheeks with gentle fingers. "What happened to them, to Peter, it's not fair."

"We have to do something about it." She clasped his hands in hers. "I want to take down my father. If we run, we'll run for the rest of our lives.

"What can we do?"

"I don't know, but we're not running. I'm not running. I understand if you want to escape."

For a moment, he didn't speak, and she held her breath, waiting. She truly understood if he wanted to leave. He could escape west and settle in Alberta or BC. Or he could head east and lose himself in one of the coastal provinces. Her father had reach in Ontario, but outside the province, he had limited power. All they'd have to do—all Hound Dog would have to do—was leave. The law would always want them for questioning, but if they turned themselves in out of province, they stood a better chance of having a fair trial and not mysteriously disappearing.

Rachel tilted her chin up and met his gaze. "What'll it be, Jack?"

"I'm not leaving you," Hound Dog said. "Whatever you want to do, I'll support you. But think it through carefully. We'll get only one chance."

"Thank you." That didn't begin to convey her relief over his decision to stay, but it was all she could manage to say.

"Get some sleep. We'll figure it out when you're rested."

"Okay. You can get a good view of the road from up here." She pointed to a window opening on the back fields. "Nothing out that way but pasture. Nowhere for grendels or anyone else to hide. Don't forget about it, but your focus should be the road."

"Relax, boss, I got this." He sounded more amused than annoyed.

"Sorry. I'm jumpy. They found us too easily before. They ambushed us."

"They can't track us. Sleep. We'll be fine."

She yawned, so tired not even the thought of grendels could keep her from closing her eyes. "All right. I'm staying up here."

His expression showed surprise but he didn't comment. Images of guards creeping into her cell in the night flashed through her head, and she flinched at the memory. Sleeping without having to be on alert, with Hound Dog to watch over her, would be a relief.

He waved at a pile of straw in the loft's back corner.

"Flake out there. Check for rodents first. I left the blanket I used below." He stood and headed for the ladder. "I'll get it for you. You're liable to fall and break your neck. How long since you've slept?"

She grinned at him as she grabbed her water bottle and strode to the corner. "Too long, Dog. Too long."

***

Four hours later, Rachel woke to rain pattering on the barn's roof and the aroma of cooking wafting up through the hole in the floor. She jerked to a sitting position, jumped to her feet, and rushed to the loft doors to make sure no one lurked outside.

Hound Dog had left his post in the loft. He'd left her alone. She'd never have slept if she'd known he'd abandoned her. Her hands shook in reaction to her sudden fright. She scowled and, with a full bladder adding to her discomfort, climbed down the ladder.

The barn door stood ajar, a small campfire blazing just inside the door. Two buckets filled with water sat nearby. A saucepan rested on a grill, which sat on a circle of rocks. Soup bubbled inside the saucepan, producing the tantalizing scent to which she'd awakened.

Her stomach growled, and her mouth salivated. Hunger almost overrode fury, but terror over what could've happened while she'd slept, oblivious and trusting, overruled all.

He left the loft. Hysteria rose, and she wanted to scream and rant and rave at him.

"Hey, I went to the house and scavenged more stuff. I also found a working well." He waved a hand at the buckets of water. "Cleaned stuff as best I could, so we've got bowls and spoons. Not too—" He noticed her expression. "What's wrong?"

"You left your post."

He scowled. "I'm always on alert. You were never at risk. As soon as it clouded over, I came inside. Haven't seen any grendels, and no cars have driven past the property, never mind turned into the driveway."

"You left your post."

"No, I patrolled the area. What difference does it make if I left the loft? I patrolled." He stopped, and realization flashed across his face. "I'm sorry."

Uneasy, she shrugged, recognizing she'd reacted unfairly. He'd done nothing wrong. Except leave her alone. Was this her new normal? Would she always need someone around when she slept or this horrible panic would build inside her? Or was the need specific to Hound Dog? That would be much worse.

"I'll be okay."

He crossed to her side. "You'll feel better after we eat something. Canned soup isn't exactly gourmet, but it'll taste great considering how hungry you must be. I had a snack while you slept, so I'm not starving, but I could eat again."

After she'd stepped outside to relieve herself, she let him guide her to a blanket he'd spread out nearby and serve her the soup. He was right: the food tasted good even if it came out of a can and boxes and packages. Besides the soup, Hound Dog had found crackers and peanut butter, and for dessert, cakes and pastries in vacuum-sealed packages. Rachel's tension released as her belly filled, and she silently forgave Hound Dog for leaving her alone in the loft. Aloud, she apologized for overreacting.

"Jack, I'm sorry." When he gave her a puzzled look, she said, "For how I behaved when I woke up."

He shook his head. "I get it. You don't want to be alone."

She winced and remained silent.

"It's okay. Whatever happened before, we won't let it happen again. Agreed?"

"We didn't want to let it happen in the first place."

He smiled and continued, "We won't let them get us." He popped the remains of a cream-filled cake into his mouth, chewed and swallowed, then said, "I understand you don't want to leave your friend, but if we try to break in, they'll nail us—quick."

When she opened her mouth to protest, he held up his hand. "I didn't say we wouldn't rescue Peter, but while you slept, I've been thinking about how best we can do it."

"I'm listening."

He outlined a plan for her, and, as he spoke, a surge of energy and excitement had her getting to her feet. This could work.

CHAPTER 44

Home. It meant different things to different people. To Rachel, home meant safety and security—and solitude. It definitely didn't mean the castle-like structure she and Hound Dog crept toward in the moonlit night. This was her father's home, her stepmother's home. It'd never really been hers.

She'd lived here on and off, but after her father and Marne had married, she'd never felt comfortable or happy here and had moved out before Marne moved in. After high school, she moved out, first to residence at university, then to the townhouse she lived in now, paid for in part with money her mother had left her.

She'd split her time between her townhouse and the base, and the base itself offered her the haven she needed—until Pattenden's treachery took that away. The base had offered something else she hadn't recognized before: a sense of camaraderie, of family, more so than she'd experienced with her real family once her mother died. She'd only returned to her father's house for major holidays, when they gathered together in uncomfortable politeness. Frequently, Stefan showed up late to these gatherings; though, to his credit, he showed up no matter how busy with work.

Busy creating monsters.

"You lived here?" Hound Dog interrupted her

reminiscences with a low whistle.

She glared at him. "Keep it down."

"Sure thing, boss." He pantomimed locking his lips and throwing away the key.

She shook her head in exasperation but said nothing more. Ahead loomed the stone porch with the double front doors. Motion-activated cameras would capture them if they got too close, so she held up her hand, halting their progress. She pointed to the bushes alongside the walkway leading to the front steps, and Hound Dog melted into the shadows.

Rachel gave Hound Dog time to get into position. She checked the time on the watch she'd scavenged from the abandoned house. Eight o'clock. A creature of habit, her father rarely arrived home from the office before nine at night on a weekday.

Marne also had her habits. Tonight, she'd be at her book club meeting, fortunately. Rachel held no ill will toward her stepmother. Whatever Stefan had done, he'd done before he'd met his second wife. The possibility that Rachel's real mother may not have been so innocent made Rachel uneasy, but she shoved aside such fears. The monsters her father had created slaughtered her mother. If she'd had any knowledge of, or hand in, their creation, she'd paid for it with her life.

All remained quiet. The air chilled to below zero as the sun went down, and she and Hound Dog would have been freezing if they hadn't found warm clothing at the abandoned house. Much of what they'd found had been overrun by rodents. They shook out the mouse crap and put them on. Hopefully, they wouldn't get the plague or whatever diseases mice carried these days.

Fewer items were available for Hound Dog due to his height and bulk, but they'd found an oversized winter coat he could wear. Doubly fortunate for Dog since it had started snowing—a light, fluffy snow that obscured the sky and coated the grass.

After another fifteen minutes, Rachel followed her partner's trail to the five-car garage at the side of the house.

At first, she couldn't find him.

Kudos to Dog.

She stayed in place, scouring the shadows, and finally spotted him ten metres from the garage entrance. He'd have to get closer than that—they both would—but the cameras watched. She'd told him where each one was, and as long as her father hadn't added more, they should be all right. Rachel crept to the side of the garage opposite to where Hound Dog crouched and settled in to wait.

***

At precisely 21:05, the electronic gates opened and headlights lit up the driveway. Rachel huddled farther down into the bushes behind which she hid and prepared to run as soon as the car slid into the open bay. Hound Dog likely did the same at his end. For a big guy, he was nimble, and she trusted he'd make it into the garage before the door closed. Once they went inside, she didn't care if the cameras picked them up. The moment her father stepped from the car, the game they played would level up.

The car paused in front of the garage, and the door rose in a slow, steady glide. As the sleek, new Jaguar eased inside, Rachel ducked in alongside the back doors, keeping below the level of the side mirror. She sensed rather than saw Hound Dog slip in on the other side.

The car stopped.

The garage door started its descent.

The driver's door opened.

Overhead, lights flicked on and the garage door thunked closed.

"Freeze, fucker." Hound Dog had his gun levelled at Stefan by the time Rachel made it around the front of the car.

She raised her weapon and trained it on her father. Pain throbbed beneath the bandages wrapped around her, but she ignored it—no, she welcomed it. It reminded her this man was responsible for the damage done to her body. She could have been mutilated or killed in the ring, and her father had put her there. Hatred for him coursed through her, and she mustered all her self-control to not pull the trigger and obliterate the face at the end of the barrel.

"Rachel. How nice to see you." Stefan fixed his gaze on his daughter, ignoring Hound Dog as if he were inconsequential. "I assumed you'd be long gone by now."

Dog reminded their prisoner of his presence with a quick elbow jab to the gut, and Stefan doubled over, air rushing audibly from his lungs. They stood over him and waited while he caught his breath and steadied himself with a hand to the Jag.

When he could finally speak, he said, "Dog." The single word dripped with contempt. "Classy as ever."

"We're going for a ride, and you're driving. Get back in the car." Hound Dog wagged his gun at the car and then turned it back on Stefan.

"Where we going?" Stefan's tone was mild, conversational. No trace of nerves or fear leaked through his façade. Perhaps, he believed she didn't have it in her to hurt him or to allow anyone else to hurt him.

Better set him straight before he did something stupid such as tackle Hound Dog. "One false move, Dad, and I'll shoot you. Get in the car."

Stefan reached for the door handle but paused. "Rachel, we can work this out." His voice soothed, reminding her of days long gone when he'd sit on her bed and tell her bedtime stories. He only knew one—at least, that was what he'd claimed. But she didn't mind hearing it night after night from the time she was two until she turned four.

"I don't know how it all turned so bad." He dropped his hand and made as if to reach out to her.

Rachel and Hound Dog steadied their weapons, their expressions turning cold.

"The car, Dad."

"Hear me out." But he dropped his hand again. "What happened to you, princess?"

She swallowed, the old nickname catching her off guard, and stared at him. Her body had gone numb, not even the pain able to cut through the haze that settled even into her brain.

What's he talking about? He threw me into the grendel ring.

Her silence encouraged him to keep talking. "We should be a team, you and me. You should be my right hand." He gave her a sad smile, one filled with longing and regret. "Why didn't you work with me when I offered you the chance? What have I done to deserve your hatred? Rachel, we're family. You're my girl ..."

"Dad," she eked out in a whisper. Clearing her throat, she said, "You hurt us—me, Mom ... Jeff." Especially Jeff. She tried to compose her thoughts, letting the silence draw out.

What does he want from me? He did all this. He's responsible. She had to remember that. He lied. He always lied.

She glanced at Hound Dog. He stood, silent and wary, his gun still at the ready in case he had to use it. Doubtless, he would if need dictated. He never flinched from necessary action. Their gazes met for a moment across the metres separating them, and it was all she needed. He had her back, and together, they had Peter's back—Peter, who even now might be dead. Because of her father. If she lost sight of that, she was a fool.

"Get in the car, Stefan." She refused to call him Dad ever again.

Without another word, he opened the door and climbed in, Hound Dog slipping into the back seat at the same moment. Rachel went around the other side and got into the passenger seat.

"Let's go," she said to her father. "I'll tell you where when we're on the road."

CHAPTER 45

On the ride to Stefan's research facility, Rachel attempted to question him, but he refused to respond, saying only that she was making a mistake. When she asked him about Peter, he shrugged and said Peter assisted with experiments in the lab.

Nothing she said affected her father. Appealing to his humanity brought no result. Why would it? He'd lost his humanity when he created the grendels. He had no empathy, or he'd never have done any of what he'd done.

Had he ever loved his family? She'd never seen him cry over losing his wife. When Rachel had confronted him about Jeff's death, he'd shown no emotion. He'd caused both those deaths and showed no remorse.

When they arrived at the gates, she directed Stefan to drive on through to his personal parking space. As his daughter and former employee, she was familiar with the layout of the underground parking and the route Stefan took to his office. They'd use his high-level security to gain entry into the building and get to the lab via a route that bypassed the main lobby and the security guard station. As long as Stefan did nothing to alert security, they should make it to the lab and recover Peter. If all went well, they could be in and out in half an hour.

As they exited the vehicle, Rachel and Hound Dog

avoided looking up at the cameras. They kept their guns holstered under their coats so they appeared to accompany rather than coerce Stefan. A guard in the control room always monitored the cameras, and the thought of it made Rachel's back itch, but she kept her stride casual and walked beside her father. Hound Dog strolled a few paces behind them.

Progress was slower than she would've liked, but at last, they arrived at the corridors where the labs resided and the scientists did the bulk of their practical research. Stefan halted before the doors Rachel had failed to breach when she'd tried to access the lab after Jeff's death.

"You can't go in." He faced her, again ignoring Hound Dog as if he didn't exist. His expression stayed neutral, but his hands had curled into fists. "You're not cleared for it. It's for your safety."

"Funny, you never mentioned that before."

"I hoped we wouldn't get this far."

That meant he'd expected security to stop them. "If security shows up, you'll tell them to clear us. The door, Stefan. Unlock it."

He pressed his thumb to the pad, and when the light changed from red to green, he punched in the numbers. Locks clicked and slid open. Hound Dog pushed open the doors and led them through. Stefan paused in the open door, blocking her path.

"Move it," Rachel said, her tone flat and low.

"Are you sure you want to do this? You should've run, Rachel. You'll never make it out of here."

He was awfully talkative all of a sudden. Uneasy, she shoved him through and shut the door behind them.

The corridor dead-ended about twenty metres down at a set of double doors. Beyond that stretched a block of rooms set up for a variety of purposes. Rachel didn't know where to begin the search.

"Take us to Peter," she ordered.

When he hesitated, she made her voice low and threatening but kept her expression mild and pleasant.

"Move. To wherever you're holding him. Now."

Did he stall to delay revealing what had happened to Peter or because he expected pursuit—or an ambush? How could he? He'd had no chance to alert anyone. She watched him carefully. He'd made no surreptitious signals to the security cameras. His pace had remained unhurried as he walked beside her. Nothing in his manner had betrayed anxiety or fear.

It made her uneasy. He'd been too cool on the ride here, and now, he'd gotten talkative and reluctant.

"Walk," she said, maintaining a steady voice. "Show us the way. And if Peter's not in the room we enter, we'll search the place ourselves, and I don't guarantee we won't shoot any grendels we find. We only want Peter."

Stefan continued walking, his pace slow but steady. He headed to another set of double doors, again using his thumb and an access code to get them in. Hound Dog pushed through the doors, Stefan next, Rachel taking up the rear. This time, Stefan didn't pause in the doorway but led them at once to one of the two doors on the left. Yet again, he used his thumb and the access code to gain entry.

As they followed Rachel's father into the lab, an agonized howl rent the silence and made them freeze. Hound Dog, a step ahead of Rachel, already drew his weapon to ready when Rachel reached for hers. He ducked to the left while Rachel went right.

Stefan stood, unfazed, a few paces inside the room. While the unholy shriek had curdled Rachel's blood and left her shaking, Stefan calmly walked toward the cages at the back of the room.

Inside one cage, a grendel leaped and snarled. It had scented them and already drooled at the prospect of fresh meat. In the other cage, Peter huddled on a cot. He'd looked up when they walked in, and the faraway look in his eyes told Rachel he hadn't recognized her or Hound Dog. He dropped his forehead to the arm he used to cradle his knees.

"Stop, Dad," Rachel said, remembering as soon as she

spoke her vow to never call him that again.

He halted midway into the room, stopping beside a desk that held a computer, a pile of papers, and an assortment of hardcover books. She hurried to where he stood.

"Dog, cover him while I check on Peter." Without waiting for a reply, she hurried the rest of the way to the cages, keeping as far away from the grendel cage as possible.

The grendel threw itself at the cage's bars the closer she got to it, but she ignored the snarls, the thrashes, and the reaching arms.

"Peter," she cried, her voice choking.

He raised his head from his arm, his eyes at first vacant.

"It's me—Rachel."

Recognition dawned and tears streamed from his eyes. "Rachel. I can't take it anymore."

"We're here—me and Dog. We're getting you out. Where do they keep the keys?" A padlock hung from the latch on the door and she scanned the room, searching for a hook or somewhere obvious where they might store a keyring. Perhaps in the desk. She covered the ground in two long-legged strides and began rooting through drawers.

"Where's the key, Stefan?" she asked.

His gaze roved around the room, his expression curious, as if this were the first time he'd ever had to think of keys. After a moment, he shrugged. "I don't know. I'm not the one who opens these cages." A smirk appeared on his face, his enjoyment at the predicament evident.

Rachel cursed and picked up the pace, searching for either keys that might open the padlock or something with which to cut the lock. She found a ring with three keys on it. "Dog, see if one of these works."

"Cover him," he said, indicating Stefan, and snatched the keys from her hand.

"Glad to." She levelled the gun at her father and said, "Don't move. We'll be out of here soon."

"We? Just want to clarify."

"The three of us. You can take Peter's place in the cage."

"It's not too late, Rachel. Work with me. This can all be yours. You have no idea how far our research has come—the good we can do for mankind."

"Knock it off, you psycho Frankenstein wannabe. I can't be bought. Nothing you offer will compensate for the horrors you've caused. I don't care if you bring Jesus back in a second coming. You've destroyed thousands of lives already with these monsters. However they evolve, nothing will make up for the damage you've done."

"I didn't mean to hurt anyone. Do you think I wanted your mother to die?"

"Honestly? I don't know."

Hound Dog interrupted them with a cry of triumph. He opened the door to Peter's cage, stepped inside, and helped Peter to his feet.

"Can you walk?"

Peter croaked out a "yes," but when he tried to take a step, he grimaced in pain.

"Lean on me," Hound Dog said.

Together, they hobbled from the cage, but before they could take another step, the door to the lab burst open. Pattenden and two security guards from the facility rushed in.

"About fucking time," Stefan snapped.

"Freeze," Pattenden ordered.

Rachel fired her weapon at her former captain and threw herself to the floor as Hound Dog shoved Peter to the ground beside her.

"Cover me," Hound Dog hollered and made for the grendel cage. In her periphery, Rachel saw him fiddling with the lock.

Rachel rose to a crouch, and even as her father shouted at everyone to hold their fire, she put a bullet into Pattenden's shoulder, knocking her backward. Rachel then took aim at the guard to the captain's right at the same moment he turned his weapon on her. The grendel leaped through the open cage door and attacked the nearest unvaccinated human: Hound Dog.

CHAPTER 46

The guard's gun fired, but the bullet skimmed over Rachel's head as she ducked. Her shot also went wide. Hound Dog knocked the grendel away with a punch to the creature's solar plexus and an upward and outward thrust of his arm. The beast flew into Stefan.

Untrained in the art of grendel combat, Stefan tried to twist away but screamed when the starving creature clamped razor teeth into his shoulder. The creature gnawed and chewed on the shoulder, his victim screaming in rage and pain. Before the guards, Pattenden, or even Rachel, the one closest to the skirmish, could react, it released the shoulder and tore into Stefan's throat.

Hound Dog hadn't been idle while everyone else had frozen in place. He used the precious seconds to reach the guards and now tussled with one of them. Blood leaking from her shoulder, Pattenden crawled toward the gorging grendel, her gun raised but trembling in her hands.

Rachel ran to help Hound Dog, shouting at Peter to get out of the room. The grendel would ignore him—his vaccines were obviously up to date since he coexisted peacefully near the grendel's cage—but the guards and Pattenden wouldn't hesitate to at least shoot to wound. He tried, but whatever he'd endured in that cage had affected him, and he staggered and fell as soon as he got to his feet.

"Crawl if you have to," Rachel shouted, and then forgot about Peter as the second guard, a burly woman who looked like she could hold her own in the grendel ring, swung a fist at Rachel.

A weapon fired and she glanced over in time to see Pattenden take another aim at the grendel. The sound of the weapon firing had attracted the creature's attention along with Rachel's, and he stopped his feast and turned on the captain. She fired again, but Rachel couldn't spare another glance in that direction. The guard she wrestled took all her focus.

They tumbled to the ground, rolling, Rachel struggling to maintain dominance and pin her opponent, the guard sweating and panting. Of the two, Rachel was more willing and skilled at fighting dirty. She'd wrestled grendels and won, week after week, and she refused to let this guard, built like a cave troll though she was, beat her. Rachel dug her fingers into the woman's eyes, and the fight ended.

The guard howled and released her hold on Rachel, and she seized the moment to knock the woman out with an uppercut. Rachel then leaped up and swung around, searching for Hound Dog or Peter.

Hound Dog, his nose bloody, wrested control from the guard, grabbed his head, and bashed it against the wall. The man dropped to his knees and then face-planted to the floor. Rachel snatched her gun from the floor while Hound Dog retrieved his, but as they turned to race through the door, a bullet hit Dog in the back of the shoulder. He yelped and fell to the ground.

Rachel ducked, flipped a table on its side, and, crouching behind it, returned fire in Pattenden's direction. All else in that area had fallen silent. Stefan lay dead—she'd seen the monster ripping him to pieces—and, based on the lack of snarling and growling, Pattenden had killed the monster.

"Dog, you good?" She needed him to say something.

"Yeah, flesh wound." His voice, drifting in from outside

the door, remained steady, but as soon as he stopped talking, he panted to catch his breath.

"Give up, Captain. You're outnumbered and we've got the door."

"Do you?"

"We fuckin' do. Anyone comes into the hallway, Dog, shoot to kill." Rachel hoped to God no one would show up. She had no desire to blast their way out of here.

How many guards watched the building at night? Two was the norm: one to watch the monitors, the other to patrol the building. After all, what was the point of all that technology protecting the place if you couldn't depend on it?

Pattenden had been on hand though. Her father had indeed been expecting them. Fat lot of good it'd done him, and Rachel doubted anyone else in the squad conspired in this with the captain; otherwise, they'd have already joined the party.

"What's the story, Dog? Where's Peter?"

"I'm here," Peter replied from the hallway at the same time as Hound Dog said, "With me."

Rachel belly-crawled to the edge of the table, grabbed the guard she'd knocked out by the ankle, and hauled her body close enough to access the holster in which she kept a cell phone. Rachel snatched up the phone, tapped "Emergency," and called 911 on the locked device.

"Nine-one-one. What's your emergency?"

Rachel told the man on the other end exactly what her emergency was.

***

When Hound Dog overheard Rachel talking to an emergency services operator, he thought she'd lost her mind. They were fugitives, as good as jailed for crimes they'd never committed if the cops caught up to them. Then she spoke, and he realized those years she'd worked for her father had taught her all she needed to know about taking control.

Sure, Hound Dog knew she was a leader—an exceptional leader. She'd led protectors into the field and always returned from the hunts successful and with all team members intact. She inspired those she led, and had Pattenden not betrayed them, Rachel likely would've been promoted to captain sooner rather than later. But he had no idea she could take charge in the outside world.

As protectors, they lived in a microcosm. The forces that hunted them after they'd escaped the arena existed in the macrocosm he'd always wanted to avoid dealing with. Hound Dog had assumed if they didn't disappear they'd be jailed. Rachel gave him hope they'd not only avoid that but they'd make a life for themselves without going into hiding.

First, she identified herself as the company owner—which she technically was now that her father lay dead on the floor across the room. Second, she provided details of the situation ambulance and police services would walk into. She made it clear crimes had been committed and Captain Pattenden would need to be interrogated after receiving medical treatment. Finally, she explained they should consider Pattenden an active shooter, contained but still armed.

Once she disconnected the call, she called out to Pattenden. "You're done, Captain. Put down your weapon, and kick it out where I can see it. Your backup piece too."

Silence.

"Captain, you heard me call the cops. They'll be here in minutes. The game's over. Between me, Dog, and Peter, we'll have all the evidence we need to put you away and reveal to the world what my father did. Give it up. You need medical attention."

"I'm not sorry, Needham. Just sorry I was caught. See you on the other side."

As Rachel shouted "no" and jumped to her feet, a gunshot echoed through the room.

"Rachel, get down," Hound Dog hollered, assuming Pattenden fired on them again. But no bullet ricocheted off the walls or the table that protected Rachel, and she continued her run for the other side of the room from where the shot had come. By the time Rachel reached the captain, Hound Dog stood and limped to his team leader's side.

At their feet, Pattenden lay on her back, the gun by her hand, her face blasted away.

"I guess that's an admission of guilt right there." He turned his gaze from the captain to Rachel.

She didn't return the look, her gaze fixed on Pattenden's body. "Maybe that's why she did it."

Hound Dog shook his head. "She didn't want to go to jail, boss, that's why she did it."

"We were friends. Yes, we were," Rachel insisted when Hound Dog opened his mouth to protest. "I don't understand why she betrayed me. She must've been sorry, at least a little."

They stood together silently for a moment. Hound Dog broke it. "Let's go, Frosty. We'll let the cops know the gunfight's over. Get help for Peter."

"And for you." She raised her head and angled her face toward him. "Peter will win a Pulitzer over this story."

"I hope so," Hound Dog replied. "He went through enough for it."

On the way out, they paused by her father's body.

"He wasn't vaccinated," she commented.

"Why?" Hound Dog asked.

"He probably didn't trust it was safe." She met his gaze. "Let's get out of here, Jack."

Hound Dog put an arm around her shoulder and together they walked from the room in silence.

CHAPTER 47

Eagle's Nest Lookout afforded a panoramic view of the York River Valley in the town of Bancroft, Ontario. Rachel, Hound Dog, and Peter stood on the wooden, two-tier platform at the top of the cliff at dawn on a frigid December morning. They'd left their car in the small parking lot and hiked the short distance to the lookout. Bundled in layers of winter gear, only their eyes and lips peeked out from inside their ski masks. They all carried handguns, and Rachel and Hound Dog each had a rifle slung over one shoulder. Grendels hibernated in the winter, but that didn't mean you could let down your guard. Rachel carried the urn containing Jeff's ashes.

They faced the west, the sun rising at their backs, but since heavy snow clouds obliterated the sky, they only knew day had arrived when they no longer needed their flashlights. Rachel made her way to the upper deck of the lookout and went to the railing overlooking the town of Bancroft.

She'd chosen this place to scatter her brother's ashes because it had been one of his favourite places to visit when they were kids—before the grendels appeared. Before their mother died. When they still believed their father loved them and wanted what was best for them. They'd been a family, loving each other, supporting each other.

"Our parents brought us up here for picnics," she began.

Peter joined her on the deck, but Hound Dog remained at the top of the stairs to stand sentry. Even for this solemn ceremony, he'd watch their backs, and Rachel's heart filled with love for him. She met his gaze in the growing light, and he smiled—not the wide, jovial grin he usually sported but one filled with affection. He'd joined them for this memorial to watch over them as they said goodbye to one they loved who he'd never met.

She swallowed past the lump in her throat and continued. "Jeff and I loved it here. No matter where else we travelled, we had to come back here every summer." This small cliff hadn't the majesty of the Canadian Rockies, and the trails weren't long and winding and remote like the ones in Algonquin Park, but this had always been their special corner of Ontario. Down below, following the curve of Hastings Street on the west side, flowed the York River. They'd spent hours playing in the park. Rachel had always assumed she and Jeff would one day return with their spouses and children.

Her eyes welled up, and the tears trickled down, but she ignored them. Head held high, hands cupped around the urn, she told Hound Dog and Peter about the little boy she'd grown to love who'd become the scientist, the activist, the young man she was proud to call brother. "He was so brilliant. God, we need him. He should be here to help us clean up the mess my father made." She stopped and gazed at Peter. His story had gone viral.

Going public with what her father had done hadn't been easy. Rachel continued to get death threats from those who believed she'd been in on the conspiracy, but the truth had come out, and it had literally set her and Hound Dog free. She inherited her father's company and vowed to undo what he'd done if it took her the rest of her life. Hound Dog had promised to help her, so she'd made him head of security at the research facility.

"Peter, you rescued us that May weekend so long ago. Without you, we'd never have made it out of the marina alive.

I know I've said it before, but it's worth saying again: I'm so grateful to you for helping two little kids in trouble. You were my hero for a long time—better than any superhero—and that's why I could turn my rage into something positive and become a protector. I was furious after you left even though I knew you had to go and pick up the pieces of your life."

He reached for her and put his arms around her. They hugged, the urn pressed between their padded bodies. Rachel buried her face in his chest and then raised her head to meet his gaze.

"I had such a crush on you by the time you got us to Peterborough."

"I know. I didn't know how to let you down easy, but I tried my best." His words brought comfort in that low and soothing with a touch of sexy voice. "By the time I left you with your dad, I thought of you as a little sister."

She smiled, the flow of her tears ceasing. "I'll always love you like a brother, Pete. I know Jeff loved you like the brother he never had. He'd be happy you're here. Will you help me?"

At his nod, she held up the urn. Together, they opened it and removed the bag with the ashes.

"Wind's from the west," Hound Dog commented.

"Thanks, Dog." Even here, he had her back. "Let's move to the south end, then."

She and Peter made their way to the edge of the railing. Below them sprawled a forest of evergreen trees, spiky and snow-covered, and deciduous trees, bare and skeletal. Rocks jutted from the uneven cliff face. When she raised her face to the sky and breathed in deeply, flakes of snow landed on her lips. Silently, Rachel and Peter tipped the bag, scattering the ashes into the wind. The powdery grey remains flew and scattered in the breeze.

"Goodbye, Jeff," Rachel whispered. "I love you. I miss you."

Beside her, Peter produced a flask from inside his jacket. "To Jeff." He took a swallow and passed it to Rachel.

Unsure what to expect, she took a swig. "Whiskey?"

"Yeah. I know Jeff didn't drink, but I figured we'd need something bracing."

She handed the flask back to him, and he walked over to Hound Dog and offered it to him. Rachel returned her attention to the ashes and saw no trace of them. Behind her, the two men talked in low voices. Footsteps heralded the approach of one of them, and she recognized Hound Dog's tread. When he reached her, he put his arm around her shoulders and held the flask to her lips.

"One more swig?"

She sipped, leaning into him as she did. "Thanks, Jack," she said, meaning so much more than simple gratitude for the gulp of alcohol.

He stroked her cloth-covered cheek with gloved fingers and she savoured the touch.

"You saved me, too, you know," she said.

"I know," he replied, his tone holding the old Hound Dog arrogance. She loved him for it and laughed, a good, hearty chuckle, but the moment had brought the tears back to her eyes, and she found herself laughing and crying at the same time.

"You've had enough," he joked. "You ready to head home?"

"Yes."

He kept his arm around her as they walked to Peter and then down the stairs to the trail that would take them back to the car. After they left the open area around the platform, Hound Dog released her, and they walked single file, their guns at the ready. They'd brought two vehicles, and when they reached the parking lot, they said their goodbyes to Peter. Rachel hugged him and kissed his cheek.

"Remember, you promised you'd visit us for Christmas."

"I promise. Frosty."

She laughed. "We'll have to come up with a nickname for you, too, before you return. Make you an honorary protector."

"Bye, Dog, take care of my sister," Peter said and jumped in his vehicle when Hound Dog replied with a "You bet."

Rachel and Hound Dog stood and watched Peter's vehicle reverse out of the parking lot, turn, and head down the slope toward the main road.

"I'll miss him," Rachel said. "He's always off chasing a story. I used to resent that. We idolized him and he never seemed to have time for us. I don't know why I clung to him. He was a stranger to us, really." She set the urn inside the car on the back seat and turned to face her partner.

Hound Dog drew her to him. "He saved your life, Jeff's life. He was there for you when your father wasn't."

"That marked the beginning of the end of our family."

"You had your work."

"Jeff's work got him killed."

"No, your father's work got Jeff killed."

"My father's work killed Coder and Foot-Long too."

Their friends had been buried with honours in the protectors' section of a cemetery outside of Peterborough. It had happened while Rachel was on the grendel-fighting circuit and Hound Dog was a prisoner. They'd visited the graves as soon as they discovered where the two young men had been buried, but Rachel would never forgive herself for their deaths.

"It's not your fault."

At Hound Dog's words, a wave of affection for him swamped her, and she took his hand and squeezed it. After she released it, she said, "Where to, Dog?"

"You owe me a dinner, boss. It's time we had a real date."

In a fit of spontaneous joy, she threw her arms around him. "I thought you'd never ask."

His lips found hers despite the ski masks they wore, and the kiss electrified her. When he deepened it, her entire body responded, and he stole her breath away. Vaguely, she reminded herself they were outside and at risk, but she clung to him for another moment. Finally, her lips formed words, and she spoke into his mouth.

"You'll get us killed, Dog."

"I always figured we'd die in each other's arms one day, Frosty," he replied as he eased away from her.

"You know," she said, "one day we will."

His mouth quirked up, and he opened the car door for her. "That was a proposal, boss."

"I know." She slipped into the driver's seat, giving him a kiss as she passed by him. "That was a yes, Dog."

He slammed her door closed, and she heard him whistling as he walked around to the passenger side. Despite everything that had happened and everything they still had to do to fix it, she felt lighter, happier. She and Hound Dog made a great team. They'd make an even better family.

The End

Thank you for reading my book. If you enjoyed it, won't you please take a moment to leave me a review?

SAMPLE CHAPTER: *EARTHBOUND*

The first thing I noticed about being out of my body was that everyone in the hospital room appeared brighter. They glowed. The second thing I noticed was that I was still shaped like me. I wasn't a ball of light floating around the room.

My spirit body, when I examined it, shimmered with an aura like everyone else's, but it was transparent. I held up my hand and could see through it—not to bones or anything internal, but to the blue coverlet on the bed where my physical body lay.

Tubes snaked from my arms, and my chest rose and fell, so it appeared I wasn't dead. However, I looked hideous: greasy, dull brown hair clumped in thick strings on my pillow or plastered against my face; dark circles under my eyes that made them look as if I'd been in a rumble; and lips that could have used ten applications of lip balm.

Which made me realize the third thing: Inside, I was still me. If I was dead—which was possible, since the machines might have been forcing my body to mimic life—then I hadn't elevated to a more saintly version of me. Judgment and cynicism still came easily.

Damn.

Shouldn't death have made me more evolved?

And where was the tunnel? The light? My dearly departed

loved ones? Shouldn't someone who could tell me it wasn't my time be here?

More importantly, where was my family?

Medical personnel were the room's only other occupants, and they were leaving. All looked as if they'd fought a valiant battle, and perhaps they had. They'd tried to save me, and, while the results were nothing to high-five about, they hadn't declared me dead.

No sooner did thoughts of my family wink out of my head than I found myself in a waiting room. Two men and two women I didn't recognize sat on a couch along the west wall of the room, staring at the floor.

My eighteen-year-old daughter, Silver, sat on a padded metal chair, elbows on her knees, face in her palms. Her long, brown hair veiled her hands. She wore the same jeans and long-sleeved, green T-shirt she'd had on when I'd last seen her.

Rory, my ex-husband, perched on the edge of another chair next to her. Also in jeans and a T-shirt, he stroked Silver's back with one hand while he held his girlfriend's hand with the other.

Clara Spencer. A classy lady. Even in what I assumed was the middle of the night, she had on what I can only refer to as an ensemble: blouse, blazer, skirt. Her short brown hair was smooth and glossy.

I liked her. She was pleasant, and she hadn't been boinking Rory while we were married, so all was good on that front.

At least my ex had found a decent replacement for me when our marriage broke apart. Clara would help him get through this as long as he didn't screw it up.

He should have already married her, though I wouldn't wish that on any woman. He's not a jerk or abusive, but life with him can be silent and lonely. Strong and silent may sound sexy, but living with it had been depressing.

The doctor who'd been at my bedside entered the room, and everyone looked up with fatalistic hope in their eyes. When he said "Rory McQueen?" the four strangers in the room resumed staring at the floor.

Rory and Silver leapt up. Clara began to rise and then sat again, back rigid against the chair.

"Doctor, is she …?" Rory choked.

"She's alive, but her heart is weak. I'm sorry. She might last the night, but it doesn't look good." The doc hesitated. His nametag read "Dr. Richler." The bags under his eyes looked almost as bad as mine.

Thanks for knocking yourself out to save me, Doc. I hoped to thank him in person one day.

Richler continued. "You can go in and see her. Take as long as you need. If there's anyone else who might want to say goodbye, you should call them."

"What do you mean? My mother doesn't have heart problems. She's only forty-six," Silver said.

"She had a catastrophic coronary." Richler checked his chart. "The paramedics revived her once already. Her heart won't take another episode and there's a ninety percent likelihood she'll have another one."

"No." Silver waved her hands at him, shooing his words away. Tears streamed down her face.

Rory hooked an arm through hers.

"Take us to her, please."

They followed Richler from the room, Clara lagging a few steps behind.

I tried to walk along with them, but, apparently, when you're disembodied, you simply think your way places. No sooner had I decided to go back to my room than poof! There I was.

My body hadn't changed since the last time I'd seen it, but I inspected it anyway.

Having one foot in the grave hadn't made me more intuitive. I couldn't tell if I was about to have another heart attack.

Death has never frightened me. I'm a risk taker, a live-in-the-now kind of gal. The idea of exploring a new dimension excited me, but I didn't want to leave my kids. If an opportunity to avoid dying arose, I'd take it.

Rory's voice approached. He doesn't talk much, but when he does, he's loud. I heard him assuring Silver that everything would be okay. Nice of him to do that, but not practical. Her mother was dying. You can't pretend that falls under the everything-will-be-okay umbrella.

I closed my eyes and tried to feel something. Love for my children flooded through me. The expected sadness didn't follow. Was it because I was still with them?

My son, Marc, was probably on his way from university. He attended the University of Toronto, so it wouldn't be a long drive to the hospital in Aurora, where I assumed I was. It's the closest hospital to my home in Newmarket.

How I'd gotten here remained a mystery.

Richler had said I'd had a heart attack, but I didn't remember what I'd been doing when it happened. The last thing I remembered was …

Oh, damn. Damn.

I'd been arguing with Silver. We'd been loud. Yelling at each other.

Oh, not that. Anything but that.

I opened my eyes.

Silver stood in the doorway, her face pale and tear stained, her eyes red. She held her hands clasped so tight in front of her the knuckles were white. The aura of light around her was white with blue and orange patches. No understanding of its meaning came to me.

The light around Rory was also white but streaked with yellow and green. Clara's light was white, red, and violet.

For once, I regretted not studying any of that new age crap people believe. Sure, I'd picked up the odd article, and when I was in university, I took a couple of philosophy courses. But I'd never cared about anything I couldn't observe with my senses.

"Dad?" Silver whispered. She crept to her father, her gaze never leaving my body.

"Yeah, honey?" Rory hugged her tight.

"Mommy's going to die and it's all my fault." She broke into quiet sobs. The sweet kid. She was trying not to disturb my rest.

"No, sweetie. You saved her when you called 911 and gave her CPR." He spoke with confidence but one look at my body in the bed belied the words.

I yearned to go to Silver and found myself standing beside her. Assuming my hand would go through her if I touched her, I gently set it on her shoulder. It hovered there. I couldn't feel anything from the contact.

She shivered. "I'm so cold, Daddy."

"It's okay, sweetie. I'm here." His arms wrapped around her shoulders, cutting through my forearm.

I winced and stepped away from them. The touch hadn't affected me—I'd felt nothing—however, the visual was creepy.

From behind us, Clara spoke. "Would you like to wear my jacket, Silver?"

"No, thank you." Her voice was muffled against Rory's chest. "It went away."

My touch had made her shiver.

Excellent. It meant there was something there for her to feel.

I moved to the machines monitoring my vitals, breathing for me, and pumping fluids into me. I touched the heart monitor.

It beeped.

"Oh, God. Oh, Daddy. Mom! The machine."

The fear and despair in Silver's voice forced me away. No time to experiment—not if it made them think there was a problem.

Rory leaned over my bed and put two fingers on my neck.

"Her pulse is steady. Maybe it's a problem with the machine."

My invisible touch had affected the heart monitor. I filed the information away for later.

Later. Hah.

Who knew what later would bring? When my body died, would I disappear? Or would that be when the famous tunnel appeared and my dead relatives came to collect me? Where the hell were they, anyway?

At the very least, my grandmother should have shown up to guide me through this. I'm certain I was her favourite—my sisters always told me so. I didn't want to think about my sisters yet, though, so I pushed them from my mind.

Another frantic cry from Silver yanked me out of my head. Any of the machines that could make noise were doing so, and my body flopped and twitched like a landed fish.

Richler shot into the room, other medical personnel right behind him. He rushed to the bed and yanked the blanket off me.

"Get these people out of here," he snapped at a nurse, though she was already ushering my family out.

I can't say why, but I followed them. The logical thing to do would have been to stay there to see if they succeeded in keeping me alive. But I was conditioned to listen to authority, and when he said get out, I left.

The last thing I heard was Richler shouting, "Clear!"

ABOUT THE AUTHOR

Val Tobin lives in Newmarket, Ontario with her husband, Bob, and Scully, their cat. She spends her days writing, reading, and searching for the perfect butter tart.
Her educational background includes a diploma in Computer Information Systems from DeVry Toronto, a B.Sc. in Parapsychic Science from the American Institute of Holistic Theology, a M.Sc. in Parapsychology from AIHT, Reiki Master/Teacher certifications, and Angel Therapy Practitioner® certifications.

CONNECT WITH VAL TOBIN

Facebook: www.facebook.com/valtobinauthor
Twitter: twitter.com/valandbob
Blog: bobandval.wordpress.com/
BookBub: bookbub.com/authors/val-tobin
Web Site: valtobin.com
ALLi: allianceindependentauthors.org/members/val-tobin/profile/

OTHER BOOKS BY VAL TOBIN

The Valiant Chronicles Series
Prequel: *Earthbound*
A spirit becomes earthbound after refusing to cross over in order to solve her murder and prevent more deaths, some of which might be predestined.

Book One: *The Experiencers*
A black-ops assassin atones for his brutal past by trying to help an alien abductee escape her fate.

Book Two: *A Ring of Truth*
A rogue assassin returns from the dead to rescue alien abductees and triggers Armageddon.

The Valiant Chronicles books are also available as a box set.

Injury
A young actress at the height of her career has her personal life turned upside down when a horrifying family secret makes front-page news.

Gillian's Island
A socially anxious divorcée confronts her greatest fears when she's forced to sell her island home and falls for the dashing new owner.

Walk-In
A young psychic woman fights an attraction to a handsome but skeptical novelist while she battles a power-hungry sorcerer determined to make her his next conquest.

Poison Pen
Three wannabe authors suffering from various mental disorders find love in unexpected places when they interfere in the investigation of a colleague's murder.

The Hunted
A monster hunter revisits her terrifying past while helping a reporter uncover the origins of Storm Lake's creatures. A sequel to the short story Storm Lake, *The Hunted* takes place twelve years later and is a stand-alone novel.

www.ingramcontent.com/pod-product-compliance
Lightning Source LLC
Chambersburg PA
CBHW011717240626
47153CB00009B/2887